KISSING ARIZONA

KISSING ARIZONA

A Sarah Burke Mystery

Elizabeth Gunn

severn
House

This first world edition published 2010
in Great Britain and in 2011 in the USA by
SEVERN HOUSE PUBLISHERS LTD of
9–15 High Street, Sutton, Surrey, England, SM1 1DF.
Trade paperback edition first published
in Great Britain and the USA 2011 by
SEVERN HOUSE PUBLISHERS LTD.

British Library Cataloguing in Publication Data

Gunn, Elizabeth, 1927-
    Kissing Arizona. – (The Sarah Burke series)
    1. Burke, Sarah (Fictitious character)–Fiction. 2. Women
Detectives–Arizona–Tucson–Fiction. 3. Illegal
Aliens–Fiction. 4. Deportation–Fiction. 5. Family
Secrets–Fiction. 6. Detective and mystery stories.
    I. Title II. Series
    813.6-dc22

ISBN-13: 978-0-7278-6961-6   (cased)
ISBN-13: 978-1-84751-289-5   (trade paper)

All Severn House titles are printed on acid-free paper.

Severn House Publishers support The Forest Stewardship Council [FSC],
the leading international forest certification organisation. All our titles that
are printed on Greenpeace-approved FSC-certified paper carry the FSC logo.

Mixed Sources
Product group from well-managed
forests and other controlled sources
www.fsc.org Cert no. SA-COC-1565
© 1996 Forest Stewardship Council
FSC

Typeset by Palimpsest Book Production Ltd.,
Falkirk, Stirlingshire, Scotland.
Printed and bound in Great Britain by
MPG Books Ltd., Bodmin, Cornwall.

ONE

Sarah blew off the phone entirely on the first ring. Her brain took grudging notice of the second ring but she just muttered 'stinkin' minute', and went on banging out her report on the Cooper homicide interviews. She was trying to state precisely why she thought the children of the deceased had given her verifiable answers but not the whole truth. For openers, why didn't they ever look at each other? She believed in the validity of first impressions, if you could get them into the record before you got too distracted by interruptions like this stupid phone. She snatched up the miserable thing on the third ring, took a deep breath to stifle her frustration and said quietly, 'Burke.'

'Sarah,' Delaney said, 'you know Artie Mendoza, right?'

'Sure. Worked graveyard with him for a couple of years.' *And he helped me last Fall, when my druggie sister went down the rabbit hole.*

'Pick up line three and see what he wants, will you? He's ranting about a box of bones.'

'A box of . . . ?' She abandoned the question because Sergeant Delaney's line had gone dead. Running the homicide division of the Tucson Police Department in a recession year kept him tightly focused on getting from one calamity to the next without blowing any new holes in his budget. Polite enough in public, in-house these days he mostly skipped frills like hello and goodbye. Sarah shrugged and punched the lighted button on line three. 'Artie?'

'Ah, Sarah, good, it's you. Listen, you coming to see about this now? Because I need to get *going*.'

'See about what? Nobody told me . . .' She began looking around for her notebook, getting ready to move. Arturo Mendoza didn't fragment easy.

'I got this call, go to the corner of Seventeenth Street and Park. That dead-end street down past the Seventeenth Street Market?'

'OK. For what?'

'Dispatch said meet some guys who claim they were hunting for a geocache in the area and found part of a body. I said, "Aw, they probably just found some old coyote bones." Went down and found three guys standing on the corner waving handheld GPS units. I said, "Show me what you got," and they told me to park in the turnaround and follow them into the alley. So I'm out in the noonday sun sweating like a hog in my vest, trying to keep up with these geezers tracking over weeds and rocks like a herd of goats. You know about this game?'

'My mother's boyfriend is a cacher. It's just an Internet version of a paperchase, right? She says it's for old guys that still miss their Orphan Annie decoder badges.'

'What, she thinks the GPS units are a little over the top?'

'Yeah, using satellite technology to find hidden treasure that's really just worthless trinkets.'

'Mom can get mean, huh? Why, does she want him to do something else?'

'Ballroom dancing. He says when hell freezes over.'

'God, Sarah, you mean love doesn't get any easier in the golden years?'

'Nope. Looks like it's a fight right down to the wire.' She gazed longingly at her computer screen. 'What about the bones, Artie?'

'They're in a plastic tub, the kind you store records in, or extra bedding? Usually has a lid, but this one's full of cement and there's a piece of something sticking up so they couldn't get the lid on. Maybe a shoulder, part of an arm? Smells terrible.'

'And you're calling me because?'

'I called the ME's office, said send a wagon to take this corpse out of here. That office manager they got down there – Ethel, you know her? Ethel got all huffy with me, said they can't be running around picking up bones every time somebody calls. Could be a dead dog, Ethel says. I said, "When's the last time you seen dog parts set in cement, Ethel?" And *she* said, "Officer *Men*doze" – she can't be bothered learning how to say my name, y'know? – "Officer *Men*doze, your story keeps getting crazier, you better get a detective down there to handle things right." *That's* why I'm calling you.'

'Well . . .' Every synapse in Sarah's brain protested leaving her almost-finished crime scene report to run a fool's errand in the ratty south end of Seventeenth Street. But she and Artie Mendoza had backed each other up during many a long night in Midtown. And on the terrible night last fall when her niece disappeared, he had stayed on the hunt, quiet and resourceful as only a good street cop can be, till they rescued Denny from her mother's neglect. There was only one way she could answer to a call for help from Artie Mendoza.

'Be right there.' She copied the next crime scene number onto a report form, clipped her Glock in its paddle holster onto her belt, and pulled on her jacket as she trotted downstairs. This errand was almost certainly a waste of time, but as soon as she agreed to it she adopted Burke's Law: *Don't waste time bitching, just do it.*

Thirteen years on the Tucson Police Force, plus a bad divorce that laid waste to her savings, had sealed her stoicism. She'd put a couple of speed bumps in her career path with a habit of speaking the unvarnished truth when a little diplomacy wouldn't have hurt anything. She was learning to be more circumspect now, in hopes of being next up for Delaney's job when he moved on. Meantime she put in her hours in the gym, did her share of dog work and guarded her reputation as a straight-ahead police detective who did not mess around. Three minutes after she hung up the phone she was pulling out of the parking lot, headed south.

They were waiting for her on a weedy strip of gravel near the corner of Sixteenth and Park, three fit-looking retirees standing by a Jeep waving electronic devices. Artie was nearby, sitting in his Crown Vic talking on the phone. He folded it up as soon as he saw her, and jumped out to introduce her to the men who had called 911.

'This is Team Low Gears,' he said, watching her face with unconcealed pleasure as he pointed to each and recited their handles. 'Huffie the Horrible,' – the white-bearded one, 'Naughty Dick,' – friendly-faced and quiet, 'and Punxsutawney Phil,' – thin, with a humorous glint.

'But that's too long to write down, isn't it? So just call

me Phil,' the third man said, smiling as he put out his hand. He added, tentatively, 'Officer?'

'Detective,' Sarah said. 'What's with the fancy names?'

'Oh, just . . . you know . . . *noms de search*. To give us a little more *profile*,' the bearded one said, smiling brightly. 'But you can just call me Huffie and this is Dick.'

'Pleasure.' She shook hands all around. Behind them, Artie was pointing an anxious finger at his watch. 'And I know you good citizens have already waited quite a while, but now I have to ask you to wait here just a little bit longer while I debrief Officer Mendoza.' She walked with Artie toward his car, saying, 'Show me.'

'Quickest way from here is on foot.' He walked a step ahead of her, pointing out the hazards among the trash heaps.

As soon as they were a few steps inside the alley, the city noises began to fade. The neglected backs of the buildings seemed older than the fronts, at once funkier and more glamorous. Looking around, Sarah imagined she could hear a distant echo of zither music from *The Third Man* theme.

'Isn't this amazing?' She looked around. 'The isolation – I don't think I've ever come in here before.'

'Looks like hardly anybody ever does.'

It was one of those spaces a big city sometimes creates and then leaves behind. Half a block south, a steady stream of customers flowed in and out of the Seventeenth Street Market, chattering happily over its astounding hoard of bead curtains, Asian produce, exotic canned goods and noodles from around the world. Twenty feet below the eastern retaining wall, heavy traffic roared by on Aviation Parkway. But here they were in a nearly moribund space, an alley between two rows of warehouses that faced north and south. All the loading docks had been moved out to the street sides of the buildings. In here the old windows were boarded up, most of the back steps had been removed and the rear doors, three or four feet off ground level, were locked up and covered with undisturbed grime.

'There's where they found it,' Artie said, 'over there where my tape is. The box is next to that pile of rubble.'

'How messed up is my crime scene?'

'Not bad. They pulled off the trash that was covering it

up – they thought they'd found their treasure, you know? But soon as they saw . . . they backed right off and called 911, and they say they haven't touched anything since.'

'You believe them?'

'Oh, yeah. They're kind of spooked. You'll see why when you look in the box. Can you smell it now?'

She could, plainly. She stepped over the tape, picked her way across the rubble heap, and peered down at the plastic tub. Her first feeling was doubt.

'This can't be a whole body,' she said. 'The tub's too small.'

'I know,' Artie said, 'but chopped up, maybe?' On that cheerful note, he looked at his watch again and said, 'Look, I got about a hundred calls on my screen, I *gotta go.*'

An hour later Sarah had parked her car on the gravel strip facing into the alley, and was sitting in it with the A/C on, chewing on a granola bar and watching a couple of crime scene techs at work. Before they arrived, she'd photographed Artie's taped square from every possible angle and noted down the distances from both ends of the alley. Now she added the names of the streets on all four sides and, thanks to the geocaching team, the GPS coordinates of the box of bones.

After Artie left she'd walked the alley with them, making notes as they explained how they'd followed their electronic tracking toys in here, looking for their hidden treasure. They tried briefly to impress her with statistics, telling her how many more than five hundred caches each of them had logged, all over the country. They gave up on that brag when they saw that her look of disbelief contained no admiration.

'Just show me what you did,' she said, and they all raised their GPS units and showed her the arrow on the face, and the digital printout of distance.

'When all our units were reading eight or ten feet we stopped and looked around,' Phil said, 'and right away we all said, "Up there on that rubble heap." You get a feel for these sites after a while. We could see it was the best hiding place around.'

'But couldn't you smell this box before you found it?'

'Sure,' Huffie said, 'and I said, "Oh, damn, there must be

something dead right close to it." So we were kind of careful how we pulled off that trash.'

'But soon as we got it uncovered,' Dick said, 'we could tell the smell was coming from the box.' He had his back to it, trying not to look at it any more.

And she believed them when they said it was still exactly where they had found it. A three-foot square tub of cement and body parts was obviously very heavy, and was not going to be easy to pull down across old splintered boards and broken glass. A ball-and-socket joint and the top portion of what looked like a humerus protruded a couple of inches above the top of the cement that filled the plastic tub right to the brim. Any flesh that had hung on the bones had been eaten or weathered away, but a few strands of hard brown tissue clung to the undersides. The stench of death was still quite strong and added to the creepiness of the alley, where decay seemed to be attacking the buildings themselves.

Phil's voice wobbled a little when he asked her, 'You think that's a human in the cement?'

'A body anyway. Or parts of one,' Sarah said. 'The box looks too small for a whole grown-up, but that bone's too big for a child.' She felt relief in her chest when she said that, and saw the feeling echoed in their faces. She was also glad to be able to add, 'But I'm no expert, so I called a crime scene unit. They'll be here shortly. In the meantime will you just go through this one more time with me? What exactly did you touch?'

She made notes of everything they said, then made them promise to call the crime lab and make a date to be finger-printed, a prospect that clearly pleased them. When she thought they'd covered everything, just as she was getting ready to send them on their way, Dick suddenly said, 'Now would you like to hear about the cache?'

'What? You went ahead and . . . you said you didn't touch . . .'

'It wasn't right by the box,' Phil said hastily. 'We all watch CSI, we knew we weren't supposed to go near that any more. We didn't even intend to look for the cache, but then . . .'

'Dick walked a few feet along the bottom of the rubble heap and said, "Doesn't that pile of rocks right there look

kind of . . . arranged?" and we both said he was right,' Huffie
added, pointing. 'You want to see it?'

They showed her where to stand, a dozen feet or so from
the box. She said, 'I still can't see it.'

'I know,' Huffie said proudly. 'It's a pretty good hide. But
if you move this rock and this one . . .'

'I still don't see anything.'

They all made little satisfied sounds, like, 'Heh, heh,' and
then Dick reached and picked a small dark box out of the
rubble heap, saying, 'Yeah, it's a pretty good match.'

'And when we saw it,' Phil said, 'we all had the same
thought, that maybe it would be helpful if we opened it up
and told you what it said.'

'Oh? Why? What does it say?'

'Well, here, we'll show you.' He opened the flat metal box
and scrolled it out. 'See, the log always says how long the
cache has been in place, and when it was last found.'

Huffie pointed a careful finger. 'This one was placed here
the first of last October, see? Four months, two weeks and
two days ago, to be precise.' His face showed her how much
pleasure he took in being precise.

'Yeah, and it's been found more than thirty times,' Dick
said, 'but for some reason, not so much lately. The last time
anybody signed for this cache, before today, was February
fourteenth. Three days ago.'

'So probably this box of cement got dumped here since then.'

'Unless somebody with a bad cold was geocaching on the
fourteenth,' Phil said.

'Have to be the worst sinus infection ever, right? Look, I
need to keep this log book for a while. I don't need the
whole cache, but I suppose it should all stay together,
shouldn't it?' Sarah stuffed the little notebook back in the
box and clipped it shut. 'Is there a way for me to notify the
owner that his site is . . . uh . . .'

'Muggled,' Phil said.

'Oh, yeah? That's what you call it?' They all nodded
happily and she laughed. 'You guys do have fun, don't you?
Listen, I don't want a stream of gawkers down here, what
can we do about that?'

'I know Aces High,' Huffie said. 'The owner of this cache.

I could phone him up and ask him to archive it and not talk about it.'

'Archived means it's out of order?'

'Yup.'

'That would be good,' Sarah said, 'but do you really think there's a chance he can resist talking about it?'

'It does seem like kind of a stretch, doesn't it? Should I tell him to get in touch with you?'

'Do that, will you? And email me his phone number. Then if he doesn't call me I'll call *him* and describe how unpleasant police investigators can get if you cross them.'

She smiled into the white-bearded face of Huffie the Horrible, and he smiled back and said, 'Bet you're good at that.'

Dick said, 'Can we log it?'

'No,' Sarah said. 'Later.'

They all looked at each other. Phil shrugged.

'Just as well,' he said. 'I mean, think about it. It's the best thing we've ever had to put in a comment box, and the detective says we can't even mention it.'

'You be good guys and help me now,' Sarah said, 'and when this is over I'll see you get a commendation and a pip of a story for the comment box.'

'All *right*,' Naughty Dick said. He put his elbow against Phil's shoulder and tapped on his fist. 'Hear that, Punxy? We're gonna be heroes.'

'About damn time,' Phil said.

Now they were gone, and Sarah was waiting for the crime scene unit to finish up. Watching the numbers on her watch scroll past noon, she washed her energy bar down with one careful sip of water and slid her seat back. There were no rest rooms within easy driving distance of the corner of Seventeenth and Park. She was counting on the sweat she'd lost walking the alley with Team Low Gears to keep her bladder empty enough to last till the ME's van arrived.

Meantime she had nothing to do but think, and no reason not to think about the crime scene report she'd left on her computer. She put her head back and closed her eyes. Traffic faded to white noise as her mind went back to Monday, when she'd first seen Tom and Nicole Cooper in front of their dead parents' house.

When the summons to a homicide scene called her out of the shower that morning just after six, Sarah woke Denny and told her she was on her own for getting to school. No big sweat, because they always did a checklist of clothes and school supplies the night before, in case of a work call like this. The upside of taking in a previously neglected kid like Denny Lynch was that she knew how to get her own breakfast and board the bus on time.

The crime scene was in Colonia Solana, a residential area that bordered on Reid Park. Built in the fifties, the neighborhood featured sprawling brick ramblers on one-acre lots with huge trees. The Cooper house was typical, hand-split shakes over red brick with a great deal of white-painted woodwork, three carports filled with a big SUV, a crossover and a sleek red Porsche convertible. Neighborhood streets were curving, and punctuated with speed bumps to keep traffic slow. The sweeping curve in front of the house was lined with TPD vehicles by the time she arrived, so she parked by the curb across the street.

The officer guarding the crime scene checked her in, held up the tape that crossed the sparsely-graveled yard and told her to go around to the back door. 'And stay on the gravel, please, we're trying to keep everybody off the brick sidewalk and away from the front door.' She picked her way around huge clumps of overgrown agave and prickly pear to the back door, where she put on booties and gloved up.

A uniform she didn't know told her, 'Press down hard on the latch, it's not locked but it opens hard.'

She entered a recently remodeled kitchen. Top-of-the-line stainless-steel fixtures and granite countertops, an island with a butcher-block top, all looked barely used. She crossed into a dining room filled with older furniture, a mahogany table and sideboard. Delaney was standing in the middle of a long dim living room with two detectives, Jason Peete and Leo Tobin. The room had a big picture window across the front, but it was double-draped with white sheers and lined chintz drapes. The sparse light in the room came from end-table lamps with small bulbs.

Delaney looked across the other two detectives and said, 'Ah, Sarah, good, you're just in time. You can go along with Jason and Leo, see the bodies first. It's through that door there and down the hall. Leo's going to be primary and Jason's got the scene. Come back here and see me as soon as you're done over there, Sarah, will you?' Not waiting for an answer, he began punching numbers into his phone.

Leo and Jason left his side and walked toward the door into the hall, where they turned and waited for her. Jason was a buffed-up black man who had sported glorious dread-locks while he worked in an undercover drug unit, then switched to an elegantly sculpted jawline beard and soul patch when he was assigned to a gang squad. Homicide rules said only conventional hair and minimal mustache if any, so Jason had gone overboard as usual and shaved every hair off his head. Now he had a nervous new habit of patting the top of his naked dome.

Tobin was in his late forties, with a retreating hairline and weathered body that he kept in reasonably decent shape by hiking in the mountains. He had a long-standing interest in local history, loved old mining claims and ghost towns, and was everybody's go-to guy for where to find petroglyphs and ancient ruins.

When she caught up with the two men at the door, Sarah, whose summons had not included much information beyond this address and 'homicide', asked them, 'Two victims, is that right?'

'Man and wife, yes. Both here in the hall,' Leo said. He opened the door and they filed in. 'Shee. Look at this mess.'

The smells were very strong in the enclosed space. Sarah took shallow breaths at first to get acclimated. After a couple of minutes, the intellectual effort to take in other impressions crowded out the discomfort. From then on she breathed normally.

They were in a long hall with doors opening along the left-hand side. The entire right wall was windows shaded by a wide overhang, looking on to a pool and bushes.

The woman's body was nearest, lying on its side facing away. There was a spray of blood up to about four feet on the wall behind her, chunks of bloody tissue stuck to the molding lower down. But most of her blood had soaked the carpet and spread out in a stain all around her.

'I can't see a wound,' Sarah said. 'Can you?' Leo was four inches taller.

'No.'

A crime scene tech, booted and gloved like themselves, was standing in an unsoiled patch of carpet beyond the woman, taking pictures.

Beyond her, the ME crouched over a second body at the end of the hall. Splatters of blood and bloody tissue, rapidly browning, clung to the walls, floor and ceiling in a great wide swathe behind that second body.

'Ah, Greenberg.' Jason said.

'Well, The Animal always claims to like a challenge,' Leo said, 'this ought to suit him fine.' Dr Greenberg owed his nickname to his liking for extreme athletic feats, hundred-mile runs and cross-country bike rides. He was so fit he seemed to vibrate if you got too close.

'Did Delaney give you a take on this?' Sarah asked them. 'Who called it in?'

'Housekeeper,' Leo said. 'She got hysterical and started to shake shortly after we got here, so Delaney had a uniform take her to Emergency.'

'The housekeeper lives in? How come she didn't hear the shots?'

'She doesn't live here. She found the bodies when she came to work.'

'At six in the morning?'

'Five thirty – that's when the call was clocked.'

'What kind of a housekeeper starts work at five thirty?'

'*I* don't know,' Leo said impatiently. 'Maybe she'll come back here after she calms down and tell us what kind of a housekeeper she is.'

'Helluva mess down there,' Jason said, squinting toward the other body. 'Lot more of him spread around, did you notice?'

'Shot standing up, looks like. In a hall with no chairs, why not?'

'But I wonder why their spatter pattern's so different,' Jason said. 'Like she was leaning over, or . . . what?'

'Let's see the other side,' Sarah said. 'Looks like they want us to walk on these pads.' They crossed by the window, in single file, and huddled in a clear spot in the middle of the hall. From over here, it looked as if the woman had been shot in the ear, or just in front of it. A thin line of blood had streaked down her cheek from there, and dripped on to the carpet until it congealed in a short stalactite off her chin.

The lower half of her head was mostly missing.

'Why, that's Lois Cooper,' Sarah said.

'Well, yeah,' Leo said. 'Delaney didn't tell you whose house this is?'

'Didn't tell me anything,' Sarah said. 'Just the address, and two victims.' The woman on the floor had waited on her years ago at the little Cooper's Glass & Paint on Grant Road. Sarah had been a rookie cop furnishing a first small apartment. And years later, furnishing her honeymoon house in Oro Valley, she would see Lois Cooper sometimes in the big new Cooper's Home Stores on Oracle, although by then she mostly managed the other big store on East Speedway.

Lois would have been in her fifties by now, Sarah figured. Her dark hair was streaked with gray, her figure thickened. Wearing her church clothes, probably, a good suit and even a hat, tumbled off to one side, the veil stuck in the gore. Purse right there, partly underneath her, still clipped shut. Not robbery, then. Very dressed, for Tucson, but she remembered hearing from someone that Lois Cooper was a traditional Catholic who took her observance very seriously. *Out all day Sunday in her church clothes? Came home and got shot.*

'So that must be Frank Cooper, is it? Did you know him?'

'No,' Leo said, 'but all the cars are here, so that must be Frank.'

'OK, entry wound in the ear, no guesswork about the exit,' Leo was saying. 'I don't understand about the angle yet, but work with what you got.'

'Slug's probably in the middle of that mess there,' Jason said, pointing to the biggest cluster of bloody tissue clinging to the wall.

'Everything still looks a little . . . sticky,' Leo said. 'We don't know yet if anybody heard this train wreck, huh?'

'No,' Sarah said. 'Add it to a long list of things we don't know.'

'And we can't learn much more about them here,' Leo said, 'since we can't get close enough for a decent look. Let's go see what Greenberg says.'

When Sarah's plastic booties appeared by his shoulder Greenberg said, without looking up, 'Step there and there and stand over there in the corner.' He turned, having glimpsed two other pairs of legs, and glared up at Leo and Jason. 'Oh, what's this now, the whole herd? Step there and there – carefully! – and go stand by Sarah.' The three detectives obeyed him wordlessly, as most people did, because an argument with Greenberg was too exhausting to include in the average working day.

'I need a few minutes of silent concentration,' the doctor said, 'before I answer any more questions. Can't get this job done with people chattering over my shoulders! Why don't you sleuths go through that bedroom door and talk to the techies for a while. Come back in ten minutes or so.'

They walked into the master bedroom and almost collided with the backside of a female criminalist who was spreading black powder along the edge of a dresser. Her badge said her name was Diane.

'Whoops!' she said. 'Hang on while I finish this lift, will you? Only take a minute.'

'No problem,' Sarah said, and stood still, scanning the room without moving.

Diane peeled off the print, looked at it critically and nodded. She pasted it into her little spiral notebook, noted the place and time, and said, 'OK, guys. I'll go work in one of the other rooms for few minutes while you have a look. I'm not done in here yet, though, so please . . .' She rolled her pleading eyes at them.

'Have no fear, dear,' Jason said. 'We are highly skilled master detectives who watch a lot of TV, so we know not to touch things.'

'Excellent plan,' Diane said, and rewarded him with a radiant smile. She fit the spiral notebook into its place in a complex basket of tools, made a mark on a list of tasks, and left carrying the basket.

They were in a sparsely furnished bedroom with white walls, gray carpet, blue drapes. A perfectly pieced and hand-quilted comforter in rosy colors, folded on the end of the bed, provided the one homey note. Otherwise the whole room looked as if it had been lifted, in a quick half-hour's decision-making, out of a store display.

Standing in one spot, Leo started a slow three-sixty turn, and the other two followed his example. Hardly less impersonal than a motel room, the bedroom had two forgettable prints on the wall. One family photograph on the dresser showed the Coopers about twenty years ago, with two grade-school-age children. Continuing the turn, Sarah saw plenty of closets and drawer space in a practical room with no books or memorabilia. One hard-looking armchair. Nobody sat in here having coffee and a chat. This was a room where you slept, got dressed quickly, and got out. It was too uncluttered to be the bedroom of a living couple.

Maybe it wasn't? Sarah pulled out a couple of drawers and looked in the closet.

'Only women's clothes,' she said. 'Mr Cooper had his own room. Connection through the bathroom?'

She stepped into the bathroom, which like the bedroom was clean, neat and impersonal. 'No connecting door in here,' she said. She came out and said again, 'Not connected. Separate.'

'OK, Sarah, I got the picture,' Jason said.

They went back into the hall and stood carefully in clean patches on the carpet, like good children in school. Frank Cooper lay in a heap. His limbs were tangled except for his right hand and arm, which lay stretched out toward the weapon that must have killed him. His face looked undamaged. The back half of his head was missing.

Still not looking up, the doctor said, 'So?'

'Looks like he stood sideways in the hall and ate his gun,' Leo said.

'Sure does. And dropped his big blunderbuss –'he pointed to the .357 Magnum Smith & Wessen revolver lying near the dead man's outstretched right hand – 'right at his feet when he fell. So convenient, right? No doubts about the weapon.' Greenberg's face wore a funny little sneer. Even for

Moses Greenberg, Sarah thought, that's an exceptionally dubious face.

Jason said, 'Sure looks like the same gun did them both, huh?'

'Well, I'll wait till I hear what you geniuses dig out of the walls here before I venture an opinion on that. But yeah, the wounds certainly appear similar.'

Leo asked him, 'You going to be able to autopsy pretty soon?'

'With a scene like this one? Bet your ass. Nothing short of a massacre's going to take priority over these two.' The doctor squinted ironically up at them. 'Any other questions you'd like to have answered?'

'I'm curious about times of death,' Tobin said.

'You are, huh?' Greenberg looked pleased. 'Damn, I do like to see signs of intelligent life in the detective division.' He pointed to two places on either side of the body. 'Step here and here very carefully, kiddies, and get out of my face. I might have something by tomorrow night, but probably not until Wednesday.'

They picked their way carefully back down the hall toward the other body. Sarah said, 'Imagine that housekeeper opening the door into this hall and finding these bodies lying here. All alone in this house in the early morning. You wonder how she had the courage to make the call.' She looked at Leo. 'Did she, by the way?'

'You mean was she the one who called us? Um . . .' He looked at Jason. 'Isn't that what they said, that she reported the bodies?'

'I think so. She was kind of babbling by the time I got here, we were all thinking about getting her away before we had to carry her, so . . . I guess Delaney knows.'

'Or we can check the tape downtown.' Leo frowned, all business now. 'Let's get on with this.'

'Does it seem to you,' Sarah said, looking down at Lois again just before they went out, 'that she's a little . . . juicier than he is? Like her bowels and bladder voided somewhat later?'

'Oh, please, can't we leave the juice to The Animal?' Jason said.

The living room looked even cleaner and more uncluttered after the grisly scene in the hall. Sarah walked back to
Delaney, who as usual was talking on the phone. He finished
his conversation with a few quiet monosyllables and said,
looking at his notes, 'Sarah, I think I'm going to ask
. . .' A loud conversation was suddenly audible outside the
open front door. Delaney stepped into the small foyer and
looked out, saying, 'What's going on?'

Sarah followed him and heard an assertive male voice
telling Shelby, the officer at the tape, 'Of course I can go
in, this is my parents' house.' A tall, strong-looking man
in hiking boots and good outdoor clothing stood on the
sidewalk, carrying a handsome black leather camera case
on a strap over his shoulder. His face was flushed and
he held his shoulders a little high and his back stiff, like
a soldier on parade. He brought a discordant note of controversy into a crowded space where many law enforcement
professionals had been moving carefully and keeping their
voices down.

Sarah thought, Well, after all he's not used to being stopped
at this door, it must feel . . .

She took back that dollop of sympathy when the man
leaned over Shelby and insisted, 'I was told to come here at
once and ask for a Sergeant Delaney. Find him for me right
now, please.'

Shelby opened his mouth to explain that he couldn't leave
his place at the tape, but Delaney walked down the front
steps saying, 'Mr Cooper? I'm Sergeant Delaney.' He stepped
off on to the gravel and walked down to the tape, where the
tall young man stood glowering at Shelby. 'I'm sorry I can't
let you come in here just now. It's a crime scene until we're
finished. You know about your parents?'

'Yes, Rosa told me. And Phyllis, I checked with her because
I couldn't believe . . . What the hell's going on here, who are
all these people?' A TV truck had just arrived and two more
squad cars; the whole street was filling up with cars.

'I'm very sorry for your loss,' Delaney said. 'I know this is
a terrible shock. But just for now . . . do you mind walking
down this row of cars here to the RV that says Tucson Police
Department? Right there, yes. And this officer –' he signaled

Ollie Greenaway who was still putting markers in the yard
–'will let you in and stay with you until we . . . till one of my
detectives comes over there to talk to you.'

'Are you serious?' Cooper kept getting redder and angrier,
his bright blue eyes glaring out of his ruddy face. 'Both my
parents are dead in this house and you're telling me I can't
go in and see them? You want me to go and sit in a . . .
trailer?' He spat out the last word. Sarah thought he might
be going to explode in a minute and walked toward him,
ready to help subdue him if need be.

But Delaney as usual got cooler and quieter as the opposition heated up. He had summoned two officers out of the
street, the angry young man was surrounded by large men with
guns now, and began to look aware of his narrowing options.

'I know this is a very hard time for you,' Delaney said.
'We want to help you all we can and I'm sure you agree the
best way to do that is to complete this investigation as quickly
as possible. And to find out what happened to your parents,
we need to get all the evidence collected while it's still fresh.'
He talked soothingly beside the yellow crime-scene tape,
doing his stolid blinking thing, and the man gradually calmed
down.

'So, if you'll just wait for us over there for a few minutes
. . . there you go.' Delaney nodded around at everybody as
if he was relieved to see they all agreed, and in a few more
seconds Tom Cooper was walking toward the department's
modified RV with his three-man escort. He almost balked at
the doorway, waved his hands and shook his head, but Ollie
had the door open and was helping him up the step with a
hand under his elbow.

Delaney walked back inside and told Sarah, 'I want you to
do the inside interviews. Besides this piece of work that was
just here – he's the son, Tom – there's a daughter, uh . . .
Nicole.' He was flipping through his notes. 'I'm told she's on
her way. You'll need to get Tom's stats and his whereabouts
yesterday and today till now. Same for the daughter. It seems
they both work in the family business, Cooper's Home Stores.
Family whereabouts first, and then who hates who and why,
and anything they'll tell you about employees, money –' he
spread his hands – 'fights . . . the whole ball of wax.'

'Sure.' Something about this set-up was making him nervous, he was telling her things he knew very well she didn't need to be told.

'There's the manager at the Oracle Road store, a woman named Phyllis Waverly who seems to be kind of the Big Cahuna of the employees. She says she can't get away from the stores right now, somebody has to be in charge, but she'll try to get to the station by afternoon if you can see her then. Try to see her today – sounds like she'll know what's been going on. There's a housekeeper we took to the ER, you know about her?'

'Leo told me, yes.'

'OK. Her name is, uh, Rosa Torres. She found the bodies so you need to see her as soon as you can, but it may not be today – she started to tell us about finding the bodies and just totally lost it, they were sedating her in the ambulance as they drove away. Here's her number and the manager's number at the store. No sign of forced entry, by the way. Rosa used her key on the front door like always, and Jason did a quick check of the other doors and windows, didn't find anything unlocked or broken. Oscar and Ray have started the neighborhood canvass.'

The department command post was a modified RV fitted out with a couple of desks in front, plenty of communications gear, photography equipment and computers. They'd kept the galley but the dining table was gone. In the back, though, instead of a bedroom there was a private space with a booth, table and chairs, which worked well for interviews. The digital recorders were very sensitive and picked up any background noise, so the vehicle had to be parked at some remove from a crime scene, in a quiet spot. They'd parked it in the driveway of an empty house with a For Sale sign.

Sarah found Tom Cooper rummaging through the refrigerator. He backed out holding a bottle of water, looked down over his noble nose, said, 'Well, so I'm going to be grilled by the lady police, hmm?' and made a small sound that just missed being a chuckle. Sarah put on her Ice Cold Cop face, led him to the interview table, opened her notebook and started the who-what-where-when questions that had to be asked.

Tom said he'd spent the weekend in Madera Canyon. 'I go there often, I love the place. Stay at a small bed and breakfast and hike on the mountain. My hobby's photography, and the flora and fauna there . . . there are several different microclimates . . .' He seemed ready to launch into a wildlife lecture.

'I know, I like it too. How did you hear about your parents?'

'Rosa called me. Soon after she called the police, I think. She was crying . . . kind of babbling, but she insisted they were both dead, I got that much out of her but I still can't believe it. Is it true? Are you sure?'

'Yes. I'm sorry.'

'God.' He took a printed bandanna out of his corduroy pants pocket, and mopped his face. 'Rosa said come right home, so I did. Now I'm here and your sergeant won't let me in the house. How long is that going to last, not being able to get in the house?'

'Quite a while, I'm afraid. It's a big crime scene and we need to process it all as soon as possible.'

'Jesus.' He looked at the ceiling and thought. 'It feels so *unreal*. Like a Kafka novel. They're my *parents*, for God's sake. I rush home after getting terrible news about them and I'm met by a lot of strangers saying, "I'm sorry, you can't come in."'

Confusion and grief were to be expected at such a time. But Sarah thought part of Tom Cooper's unhappiness stemmed from the fact that he was accustomed to having his own way. He seemed determined to stay on the attack till he got it. She decided to shake him up and see what dropped out. 'Do you think it's possible that your father killed your mother?'

'What?' He was startled right out of his chair, jumped up, staring. 'Of course it's not possible.' He paced around her, waving his arms. 'Whose crazy notion is that? You shouldn't be repeating it, I won't put up with that kind of talk!'

'You weren't aware they might be fighting or—'

'No, of course not. And I want you to stop spreading this terrible lie right now! You should be ashamed of yourself, insulting my parents when they're not here to defend themselves!'

'Will you sit down so we can talk, please?' He sat on the edge of a chair, crossed his legs, wagged the top foot. He looked ready to fly off again at the next thing she said. 'When did you see them last?'

'Saturday afternoon. We have a rule that we all go our own way on Sunday, and sometimes I start a little early. I said goodbye to my father at the East Speedway store about two o'clock, went home and packed my gear in the car and drove to Madera Canyon.'

'Did he seem at all upset when you said goodbye? Anything unusual?'

'No. My father was never upset. He was exactly the same every day of his life, always in charge.'

Must have been some store when the two of you were in it together.

'Has the house been broken into? Is that what happened, he found somebody stealing something? He was always fierce if he caught anybody stealing anything at the store. If he caught somebody in the house—'

'We haven't found any sign of a break-in, Mr Cooper.'

'See, but I'd know right away if anything was missing or out of place. That's why you should let me in, so I could look around and see . . .'

'Mr Cooper, there was no forced entry. Rosa used her key to open the front door just as she always did.' Cooper looked puzzled and dissatisfied. 'What about employees? Any of them have a grievance?'

'Well, it's always possible somebody could be mad at the boss. My father was pretty strict, and he wasn't very tactful if somebody screwed up. Nicole would have a better idea of that, I don't do much in the merchandizing end.'

'Oh? You just do the buying?'

'No, no. I don't do any buying.'

'What other part is there?'

'The money part. I'm the money man.' He ducked his chin and showed a small, self-satisfied smile.

'What does that mean?'

'Just what it says. I manage the money.' She waited. Silence, she had learned, sometimes elicits its own answers. She kept her eyes on his face until he added, 'We run a big organization, two warehouse-type stores and a third in the planning stage. My parents have always been too busy making money to think much about investing it. So gradually I've taken over that end.'

'I see,' Sarah said. She didn't, exactly, but decided she had more important questions now. 'I'll need to see your receipts from the hotel where you were staying, please, and the pictures in your camera, they'll be dated and timed. Anything else that will confirm you were in the canyon.'

'Dear me, what else? Charges on my gas card, I suppose?' His sarcasm made it plain how insulting he felt it was for her to ask for proof. His pomposity was so annoying, Sarah caught herself thinking how satisfactory it would feel to slap the cuffs on him and read him his rights.

But in the next minute the door of the RV squeaked open, and the floor gave the little bounce that signaled somebody standing on the step. Tom Cooper, whose chair was facing the door, said softly, 'Oh, God, here's Nicole . . .'

His sister stood motionless in the doorway for a long couple of heartbeats. Then her eyes moved, but not toward her brother. Sarah found herself being assessed. Apparently that didn't take long. Nicole closed the door and moved toward them along the narrow aisle. The small space felt colder with her in it. She said, 'Detective Burke?'

Despite being six inches shorter and a hundred pounds lighter than her brother, Nicole Cooper exuded self-confidence in a way he didn't. She wore blond-streaked straight hair in a chic cut, discreet make-up in desert tones and a simple, expensive-looking pale gray suit. Her voice was so quiet Sarah had to lean forward to hear her ask, 'Are my parents still over there, in the house?'

Sarah said, 'Yes. I'm sorry you can't see them yet – it's a crime scene, and we have to protect the chain of evidence.'

'I understand. Where's Rosa, do you know?'

'Last I heard, still in the hospital.'

'In the hospital? Rosa? What happened to her?'

'I understand she had a sort of breakdown while she was telling the first responders about finding your parents this morning.'

'Breakdown? I can't imagine Rosa breaking down.'

'Well, she had a pretty bad shock. And look, the rules say I need to talk to you and your brother separately the first time.' Her instincts were telling her to get this odd couple apart and see if she could find out why they didn't speak to each other. 'Do you mind if we go across the street and sit in my car?'

'Not a bit.' Nicole walked back to the tinny door at the front of the RV and pushed it open. All her movements were lithe and decisive.

Sarah turned to Tom in the chair beside hers and said, 'Will you just wait right here, please?'

'For what?' He was getting red again, hating to be told what to do.

'For me to come back,' she said, keeping her voice level and her eyes fixed on him in a neutral stare.

'Oh, well, hell yes, where am I going to go anyway?' He rattled the coins in his pockets. 'I just feel as if I should be doing something!'

'You are. You're helping us find out what happened,' Sarah said, to the top of his head.

He looked up quickly at that and said, 'Oh, I know!' and went back to scanning his shoes.

Like most homicide investigators Sarah sometimes claimed that nothing surprised her very much any more. But she thought, as she caught up with Nicole and led her to the department car, that if Delaney thought Tom Cooper was a piece of work on his own, he should really see him with his sister.

Meeting each other for the first time after hearing about the death of both their parents, most siblings would rush to each other, hold on hard and try to give comfort. Sarah and her sister had often ridiculed the stand-offish behavior of their brother, but now she thought, Even Howard the Stick would give me a hug at a time like this. The Cooper siblings had stood half an RV length apart without saying one word to each other. Didn't say hello, never met each other's eyes. The mutual avoidance was so total it didn't even convey anger. Loathing? Maybe, but it seemed more like dread. As if the sky might crack open and rain lava if they spoke one word to each other.

The contrasts were interesting, too. Tom Cooper was

aggressive in a pushy, sneering way that Sarah thought might be a cover for insecurity. Nicole moved and spoke with the quiet authority of a person accustomed to having the final say. Right now, along with her self-assurance, she had the slightly distraught air of someone who has mistakenly locked herself out of a house in a cold rain – an obviously intelligent person taken aback by a shocking event. Sarah thought her demeanor seemed much more appropriate than her brother's, except that she hadn't offered him any more comfort than he'd given her.

She had been driving home this morning after a Sunday in Phoenix with friends, Nicole explained, when she got word 'from somebody at the police department, I didn't get the name,' that there was a 'problem' at her parents' house. 'Neither one of them answered their cell, so I called Phyllis. She told me to pull off the road, and as soon as I was parked she told me what had happened.' Nicole rested her forehead briefly on two fingertips. When she raised her head and looked at Sarah, her eyes were bright with unshed tears, but her voice was steady.

'She asked me if I wanted to close the stores for a couple of days, to show respect. I said, "What would they have wanted?" and right away we both said, together, "Keep 'em open, take care of the customers."' She gave a little dry bark of a laugh, halfway between irony and pride. 'She said she'd see to it, and I should go ahead and take care of . . . whatever there is to take care of. Every organization,' she added thoughtfully, 'should have at least one Phyllis.'

'Reliable?'

'Like a rock. And smart and tireless.'

'Do your parents . . . were they still working in the two stores?' Sarah remembered them well, the busy, capable couple to whom she'd paid so many dollars when she was decorating her big honeymoon house in Oro Valley.

'My mother still manages . . . managed East Speedway. Dad's been acting as CEO of the entire operation for some time. We share an office downtown, I supervise the accounting for both stores. Which means I do the lion's share of the ordering too, because the system's set up for reordering to be automatic till we change a line. Just-in-time supply systems, that's the name of the game today.' She perked up a little, began to look better fed and warmer, when she talked about the business.

'Have you always worked for your family?'

'Yes. Even in grade school we were expected to run errands and do odd jobs around the store – the first one, the little one on Grant Road. By the time I was in high school we had the big store on Speedway and we built the second one on North Oracle while I was in college. I put in thirty hours a week, split between the two stores, while I got my degree at U of A.'

'That must have been hard.'

'Sometimes. But it was also motivating. I was always at the top of my class because I knew exactly what I was studying for.'

'What's that?'

'Control.' *I think I'm hearing her power-point speech to Rotary.* 'Control is everything in business. Information. Knowing what your costs are, where everything is, how to move it, what to charge.'

'And you know all that?'

She shrugged. 'That's what I do. Yes.' Then she seemed to realize how much of what she had thought she controlled was gone. She said, 'Will you excuse me for just a minute?' and without waiting for an answer she opened her door and got out. She walked along the sidewalk for half a block to a corner, stared into the middle of the street for a few moments, took some deep breaths. When she got back in the car, she opened her mouth and closed it a couple of times and finally said, 'I still can't . . . are they really both dead?'

'I'm afraid so, yes. I'm sorry you can't see them yet. Later today, though.' Sarah let a little tick of time go by and added, 'I know this is very hard for you.'

'Yes.' She closed her eyes briefly, swallowed, and said, 'Thank you.' She took a tissue out of a box on the console and blew her nose. 'What else do you need to ask me?'

'Did your father own a gun?'

'Yes. A big one, uh . . . I don't know much about this subject, but . . . some kind of a big revolver. Does Smith & Wessen sound right?'

'That's what's in the house there, with his . . . beside him. Yes. What about your mother, did she own a gun?'

'Yes, she did, because Daddy insisted. He bought two just alike for us, tiny things, from . . . let me think . . . Beretta? I forget because I never look at mine, it's in a drawer in my house.'

'But you know how to use it?'

'Yes. Or I did at one time, I guess I'd need a refresher now. He managed to drag us both out to the practice range a couple of times to practice. But we both hated it. Mom kept telling him, "Frank, we're not going to shoot anybody, no matter what you say."'

'Your mother kept hers in her bedroom?'

'Last I knew. Daddy wanted her to carry it in her purse, but she wouldn't – she was afraid of guns. Was she really shot?'

'It looks that way.'

'That's so . . . obscene. Who could have . . . somebody got in the house? How?'

'We don't know yet. Was your father a good shot, did he practice?'

'Yes, routinely. He got sort of fanatical about self-defense as he got older, joined the NRA and got all passionate about the Second Amendment. That's the other thing that's so hideously ironic about this. All those hours of practice, big talk about being prepared to protect yourself – why would he let them both be killed?'

'You never know how you're going to react till you have to do it,' Sarah said.

'I suppose. He belonged to a gun club, competed in shoots. Practiced at a range south of town. There's a whole shelf full of trophies in the house there – in the den. My mother always wanted to call that room the library, but they never got around to buying any books, so Daddy called it the den and kept his shooting trophies and his biggest TV in there.' Nicole closed her eyes for a few seconds, opened them, and said, 'Families are the hardest thing to figure out, aren't they?'

'Yes. When did you last see your parents?'

'We all had lunch together Friday at the Machiavelli's near

the North Oracle store. We were contemplating another expansion, a third store in Phoenix. It's a risky year for it, but by the same token bargains are available that you don't see every year so . . . my father and I agreed it was worth the risk, to get ourselves positioned in the market before the turnaround gets started. We went over some of the numbers.' She licked her dry lips. Sarah pulled a bottle of water out of the cooler in the back and handed it to her. She drank it thirstily.

'My mother was dubious. She thought it was too soon to make this move. The discussion got . . . pretty heated.' She drank some more. 'That's too bad, isn't it? Big noisy fight at our last lunch? And now the whole subject is moot.'

'I suppose. How did your mother seem to you? Anything unusual about her behavior?'

Her pale face showed a quick flash of irony. 'No, Mom was pretty much her usual self.'

'Which was?'

'Loud, argumentative, occasionally abusive toward my father.'

'Oh?' Sarah thought it was the most unsuitable comment she'd ever heard from a newly-bereaved daughter. The Cooper family wasn't getting any easier to understand – every time you moved, you sank into a new swamp. She was trying to wade carefully. People said things in emotional moments they didn't quite mean. Reminded of the statement later, they often turned their anger on the detective. 'So . . . she didn't have a quiet voice like yours?'

'No, I guess everybody within two blocks of Machiavelli's that day knows she thought her husband was getting ready to launch a folly. Risking everything they'd worked so hard for, she said, in this terrible year for the building industry. She kept saying, "What are you thinking?" She wanted the whole idea put on the back burner till she agreed it was time to go ahead.'

'So would you say your mother was extremely unhappy?'

'Not exactly. She liked to get her own way and in the end she would certainly have got her way about the new store, if she really wanted to. My father couldn't get any of the loans he was talking about until she was ready to sign for them.'

'You said, "if she really wanted to", but you make it sound as if there wasn't any doubt what she wanted. Was there?'

'Maybe. Sometimes she liked to play devil's advocate – make him really fight for an idea, see if he could convince her. It wasn't pretty but she was shrewd about spotting the holes in his reasoning. Daddy often said, if he could get it past Mama, he could be pretty sure he had a winner.'

'How did your father behave at that lunch?'

'He wasn't exactly in top form. He'd been out talking to bankers, and the news wasn't good.'

'They didn't want to lend him the money?'

'No. He was pressing them hard, talking about his track record. He said, "Those bastards have made a lot of money off me, now when I need them they go soft." But the market is pretty spooky right now. And they kept telling him, "With your cash flow, you should have a bigger bottom line." That made him angry – he hated being criticized.'

'Ah. Was your brother at that lunch?'

'No.'

'I thought raising money was his job.'

'What, Tom find capital? No, no.'

'But he said—'

'That he deals with the money. I know. But Tom just deals with the *leftover* money.' A small, secret smile curled her pale mouth.

'OK.' Giving up on understanding this family circus for now, Sarah decided on the direct approach to the crime. 'Was this fight serious enough to make your father want to kill your mother?'

'To kill . . .' She stared at Sarah, swallowed a couple of times. 'Is that what . . . ?' She finally managed, just above a whisper, 'Is that what you think happened?'

'Some evidence points that way.' Sarah watched Nicole's thin, pale face as she closed her eyes again and swallowed several times. Was she going to vomit? Sarah got ready to grab a plastic bag. But Nicole drew a few careful breaths, took a small, cautious sip of water and fitted the bottle carefully into the cup holder. Sarah gave her a few seconds to collect herself before she said, 'Do you think it's possible? Were they just arguing, or were they really fighting?'

'Were they . . . ?' Nicole uttered a laugh that ended in a choking sound and mimicked, 'Were they really fighting?' Color came up in her face. Sarah watched her warily. 'Of *course* they were really fighting! Fighting was who they were, it was what they did!'

'Oh?' She thought about the industrious couple she'd known at the store. 'Funny, I've known them a long time, and I never saw that.'

'Probably not. They saved it for the planning sessions, out of sight of customers. In twenty-five years, they grew from one tiny store to two huge ones with a contracting division on the side. All those years, they expanded or rebuilt something every couple of months, and disagreed about damn near every item on the shelves. Whether they should carry it, how it should be displayed, which colors – and after everything else was decided, there was a constant struggle over how much to charge. She wanted margin, he favored undercutting the competition and going for volume. So yes, indeed, if this is still Tucson, Arizona, on the planet Earth, you can be pretty certain they were really, really fighting.'

The memory of Nicole's bitter laughter was still in Sarah's mind as she raised her seat-back at midday Tuesday, and pushed her review of the Cooper case to the back of her mind. The medical examiner's van had just parked beside her, facing the weedy alley where an unknown body waited in its cement cocoon.

TWO

Victoria Nuñez came to Arizona the first time riding on her father's back across the Tohono O'odham Nation. She was two years old. Her family had not been invited to that section of the Sonoran Desert, but luck favored them for a change, so they were not escorted out either. Their footsore little band took four more days to find Tucson than their coyote had predicted. They would have died of thirst in the desert had they not found a water station put there by an organization of Christians called No More Deaths. When they found the water by a wonderful accident, the devout of the party wanted to say a rosary of thanks. The man who was being paid to lead them said, 'Drink now and pray later,' and hurried them away. Water stations, he said, were a favorite place for the Border Patrol to find crossers.

The coyote scuttled unceremoniously away from them in a grocery parking lot near the south edge of Tucson. Pablo Nuñez found the public phone and called the number he had carried all the way from Ajijic. Soon they were picked up by Tío Rafi, who was not really an uncle but close enough – a friend of an old family friend. He gave them food and sleeping space on his floor for three days till they found a cousin of a cousin.

Victoria couldn't really remember the trip, but felt she knew all about it because her parents told her the story several times, embellishing the details as she got older. It was the biggest adventure of their lives, and they were proud of it. Her mother remembered especially how thirsty she got after the water ran out – she was already pregnant with Victoria's sister and was afraid the baby would die before they found water. But Luz was born, healthy and squalling, a few weeks after the trip ended, and gained the lifelong advantage with which she always taunted Victoria: Luz was an American citizen.

Her father's version of the story was the one Victoria liked best. He told her she was so heavy that the canvas backpack she rode in wore big holes in his shoulders.

'You grew heavier as the trip went along,' he said, 'and you were without pity even then. You beat on me like a demon child and demanded I go faster even when I told you I was exhausted.'

'Why do you tease her like that?' Marisol would say, shaking her head. But she could see that the grotesque joke worked in some way for both of them. Pablo liked playing the martyred father, more and more as he became a mostly absent one in reality. And Victoria enjoyed the feeling of power it gave her to imagine she had once dominated her father, forcing him to carry her quickly across a desert.

'Did I yell at you?' she would ask him. 'Was I fierce?' And when he answered, Yes, yes, you were the very devil, she would cackle with glee.

She was six by then, walking to school every day with the children who lived in the other half of their small house in South Tucson. Pablo had a job with a gardening service that managed the grounds at big resorts – a distant cousin on the crew helped him get the job and the fake work permit. Marisol stayed home and cared for the children of all the maids and housekeepers who lived nearby, until Victoria and her sister Luz were both old enough for school. Then Marisol too got a green card and a job on a house-cleaning crew.

The crew was run by Tía Luisa, Marisol's mother's sister. She had left home long ago and was presumed lost because the family never heard from her. Luisa was illiterate in both Spanish and English, and too ashamed to admit it. She would never ask for help with letters, as many others did. She worried about this a great deal for the first year she was in Tucson, but as she saw how much trouble and expense many immigrants went to for later-arriving relatives, she began to think it was not such a bad thing to be out of touch. When Marisol found her by accident in a market, Tía Luisa was rather cool at first. But when Marisol told her all the news from home she began to cry, embraced her niece and invited her for a meal. Soon they were close.

The girls learned English fast in school, and when she

heard them beginning to speak English to each other at home, Marisol said, 'Teach me,' and tried to keep up. But with work and her own housework she was usually too tired to study. She quickly learned the names for most vegetables and several bus stops, and took Vicky along when she needed something more complicated than groceries or a ride to the store.

The family had a couple of golden years, then. With two paychecks they got a TV set and a futon that made into a bed at night so the girls no longer slept on the floor. They got good clothes, too, and some toys, and learned to behave like American kids, critical and demanding.

Pablo made new friends among the groundskeepers, who were mostly single and hung out in the bars. It felt good to sit in the sun with them after work, trading jokes and drinking. He came home later and later to an angry wife and two bickering kids. Soon he began to say, of the situation he had himself created, 'Who needs this?'

After a big noisy fight in which he threatened her with his fist and she hit him with the pan she was washing, he stayed away a week. Finally he came in the afternoon with two friends in a pickup, put his clothes in one plastic trash-bag and his tools in another. Marisol followed him around the house, yelling at him, asking him what he expected her to do. Luz followed him too, crying, 'Daddy, I love you!' He never answered either one of them, just kept his head down and gathered his gear.

Victoria would not cry. She stood by the door, furious, watching him pick out his skivvies and socks from the drawer where the parents' underwear was mixed together. The final coldness of the way he separated his clothing from his wife's was somehow more insulting than his staying away had been – that was neglect; this was indifference. When he walked toward her dragging his two bags she stuck her tongue out and gave him the finger. This so shocked both parents that for one galvanized moment they cried out in unison, 'Victoria, *que verguenza!*'

Her father raised his hand to strike her but she dodged away, screaming, 'I hate you both!' That shattered the last moment when the couple might have said anything to one another. Pablo threw his bags in the back of the pickup and took off with his friends.

Marisol was devastated. She cried non-stop for two days, collapsing onto beds and even, once, into the recliner. She quickly sprang up from there, tearing her hair, shrieking that it was Pablo's chair. They had picked it out together, she wailed, and all the saints could see that now he had broken her heart. When she threw herself on the bed instead, Victoria climbed into the chair, adjusted the backrest and made herself at home. She took possession of it entirely, refusing to share it with Luz.

The girls watched TV the entire weekend, snacking on cookies and chips. Their mother, who had never before spent a day in bed, lay weeping and indifferent to them. They had no idea what she might do next. Growing crankier as their sugar-and-salt-loaded diet clogged their digestive systems, they wallowed in game shows and cartoons, and waited.

On Monday morning, Marisol got up early, washed her bloated face in cold water and started the coffee, got dressed and woke the girls.

'Get up,' she said. 'You have to go to school. I have to get to work.' It was as close to a plan as they would ever hear from her. Fatally humiliated, Marisol became essentially unreachable. Her answer to almost every question became 'Quien sabe?' Who knows? Her other favorite answer was 'no'. Soon even that was unnecessary, as her daughters quickly understood that with their father gone, their situation was desperate.

The girls coped in their different ways. Vicky got in every food line she could find and in time learned to do a little careful shoplifting. Luz hung around the neighbors' houses looking pitiful until they fed her and worked the school system for everything she could get. As she grew, she became as American as possible, worked hard to keep her clothes clean and neat, and copied the hairstyles in *People* magazine. As her mother sublet most of their rented duplex to noisy new arrivals in order to keep a roof over their heads, Luz drew an invisible bubble around herself and was soon as unreachable as Marisol. Her English became textbook perfect, her grades went to the top and stayed there, she learned to suck up to teachers for attention and prizes.

Emotionally abandoned, Victoria became an insolent stray named Vicky. She ran with the wild kids, grew a bad attitude. By shoplifting the toiletries aisles in the grocery store, she was able to style herself Gothic, with green fingernails and spiked hair. She slouched around the house scowling and swearing; when she bothered to come home at all, her mother complained.

Marisol began to transfer her anger, and with it her talent for nagging, from the husband she had lost to the daughter she could no longer control. *You want to eat my food you gonna help with the cooking,* she raged. *No you can't go to the movies, I been cleaning Anglo shit all day, you got to do the dishes.*

Vicky had always resisted her mother's discipline, and after Pablo abandoned them, her rebellion slid gradually toward open warfare. She turned twelve, and then thirteen, flunked sixth grade and began to menstruate. 'One more expense,' Marisol groaned as she showed her how to use the pad. It was all the sex education Vicky would ever get at home, but of course there was plenty to be had at school, much of it from the boys who had begun to taunt and tease her.

During the depressing boredom of the summer remedial classes she had to take after failing sixth grade, Vicky discovered the refuge her imagination could provide. Her reading was still too poor to escape into literature, but her spoken English was fluent. Her best friend in the world became the TV set. By the hour, she watched the competitive posing of reality shows, Masterpiece Theater channel with its elegant accents and period costumes, cop shows featuring tough, smart American women who could run and shoot without smearing their make-up.

Luz got a scholarship to a math-and-science camp for poor kids that summer, and Marisol worked her two jobs and slept. Vicky, ignoring Marisol's demands that she clean the house, curled in Pablo's chair, happy in her dream world. In bed at night she played the stories over in her mind, identifying with the smoothest-talking, smartest women, the ones with the power. Her inner view of herself became more and more at odds with her squalid surroundings and low test scores.

On the first sizzling-hot day in August, Immigration and

Border Protection agents staged a sweep on the house-cleaning staffs at several motels just as Marisol was starting the morning shift. Her green card proven fraudulent, she waited, weeping, in a detention center till her children could be brought to join her.

Vicky, malingering through remedial math class in Wakefield Middle School, looked up from passing a note to the boy in the seat ahead of her and saw a man in a blue uniform in the doorway. She went with him willingly, glad of a break from the tedium of class. When her mother told her what was happening, she was first unbelieving, then indignant. Her reactions were all met with demeaning indifference by the authorities at the center, which reduced her to sputtering rage.

'Shut up,' Luz hissed at her, 'you're making it worse.' Luz had memorized the number on her Arizona birth certificate. She made them look her up in the computer and acknowledge her American citizenship.

'But you can't stay here by yourself,' the social worker said, 'You're only ten years old.'

'I can stay with Tía Luisa,' Luz said. 'Can't I?' she petitioned her mother. 'Ask her!' Marisol didn't want to leave her younger daughter behind but Luz insisted, standing by the phone with her jaw pushed out till Marisol called Tía Luisa's house and begged for the favor.

'You should have kept your mouth shut and hung onto your husband,' Luisa said, blaming the wife as usual.

'Wouldn't make no difference now, they sending me back,' Marisol said. 'But Luz is American citizen like your girls. Won't you sign for her till we see—'

'See what? I got my hands full to feed my own. She's too young to work on the house-cleaning crew and I can't keep her for nothing, you hear?'

Luz, who was hanging by her mother's ear to hear as much as she could, said, 'Tell her I can learn, I will do any work!'

Marisol repeated Luz's promises and added, 'This one is determined to succeed, you will not lose on her.' Luz got a ride home to pack and came back with Tía Luisa and her husband, who scowled and groaned but signed the paperwork. Marisol surrendered herself and Vicky to the agents at IBP.

That year the Border Patrol tried returning as many illegals as possible to Mexico by plane, trying to get them resettled in their home communities, away from the border so they would not keep coming back. Marisol and Vicky got airlifted to Guadalajara.

Marisol tried to get Vicky to agree that at least the plane ride was a treat. But Vicky was so outraged that her rotten little sister got to stay and be a US citizen while she got thrown out, that for once she was almost speechless. Anger filled her chest and throat so she could hardly breathe. She had built up a very good opinion of herself; she knew she was cute and clever, whatever the teachers said. Boys already teased and chased after her. She had one almost-boyfriend named Chaco who would do anything for her, or said he would if only she . . . but she was still holding off on sex, hoping to find somebody strong and brave, a leader. Older men winked and made jokes, and she knew they were not just being kindly as they pretended. If even grown men wanted her, who were these people now who said she wasn't good enough to stay in the United States?

At the back of her anger was the shrinking fear she was too proud to admit – that her Spanish was not good enough, she would be awkward and make stupid mistakes. Kids her age would laugh and mock her, she thought – and besides, she had heard that the food in Mexico would make you sick if you weren't used to it. At the same time, oblivious to the irony, she feared they would be too poor to eat at all, and would starve.

At the Guadalajara airport they caught a bus to Ajijic. Marisol taught her how to say it, Ah-hee-heek. It was Marisol's home town, a small suburb full of artisans' factories and shops, near Lake Chapala. For generations, the men of her family had been glass-blowers here and in Tonalá, the even smaller village nearby. The women painted designs on the pottery, or were weavers, or worked in one of the shops that sold the goods. 'In the old days,' she told Vicky, 'before all the young men left, this was a good place to live. If I can find some of the people I worked for . . . or my sister Yolanda . . .'

But Marisol had been gone almost twelve years. Both her

parents had died. None of her family wrote or read well – she had exchanged a few Christmas cards with her sisters and brother, had heard about a wedding and a couple of babies. She had very little money, and no idea of the right price for things now. Marisol was plenty jittery herself, but was counting on the goodwill of relatives to get her started at something. She had tried to find family members by phone while they waited for their flight, but was not too worried that none were listed – nobody in her family had ever had a phone.

They got off the bus near the town square, checked their bags into a locker and walked around aimlessly at first. The streets were quiet; it was summer, there were only a few tourists. All the small merchants were out, though – the ones for whom their own body was the store. They piled hats high on their heads or draped lace tablecloths over their shoulders and arms. One man was almost invisible behind the dolls he had hung all over himself.

Marisol walked into shop after shop, asking questions. Her Spanish was fine, she had used it every day in South Tucson. Vicky understood some words but not many whole sentences; people talked so fast! She stared at her toes, growing more and more surly. Marisol got sick of her attitude quickly and yelled, 'Nobody gonna help me with you there looking like death! Go sit on that bench and wait for me.'

'How long . . . ?'

'Till I come get you! Just wait!'

Vicky sat pouting on the shady end of a hard wooden bench. What was wrong with her mother to give in so easily? There had to be some way back to Tucson and they could find it. She watched a man lead a burro across the cobblestone square, pulling a cartload of clay pots, and promised herself, 'Damn if I'll stay in this one-burro town.' The expression pleased her and dampened her anger a little, as she thought about saying it to Chaco, making him laugh.

Then Marisol burst out of a shop door, transformed by happiness, yelling, '*Ayé a Yolanda!*' Chattering in excited Spanish, dropping in some English words when Vicky demanded it, she told about the clerk in the store who knew her sister and let her make a phone call. 'She told me which bus to take, too. *Vámanos!*'

When Marisol's sister Yolanda opened her door to them, and her other sister Sophia brought her daughters with food to welcome them, Marisol began to wonder why she had ever left this place. They were poor, she told Vicky, but they had enough to eat and they looked after each other. She could manage here, it was a kinder place than Tucson.

There was no money for school, though. Vicky had hated school in Tucson, but was indignant when she learned she had no chance for it here. She was an adult-in-training now, expected to carry her share. Marisol used all the family connections to get Vicky an apprenticeship in a pottery in Tonalá, where skilled artisans threw the pots on a wheel, fired them and painted the patterns. Vicky was put to work with the other beginners kneading clay and mixing glazes. Her pay was so little it felt like an insult, and her mother made her give most of it to her aunt for board and room.

'Room!' Vicky sneered, 'I wish!' She had one end of a tiny cot, with her smallest cousin at the other end and her clothing underneath in the small suitcase she had brought along.

'*Ya basta!*' Marisol hissed, afraid her sister would be offended. 'Enough now. Be nice with your cousins, they will take you with them to the *paseo* in the evening so you can find friends your own age.'

'Who needs cousins? I know where the plaza is.'

'You can't go alone, girls don't do that here. Vicky, here the family is very important, girls especially must be well-behaved. We are lucky to have Yolanda, so *firme la boca,*' – she drew an imaginary zipper across her mouth – 'and follow the rules.'

Making pots was hard work and Vicky saw in the first week that she would never be one of the ones who learned to coax beauty from the clay. Soon she understood fully how boring real poverty could be, how dismal it made her to work hard for bare survival and see everybody around her doing the same. At least in Tucson you could see other people living well, so you could dream of some day having what they had.

Marisol got a job in one of the shops in Ajijic and quickly became a valued employee. She was proud that her employers valued her few words of English, which enhanced her ability to deal with tourists. Vicky sneered when Marisol told her they admired her *'estilo Americano'*. In Tucson her mother had made beds in a motel, the most menial job, and still sometimes said *'zanahorias'* when she wanted carrots. She had depended on Vicky to find things in the mall. Now she thought she was doing a big favor when she offered to escort Vicky to an evening at the stupid plaza. Walking around in a brain-dead circle, what fun was that? Still, it was better than staying home in Aunt Yolanda's tiny crowded house, so she went.

She walked beside her mother with her nose in the air, pretending to ignore the curious stares of the local boys. All these quaint local customs that the tourists loved; they made her realize that from now on she had to think for herself. What use was advice from a mother who thought Ajijic was a sweet place to live? Under her lashes, she watched the boys and men who came on to her, more of them every week now. She was looking for the discontented ones, the ones most likely to jump the wall.

THREE

The first thing the detective division taught Sarah Burke was that word processors, contrary to predictions, had not eliminated paperwork. If anything, they allowed detectives to burn through trees faster than ever, because electronic keyboards made report-writing faster. And better forensic science meant there was more to report every year.

More reporting meant that the secret to staying afloat in Homicide was keeping your emotions under tight control so you could transition quickly from one task to another. Been out on the street for two hours, talking to some nutcase through a door? Feeling maybe a little roughed up because he kept promising to shoot you? Tough cheese. Because as soon as you walk back in the station, you had better get your tushy on a chair and start typing, or you will find yourself woefully behind in your reporting chores, where you do not want to be if you value your slot in Homicide.

Sarah set great store by her slot, so as soon as the box of bones was tagged and loaded onto the ME van, she hurried back to her desk and finished the report of her interviews with the Cooper siblings. She put down what they said and left out any speculation about their odd relationship, because she still hadn't figured that out. And as interesting as it might turn out to be, she was out of time now and had to get cracking on the employee interviews. She took them in the order they came up in her notebook, the store manager first.

Three uniformed officers had watched as Phyllis Waverly strode across the lobby at the station, and who could blame them? She was hard to look away from, a big woman with gleaming tawny hair and the confidence of a first-string quarterback. Sarah had seen her a couple of times in the North Oracle store, and remembered thinking that even a statuesque woman should give up skintight pants when she left her thirties behind. Maybe tone down the make-up a little too. But it was clear that no such doubts ever assailed

Phyllis Waverly. The woman waded in her own river of high
self-esteem, strutting around the store in high-heeled boots
and clingy tops, yodeling friendly hellos to busy contractors.

And you had to give her this: none of her male customers
looked anything but pleased when she swung her ample backside around a counter to help settle a question about the tile
samples. She combined super-efficient sales technique with
enough gleaming smiles to make people feel clever and special.
And she knew, as they said, the territory; she got the customer
together with the merchandise with no time wasted but no
hurrying either. 'Everybody's go-to gal,' Nicole had called her.
It was easy to see why she got picked to manage the newer
Cooper's Home Stores.

She apologized for being ten minutes late. 'But I'm sure
you can appreciate what a helluva mess I've got on my hands
today.'

'Of course.'

'All the employees are coming to me for advice – what
shall we do about this, how do you want to handle that?
They don't want to bother the kids and there's nobody else.
They all feel like Nicole and me, that the best way to honor
the Coopers is to keep the stores running the same as always.'

'I understand. Thanks for taking the time. This crime is
very shocking and hard to understand, so . . . we're hoping
the people like you who were close to them can fill in some
of the gaps. Can I bring you anything? Soda or ice water?'

'No thanks, I'm fine.' She sat down, sighed, and took off
her dark glasses. Her eyes under their ample make-up looked
red-rimmed and a little puffy – as if she had done some
weeping earlier today. *Now there's a surprise*. Everything
Sarah had heard from the Coopers' children suggested that
the dead couple had cold personalities and very few personal
relationships. So was Phyllis crying over them, or herself?

'Now, Ms Waverly—'

'Oh, please, call me Phyllis, everybody does.'

'OK. Phyllis. Nicole tells me you're the only one who
goes all the way back with this family. Is that true, that you're
the one employee that knows all there is to know about
Cooper's Home Stores and the family that built them?'

'Well . . . yes, I guess . . . certainly if you're just talking about longevity, there's Willy, the maintenance man at the east-side store, and there's me. Both of us go back almost to the beginning. Makes me sound like a duffer, huh?'

'Oh, I can't imagine anyone would describe you as a duffer.' Phyllis licked her lips and smiled, as pleased by the compliment as Sarah had intended. 'But you've had a hand in the success of the stores all along, haven't you? And the business has grown steadily?'

'Yes. That first little one-room store on Grant Road just sold paint and wallpaper. Now it's two warehouse-sized buildings dealing in lumber, tile, glass, carpet – and besides the retail business we wholesale to contractors.'

'Were you working for them when they started?'

'No, I was still in high school then. Lois hired me the day after I graduated.' She sighed, remembering. 'They'd been doing all the work themselves for a couple of years, can you imagine? Open six days a week, and I think they restocked and paid bills on Sunday. Lois said, "I feel like I need a day off." They had an apartment back of the store, and she was pregnant.'

'That would be Tom?'

Phyllis shook her head. 'Nicole. I know, Tom looks older. But Nicole came first, she was twenty-five in November. Tom's a couple of years younger.' She closed her eyes and whispered, 'Poor Lois.' She swallowed and her mouth twitched, as if she might be going to cry some more. But her wide hazel eyes were clear and dry when she opened them.

'I was married for a while myself, to my high-school sweetheart. We divorced after five years,' she said. 'I was always working, trying for a better life. He wanted a better playmate, so he found one.'

'Were the Coopers hard to work for? Is that why you're the only employee who lasted?'

'Well . . . most retail stores have a high turnover. It's hard work, on your feet all day, and the starting pay certainly isn't the best. And then, yes –' she cleared her throat – 'Frank and Lois have always been a hard-driving pair. At Cooper's a ten-minute break meant ten minutes, not eleven.'

'But you didn't mind the pace?'

'No, I guess I'm a little driven myself.'

I think that's a safe guess. 'When did you last see the Coopers?'

'Well . . . Lois, I haven't actually *seen* since . . . let's see . . . early in the week sometime. But we talked on the phone and emailed every day, sometimes five or six times a day.'

'Including this last weekend?'

'Saturday. Not Sunday. I work Sunday, but I'm the only one in top management that does – all the Coopers take Sunday off. They're Catholic, I'm not. I take off Monday. Usually. Not today, obviously.'

'All that talking and emailing every day was about the business?'

'Sure, what else? Oh, you mean were we chums? Did we join a book club or go to movies together or something?' She smiled broadly. 'You didn't know her, huh?'

'Just in the store. I was quite a good customer at the east-side store for a while.'

'Well, if you knew her in the store you knew her as well as anybody did. Lois cared about the business and her family, and that was about it. She had one hobby, quilting with her sister on Sunday afternoons. Well, and Bingo at the church Wednesday night. She did that with her sister too – and slept over at her sister's house after, so she wouldn't have to drive home in the dark.'

'Kind of narrowly focused?'

'Tunnel vision, all the way.'

'All those messages you exchanged, were they pleasant? Or was she on your tail about a lot of things?'

'Not mine. She could be rough with employees who screwed up, but I knew how to please her. She was a hound for details, I suppose everybody's told you that? She wanted answers, fast. And not just stats, but "what do you think of this? How is that working . . . ?" Thought all the time about the business, never stopped.'

'Do you remember the last message you got from her?'

'Let's see.' Phyllis recrossed her legs and thought. 'Saturday afternoon about quarter to six, she called and said, "What's with blush all of a sudden?" I said, "You mean somebody's embarrassed, or are you talking about the color?" and she said, "The color, why does everybody want it this week?" I said,

"Lois, how many orders have you got for blush?" She said, "One yesterday and one today. We can mix the paint, but we don't stock tile in that color. I had to special order it." See, two orders, that couldn't just be a coincidence, that might be a trend, and we'd be way behind the curve if we didn't climb right on top of it, tell people about it, sell the hell out of it. *That* was Lois Cooper.'

'So, a little obsessed?'

'Fair to say.'

'But you were used to it?'

'Totally. Lois and I,' Phyllis said, with a smug little smile, 'got along like two turtle doves.'

'Was anybody in the stores bearing a grudge?'

'Not that I know of. In the east-side store you either got along with Lois or you were gone.' She tapped her glossy nails on Sarah's desk a few times. 'She was right, too. Consistent service has been the biggest reason for Cooper's success.' After a couple of heartbeats she gave a funny little half-laugh and added, 'And besides Lois liked being in charge so much she probably couldn't stop even if it was bad for business.'

Sarah turned a page in her notebook. 'Was Frank as focused on the business as his wife?'

Phyllis Waverly stared into the middle distance for a few seconds and her lips moved a couple of times before she answered.

'In a different way. They both liked being in charge but they went about it differently. She just did the chores, one day at a time. He was always thinking ahead, innovating. Didn't want to be bothered with store-keeping routines any more, wanted to talk about was the next big thing.'

'You saying he wanted out?'

'What? No! He wanted to be a tycoon! A mover and shaker.'

'Well, he was getting there, wasn't he?'

'Yes. He was on several boards and a city planning commission and so on.' She uttered what was evidently meant to be a good-natured chuckle. 'Which left him plenty of time to keep three women busy!' Sarah watched, fascinated, as Phyllis Waverly described her dead boss's brilliance. 'He got about three more bright ideas every day than we could possibly get around to trying.' *Is she composing her funeral tribute?* 'Always wanted the latest hot thing in the store. Then Lois and Nicole and I had to figure out the details – how to display it, advertise it, turn a profit on it. You know how easy it is to go broke selling Corion if you don't keep your staff trained?'

'No, I'm afraid I—'

'Or how hard it is to get everybody who works in two big stores to say the same thing about granite countertops? And about the time we'd get granite moving smoothly, Frank would waltz in with a new salesman and say, "Enough about that, come and look at these samples of slate."' She stopped suddenly and favored Sarah with an intensely sincere look. 'Please don't think I'm complaining. I don't mean to speak ill of the dead.'

'I understand. You're saying he could be quite demanding.'

She chewed her lip a few seconds and said, 'I'm saying he was just a remarkably energetic guy.'

'OK. And the business prospered from all that energy?'

'Oh, you bet.'

'Did the relationship prosper too?'

'Well, it wasn't always . . .' She stopped, took out a tissue, and wiped sweat off her upper lip. She looked as if she'd just had an alarming thought. Sarah waited, but after a couple of seconds Phyllis took a deep breath finally and said, calmly, 'Naturally, with two people as different as Frank and Lois . . . they didn't always agree.'

'Nicole told me her parents fought a lot.'

'Fought is maybe a little . . . harsh. They argued.' She thought about it and added, 'More lately, of course. Because of the proposed expansion.'

'You mean the Phoenix store?'

'Yes. Frank wanted it badly and Lois was determined to stop him.'

'How did you feel about it?'

She shrugged. 'Ready to swing with whatever they decided, of course. But I was hoping it would fly because I was slated to manage it.'

'Would you be surprised to learn Frank Cooper killed his wife?'

'What? Of course I'd be surprised.' Phyllis sat up straight,

staring. 'Is that what you're thinking? I haven't heard this
before!'

'It's one possible theory.'

'My God! You're suggesting Frank killed – really? What
makes you think . . . well, I suppose you can't tell me.'

'If he did kill her, would you expect him to commit suicide?'

'I wouldn't *expect* any of this, it all sounds *crazy* to me.
I thought you were going to tell me something was stolen
from the house. Have you looked into that? I thought you'd
ask me . . . you know . . . who I thought might have been in
their house when they came home and . . . have you checked
all that? Are any of the locks . . . ?'

'We haven't found any evidence of forced entry. Is there
somebody you're suspicious about?'

'Well, no . . . nobody in particular. But this is Tucson, after
all, aren't we always reading about break-ins? And the drug
thing, you know, people who . . . but you haven't finished
your investigation yet, have you?'

'No. It's still in the preliminary stage. And there could
have been someone else in the house. Who else had keys
besides the family?'

'The housekeeper. Rosa something? I don't know who
besides her, why don't you ask the kids?' It was the second
time she'd called them that. Her attitude would need a little
retooling if she was going to be working for them.

'You never got a key? To water the plants when they trav-
elled or . . . ?'

'Didn't water any plants, didn't feed any cats. Don't do
windows. I was a clerk and then a manager – I was never a
servant.'

*Ooh, touchy. Who hasn't been giving this woman enough
respect?*

'Apart from the business, was there any other reason he'd
want to kill her?'

'Well, I wouldn't know anything about *that*.'

'You didn't share any confidences with Lois or Nicole?'

'Confidences?' She looked at Sarah with something like
distaste. 'I wasn't a friend. I was just the paid help.' She considered the ceiling for a few seconds. 'You can work a long
time in somebody's store without really knowing them.'

Her eyes came down from the ceiling and landed on Sarah
like two hazel searchlights. 'But as far as I know, Frank
didn't have any more reason to kill his wife now than he's
ever had. And they'd been married over thirty years. They
worked together for the last twenty-seven, raised two children and put them to work in the business. Doesn't that
sound like a successful marriage?'

'Yes. And you're sure the business was doing all right?
Nicole said some of the bankers thought it should be showing
more profit.'

'Oh well . . . bankers.' She pushed some of her bright hair
off her face and turned into a corporate booster. 'This firm
is very successful. Even last year when so many stores went
out of business, Cooper's showed a small profit.'

'I hear you.' Sarah decided to touch where she thought
there might be another sore spot. 'Will you be working for
the children now?'

'Well.' Her arms and legs became restless. After some
switching around she said, 'Nicole's a tiger for work. I think
she'd like to keep the stores, if she can.'

'Would you be pleased if she did? Does she have enough
experience to run such a big business?'

'Oh . . . I think . . . with the right kind of help, yes. She's
been at it all her life.'

'And you'd like to stay and be the right kind of help? You
wouldn't mind working for Nicole?'

'For . . . with . . .' She rocked both hands. 'I think we can
work something out.'

'How about Tom? Would you be happy with him as a
boss?'

She shrugged, flouncing and tossing her head the way a
woman does when she doesn't want to answer. 'He's never
done much merchandising, so I don't see . . . I don't know
what part he would play.'

'So you don't have any impression about his work?'

'Everybody says he takes care of the family money. That
doesn't – I don't know anything about that.'

'Do you expect him to take a more active role in operations now?'

'I don't know anything about that either.'

'Do you anticipate a power struggle now between the siblings?'

'Oh, no, no.' She waved dismissively. 'Nicole and Tom are fond of each other.'

They are? Phyllis must have seen something I missed. Of course, since Phyllis's career now depended on the goodwill of the two remaining Coopers, she wasn't likely to say anything damaging about them, even if she knew it.

She checked her list of questions, found one she hadn't asked. 'Do you own any firearms?'

'No.'

'Oh? Nicole said her father went through a stage of insisting that she and her mother ought to keep a gun and learn to use it. He didn't try to get you to carry?'

'Oh, he suggested it. Even offered to buy one for me and pay for the training. I didn't want to do it, so I refused.'

Sarah's interview summary read that Phyllis seemed ambivalent about Tom Cooper, friendly toward Lois and Nicole, and almost ready to write Frank's eulogy.

It was odd, she thought, looking over her interviews, how opaque the Cooper family appeared. They had lived a very public life as successful Tucson merchants for a quarter of a century, yet their personal relationships seemed clouded in doubt. It was also interesting that Nicole and her mother, though they protested and evaded, in the end had given in and accepted the guns Frank wanted them to have. But Phyllis Waverly, 'just the paid help', had said, 'I didn't want to do it, so I refused.'

She was beginning to be glad it was Leo Tobin's case. She turned to her last report, the interview with the Coopers' housekeeper.

Rosa Torres had come to the station late Monday afternoon, clinging to her husband's arm. He walked her into the lobby, stayed with her until Sarah came down to fetch her, and told Sarah he would wait right there till she returned. His look implied, 'And when I see her again she had better not be crying'. His wife was only a few hours out of the hospital and he was deeply worried about her, he said, because Rosa Torres was not in the habit of giving way to hysterics.

Upstairs, in Sarah's little workspace, Rosa said he was

right about her. 'I never cried like that before in my life.
Even in those tough times when I was a widow with two
little kids, I never lost my nerve like that.'

Looking at her plain brown face, her straight dark hair
gone mostly to gray and pulled back in a bun, Sarah believed
her.

'But coming into that nice house the way I always did on
Monday morning . . . and finding them there in the hall – so
much blood. I'm sure I screamed, but you know how far
apart the houses are there . . . nobody came. I wanted to run
but at first I was too scared to move. When I found enough
nerve I ran outside as fast as I could go.'

'That was very brave of you.'

'I sure didn't *feel* brave. I ran screaming to the house next
door and got the neighbors to call the police. Good thing
they knew who I was. Strangers wouldn't have let me in –
I must have looked crazy by then. That Mrs Cramer was so
good to me, put a blanket around me and held my hand till
the police came. She was shaking too. I mean, we didn't
know if maybe the people that did this were still in there.'

'I spoke to the officers who took the call. They came as
fast as they could.'

'I'm sure they did, but . . . no offense, it felt like an hour
to me. Even so, I was pretty well calmed down by the time
those detectives came to question me. But then telling them
about going in there . . . something about going over it again
made it more real to me and I just couldn't *stand* it, you
know? Those two hard-working people that have been good
to me so many years . . . and somebody to just come along
and . . .' Her face twisted. 'It was so ugly.'

'I know.' Sarah waited a couple of ticks. 'Are you all right
now?'

'Yes. I want to go right ahead with this, OK? Don't want
to keep him waiting down there.'

'I'll try to be quick. First tell me, did you always come
to work that early?'

'Just on Monday. Last year when Enrique got put on four-
day weeks, he said, how about you take Mondays off too
and we'll work in the yard that day? He had an idea for a
container garden he wanted to try. He's so good to me I

don't like to refuse him anything, but then Lois, when I told her, was very unhappy. Monday's the day we clean up after the weekend, she said, I like the house squared away on Monday. And what Lois likes, you know . . .' She stopped, took a deep breath and shook her head.

'I keep saying it that way. *Likes*. I still can't believe she's gone. Such a strong woman, you know, and stubborn, never quit talking till she got her way. That sounds like somebody you wouldn't like, doesn't it? But Lois and I got along fine. She valued my work, she always gave me my due.'

'So you worked it out about Mondays?'

'Yes. She said, "We go to work at five on Monday so why can't you?" I wouldn't do it for anybody else but . . . all these years, you know, and they pay me good. So I been going to work a few minutes after five on Monday mornings. It's a little crazy but it works out. By eight thirty or nine I'm done, Enrique and I go have second breakfast someplace and still have the rest of the day for the yard.'

'That must be some yard.'

'You'd have to see it to believe. He's a wizard with plants, that man of mine.'

Rosa told her about coming to Tucson, a legal immigrant, just married, thirty-four years ago. 'We rented a room . . . thought we was rich when we both got jobs and moved into two rooms.' They had two toddlers, and were hoping to rent a house soon, when he was killed in a traffic accident.

'Me and my kids was very hard up for a while after that, lived in one room and ate very skimpy. I couldn't find work because I couldn't read English yet.' A tiny shrug. 'Couldn't read Spanish much better. I got a friend to read the "help wanted" ads for me, the day Lois Cooper advertised in the paper for a housekeeper.' She mused. 'Just luck. That job with the Coopers saved my life.'

One reason it went as well as it did, she said, was that her children and Lois Cooper's were about the same age. 'So even though we were crowded, I managed to take care of her kids and mine in that first little apartment behind the store on Grant Road. Did the laundry and cooking back there too while she ran the store out front.

'All those years of work, you know . . . we was never

friends, but in some ways Lois Cooper and I understood each other better than we did anybody else.'

'Did she enjoy her children?'

'Nicole she was proud of but kind of strict, expected perfection. Tom, oh my, he was her baby and he could do no wrong.

'After they got the big store and moved to the house they got now in Colonia Solana, by then all the kids were in school and for a while I cleaned Lois's house and two other big ones in that same part of town. Then I got lucky again and met my second husband. Enrique Torres, the man you met downstairs. He was good, treated my kids like they was his own. When he got on steady with the power company he said, "Why don't you take it a little easier now?" So since then I just do Lois's house two days a week and Nicole's every other Thursday. Well, and Tom's little place near the university, that don't take much time.'

'No cooking any more?'

'They mostly all eat out now. And they're gone a lot on weekends, all but Lois. She spends most of her free time at church or her sister's house, I think.'

Sarah said, 'There's some evidence to suggest that her husband killed her and then himself. Do you think that's possible?'

Rosa raised her shoulders, then her arms, and turned her hands up – a three-stage shrug that said life had become too incredible for words. 'Since this morning I am not sure what is possible.'

'Sure. But . . . you knew them a long time. Everybody says they fought—'

'Argued. They disagreed, as married people will.'

'OK. Did they disagree enough to want to kill each other?'

Rosa Torres watched her toes sadly for a few seconds before she said, 'Maybe about the boy.'

'The boy? You mean Tom?'

'Sure, Tom. Only boy they got.' After a couple of seconds she said, 'Had,' and her eyes grew bright. Sarah got ready to pass the tissue. But Rosa sat up straighter, sniffed once, and gave her a back-to-work nod.

'Are you saying the arguments about Tom were worse than the ones about the store?'

'Oh, the store.' She dismissed the store with a backhand wave. 'That was just how-to stuff. They both felt the same about the business. It was the center of their lives, and they each wanted to be the boss.' A little sound, almost a laugh. 'Not so unusual. But the boy –' she shook her head – 'Frank wanted him *gone*.'

'Why?'

Rosa shrugged.

'Were they competitive, was he afraid—'

'Competitive?' Her expression was amused for a second and then sad again. 'If only, as my grandchildren say. Nobody told you nothing about Tom yet?'

'Everybody's kind of evasive about him. He says he invests the family money.'

'Yeah. With Lois checking every penny before he makes a move, and Nicole keeping close track of what happens after that. They probably only have to spend twice as much time on it as if they kept him out of it.'

'Then why . . . ?'

'To give him something to do! Because he's a disaster in the store. He's messed up everything he's ever tried. All the employees know, they've always known since he first started trying to "help out" – don't let that Tom help you out, they tell each other, pretty soon you're getting yelled at by Frank for some dumb mistake. And Tom will be hiding at the other end of the store pretending not to know anything about it.

'When Lois saw he was hopeless behind the counter, she made up this nothing job for him and enlisted Nicole to help her keep an eye on it. I'm not sure how much they ever talked about it, they just did it. Because Lois loved him, he was her baby. He never went past the first year of college, couldn't do the work. She saw he couldn't survive in the world outside the stores, so she kept him near her and made it seem as if he was doing something important. You see?'

'Finally,' Sarah said. 'Yes.' *No wonder nobody wants to talk about it*. 'But Frank didn't like the arrangement?'

'He just saw it as a waste of money. Let him go out and find a job like everybody else, Frank kept saying. Maybe it'll wake him up.'

'Does Tom waste a lot of money?'

'Probably not so much. He don't do any good but he don't do much harm either, Nicole sees to that. But Frank was always looking out for Frank. Got so many good things, but always wanted more. Worked his wife half to death, never said a word of thanks. Some kind of a husband.'

'You saying he abused her?'

'You mean beat on her? No. He was just inconsiderate. Like most husbands. I got one of the good ones but I know I'm just lucky.'

'I'd say you're both lucky.'

'I guess. Lois and Frank as a couple I don't think they had much going on for quite a while. Away from work, they spent very little time together. Slept in different rooms. Had their lives arranged so they didn't bump into each other much any more.'

'Did Lois complain to you about him?'

'Never. She had her pride. She had her church. And he gave her the chance to be who she wanted to be, the boss-lady who told everybody else what to do.'

'That's what turned her on, huh?'

'Yes. Well, she was good at it, I guess we all like doing what we're good at.'

'So you think things were basically OK between them except for their son?'

'And if they argued for a hundred years,' Rosa Torres said, 'they would never have agreed about Tom.'

'OK. I know you don't *know* whether he killed her, but I'm going to ask the question in a different way: in your opinion, *could* he have done it?'

Rosa watched the ceiling fan for a few seconds. 'I suppose it's possible.' Her hard-worked brown hands found each other and nested in her lap. 'Killing himself afterwards, though –' she gave a couple of tiny thoughtful shakes to her head – 'I can't imagine Frank doing that.'

'I'm very grateful to you for coming in, Rosa,' Sarah told her when they said goodbye. 'Will you keep my card and call me if you think of anything else? You've helped me understand a lot.'

'Well, like it or not,' Rosa said, 'housekeepers know where all the dirt is.'

*   *   *

Finally, at a few minutes before five on Tuesday afternoon, Sarah hit 'save' and added her reports to the Cooper case file. The minute the screen faded she started the multitasking that always closed her day now, neatening her desk with one hand while she dialed her house with the other, to ask her mother if she should stop at a store for anything. Aggie drove in from Marana every weekday afternoon to be at Sarah's house in midtown when Denny got home from school, to share a snack while Denny vented the first windy blast of grade-school angst or triumph. Then Denny would start on her interminable fifth-grade homework and her grandmother would start dinner. Aggie was filling holes in Sarah's budget, too, buying school supplies and clothes. They were in league to rescue Denny, the child Sarah's drug-befuddled sister had left stranded four months ago, when her addictions claimed her.

The arrangement had some hidden costs Sarah hadn't anticipated. Normally a neatness freak, now she bit her tongue as she watched her house sliding out of her control. She told herself she always found the mixing spoons eventually and it didn't really matter how anybody stacked the dishwasher. She wasn't overdrawn at the bank today and Denny was getting through fifth grade. *Close enough, call it success*. It helped that Denny was bright and able and determined to make it work.

It also helped that Sarah's new boyfriend was steadfast and handy with a hammer. Aggie had said more than once that she thought Will Dietz 'looked like a keeper'.

Which he certainly did if only she had space for him. But having already shoehorned Denny into her little duplex, it was all she could do to make space at the table for Will when he came to hang out for a couple of hours ahead of his night shift. Dietz's other obstacle was Denny, whose default reaction to boyfriends was that they should all be drowned in a sack. In an effort to show her that not all boyfriends were like the ones her mother had brought home, lately he was teaching her the many uses of his Dremmel tool. He had noticed, he told Sarah, that Denny liked to learn useful skills.

'Burke's.' There he was now, answering the phone like one of the family. 'Aggie got feeling kind of rocky about an hour ago,' he told Sarah. 'She's been resting on your bed for a while, and as soon as she feels a little better I'm going to drive her home. She thinks she might have a touch of the flu.'

'Bummer. What about dinner, you want me to pick up some deli?'

'Fret not,' he said, sounding amused. 'Denny remembered there's a big can of chili in the cupboard and we're baking some potatoes to go under it.'

'Now there's a creative menu. You two are turning into the little kitchen crew that could.'

'Hell on wheels with a can opener. You on your way?'

'I am. Be there in fifteen minutes, if the traffic gods are smiling.'

They weren't smiling much in midtown Tucson at five o'clock. But Sarah knew all the side streets that kept her out of major bottlenecks, so she was two minutes ahead of her ETA, thinking about a green salad to offset the chili, when she pulled under the carport.

Denny was frowning at her math problems under the light. Dietz had thought of green salad on his own and was standing at the end of the kitchen counter, wearing her big red apron over his clean shirt as he diced a cucumber on the cutting board. His shift with the night detectives ran from ten to six. Sarah sometimes worried that the chores he took on at her house left him chronically short of sleep, but he claimed he did fine on five or six hours.

Sarah walked into her bedroom to change and found Aggie lying under a quilt, looking grey-faced and exhausted. Her try at a cheerful hello came out a gravelly croak.

'Some bug's gone and bit you, huh?' Sarah locked her weapon and badge in the wall cupboard by the door, walked over and sat on the bed. 'I'm so sorry. Are you feverish?' She put a hand on her mother's forehead and felt the first stirring of alarm. Aggie was clammy and cold.

'Will says he'll drive me home. I'll leave my car here and Sam can give me a ride back tomorrow.' Aggie swung her legs over the side of the bed, but then sat still, staring dully at the floor, looking beat.

'I wonder if you should go home,' Sarah said. 'I'd kind of like to keep you here and feed you chicken soup.'

'No, no. You're crowded enough. I'll be fine.' She stood up and tottered toward the bedroom door. Passing the mirror, she smoothed her hair and made a face. 'God, I do look like death warmed over, don't I? It's not as bad as it looks, honest.'

Dietz put down the knife and watched Aggie walk out of the bedroom. 'You feeling any better?'

'Some,' Aggie said, not sounding any better at all. 'Listen, though, if I have to leave my car here, maybe it ought to go in front of Sarah's . . .' The last three words came out slurred, on three deepening notes like a hand-cranked phonograph winding down . . .

Luckily, Dietz was quick. He got across the room in time to help Sarah catch her mother as she fell.

FOUR

The second time Victoria Nuñez set out for Tucson, she was holding hands with a thin young man named Jaime Sandoval. He was nineteen years old, with glossy black hair, a good start on a mustache and a macho swagger.

She had found him by accident, when she walked past a glass-blower's workshop and happened to glance inside. Watching the way he fetched a glowing nugget of molten glass to his uncle's blowpipe, she decided he might be the one she was looking for. He was taller than the other apprentices and more suave in his movements; he looked about ready to take his place on the pipe and start making the blue-rimmed glasses himself. His confident posture when he transferred his dangerous dollop to the blower's pipe, and the resentful way the older man watched his work, told Vicky that this apprentice was not perfectly adjusted to waiting his turn at the glass factory.

She watched while he made his next trip from furnace to pipe, making certain she was standing in his line of sight. During the short interval after he poured out the bubbling mixture, while he stood waiting to see if he was needed to catch any overflowing drops, Vicky brushed a stray hair back from her eyes with a gesture that let her sleeve fall back from her bare arm. The apprentice looked across his uncle's glowing pipe and their eyes met.

That night during her clockwise promenade around the plaza with her cousins, she saw the handsome apprentice walking counterclockwise, and smiled. As their paths converged, he smiled back. By their third circuit he had reversed course and was walking with Victoria, laughing and taunting, while the cousins trailed behind.

His name was Jaime Sandoval. He knew very little English and Vicky's Spanish verbs wandered uncertainly amongst the tenses. But they had understood most of what they needed to know about each other during their first exchange of

glances, and a band was playing, so with smiling and shrug-
ging and this glorious flirtation of the eyes, who needed a
lot of talk?

Jaime knew who she was, he had heard about the
'Americana' newly arrived from Tucson. During a couple of
nights of strolling, while her mother and aunts looked on
from a nearby bench, he told her how excited he was to be
near her. He said she was not like the local girls.

'You are very different,' he said, '*muy interesante.*' She
was bolder and more direct than the girls he usually walked
with. He asked her, 'Is this how girls behave in *el norte?*'
Soon he was talking about how much more *interesante* this
friendship could become if they were ever alone.

What a dork, Vicky thought. But she looked up at him
through her eyelashes like girls in the movies, and said,
'Perhaps when we meet again you will tell me a little more
about yourself.'

He used two circuits of their next stroll for an intensely
boring recital of his family relationships and his promised
future in the glass factory. 'Unless, of course,' he added, making
fun of it but not entirely disavowing the dream, 'Hollywood
calls me first.'

Vicky told him he was better looking than many of the
boys she knew in Tucson who were studying for an acting
career. Actually most of the boys she knew in Tucson were
studying the hand signals of the gang they were trying to
get into, but the story she told worked better for Jaime. On
their third time around the *paseo* Jaime began to beg for her
mercy – he was going mad, he said, with the pain of his
longing for her. He told her she was doing great damage to
his poor *corazon*.

Vicky pointed out that her mother and both her aunts were
nearby, and so very vigilant. But perhaps, at the darkest point
in the plaza, by that biggest azalea bush . . . they ducked
behind the blossoms for a couple of passionate kisses. Jaime
was ready to consummate his love right there on the cold
stones beside the bandshell, but Vicky pulled him back into
the light before Marisol and Yolanda, deep in conversation
about the cruelties of Yolanda's employer, had noticed their
absence.

Their brief embraces so consumed Jaime's attention that
the next morning he nearly incinerated his employer, with
an awkward spill that barely missed the old man's foot. A
delighted huddle of tourists enjoyed watching as Jaime's boss
spat rage at this worthless *sonso*, this quivering *idiota*.

By the next night's *paseo*, Jaime protested that he had suffered
enough. He had declared his love, should he not be granted a
little consolation? They should sit down and talk a while, Vicky
said, she was very fatigued after a hard day's work. She chose
a bench under a bright light in full view of their elders, where
they held an intense and candid conversation, mostly whispered. Her most urgently repeated question was, *'Comprendes?'*
She wanted to be sure he understood what to buy at the drug
store. If what he really wanted was trips to heaven – his expression told her he understood that part – he must be sure to buy
the right things at the drug store.

Even so, it was not an easy conversation. *'Que?'* he kept
saying, *'Que necesitas?'*

She was not experienced at seduction. Her suitor was
equally naive and, she realized with dismay, a little slow.
Then there was the language barrier, and she had to keep
smiling and shaking her head the whole time so Marisol, on
a nearby bench, would think she was still flirting and
protesting instead of calling the shots.

By the time Marisol began signaling time to go home,
Vicky was so exhausted she jumped up at once, cried, *'Adios!'*
and trotted to her mother's side pretending to be too shy to
look back. But she was pretty sure, by then, that the glass-
blower's apprentice understood that the price of the prize he
sought was Vicky's brand of birth control pills. (Actually
she'd never had a brand before, but she had researched the
subject carefully on the Internet before she left Tucson.
School librarians would have been amazed to see how well
Vicky could work a computer when the information she was
after was important to her.)

There was still a lot to arrange. The one small suitcase
that held everything she owned was on the floor under her
end of the cot. Hiding the pills, swallowing one daily without
Marisol noticing, and keeping them out of the reach of her
many small, marauding cousins was a constant worry. But

all that, she knew, was going to seem like a walk in the park when the time came to get her mother to agree she was old enough, and knew Jaime well enough, to go on a date alone with him. The house they were living in was crowded with people and no part of it was their own. A decent argument was out of the question. And she dared not stage a rebellion until she was sure she had Jaime ready to go.

In the end the laundry came to her rescue. Keeping their few clothes clean and managing an occasional change of bedding was one of the hardest chores for the poor women of Ajijic. Dirty laundry had to be carried to the lake in baskets, soaped and rinsed on the boulders there, hauled home wet and hung up on lines in the yard. It was back-breaking labor, nearly impossible to face after a day at the pottery, groaned over as the most unwelcome task of their Sundays off. There were laundromats in the town but they rarely had coins to spare for them.

Marisol had been doing her share of the laundry since her first week in Yolanda's house. Vicky went along to help when her mother insisted, constantly honing her insults about the 'high-tech sanitation system' in Marisol's home town. But as soon as she had her birth control pills, she began volunteering to do the family laundry by herself. Before long, she was offering to do some for Tía Yolanda too, 'since I'm going,' she'd say, and her mother was proud when Yolanda said, 'Victoria is growing up, no?'

She certainly was. Jaime always met her by the fish taco stand two blocks from Yolanda's house, carried the laundry basket to the lake and helped her hurry through the washing. He got his reward, after a couple of frantic kisses and some fumbling with undergarments, in the back seat of a derelict Dodge behind an auto repair shop two blocks from the lake. He was ardent and new to the game so his climax came quickly, which was all Vicky asked of it.

Carrying the heavy basket of wet clothes back to the taco stand, he would ask her happily if it was good for her too and she assured him that it was '*esplendido, glorioso.*' It was not at all glorious but it was a revelation. She had not realized how quickly a man could be enslaved by the pleasure of sex.

But now that he was her slave, she decided as she hung the wet clothes on the line at home, it was time to move the plan along. The next time they crept furtively out of the old car body and made their way back to the dirt lane that led home, Vicky said, 'Let's sit on this rock and talk a while.'

Jaime said, 'Talk?' Even a novice lover has instincts. 'About what?'

Vicky looked around casually, saw they were not being watched, and put her hand under his shirt, on the side near her, just above his waist. 'Let's talk about fun.'

'OK,' Jaime said, 'but I'd rather do it than talk about it.' He reached for her.

'Wait, wait, wait!' She drew back, moved away.

'For what?'

'We have to be so careful here,' Vicky pouted. 'My mother will stop letting me out alone if anybody tells her I'm meeting you. But what I keep thinking, we could have fun all the time if we were in Tucson.'

'Whoa,' he said. 'You planning a trip?'

'I'd like to. With you.' In a flash, she leaned over and put her tongue in his ear. He groaned and reached for her again.

'Think about it,' she said, standing up. 'We have to go.'

As they walked home carrying the basket between them, he said, 'You really want to go back up there? Why?'

'Think how sweet it could be if we were alone together. And the possibilities for work are endless there.' She knew they were not, but she also knew they were better than here. So the next time they did the laundry she asked, during their quiet post-coital stroll home, 'So, when we going to Arizona?'

'That's kind of dangerous,' he said. 'How about a couple of days in Guaymas?'

'*Oh, por favor.*' She let him see her contempt. 'And then come back here and take a beating from everybody, get fired and grounded? *No, gracias.*'

'Well, what? You talking about really going for it? *El norte?*'

'*Exactamente!*' She put her end of the basket down and danced around him. 'I want a man with the *cojones* to get me over that wall!'

'You are so crazy,' he said, but laughing – it excited him

that his woman, as he now called her, was wilder than the girls he had known.

'This hurts my back so much,' she told him over the soapy shirts on their next trip to the lake. She was tired that night, grumpy. 'I ever get back to Estados Unidos where I can live decent, I am going to kiss the ground.'

'Aye, Querida, why would you kiss that old desert when I am here?'

'I have plenty of kisses,' she said. 'When we finish this rinsing you will see.' She gave him a ravishing hot look like the girls in the movies, and a few minutes later in the Dodge she was pleased to hear him groan.

'Wait till you walk through those big malls they got up there,' she told him on their next laundry day. 'You can buy shoes in a store where they got hundreds of pairs to choose from.'

He looked at her sideways. 'You talking about spending real money now.'

'Anything wrong with that?'

'Only that . . .' He wrung out a garment. 'We have no money at all.'

'We'll make it after we get there, don't you see?'

'*Quizás*,' he said. 'Anyway,' he finally admitted, 'anything would be better than rinsing your auntie's panties twice a week.' He wrung out a pair and held the leg openings up to his eyes like goggles. Vicky laughed so hard she fell into the water.

Pulling her out, Jaime noticed the women at nearby boulders watching them, and hissed, 'Stop laughing, quick.' They finished up silently and packed the basket. As they walked home, slower than usual to give Vicky time to dry off, Jaime said, 'I know a guy named Carlos who says he's thinking of going soon . . . I'll talk to him.'

'You see?' She ducked her head to plant a furtive kiss on a side of his arm. 'Already we begin to have a plan.'

FIVE

'Sarah,' Ed Cokely said on the phone Wednesday morning, 'you got a minute?'

'Just about,' she said. Ed Cokely was an experienced detective and decent guy with a well-earned reputation for telling the longest, dumbest cop jokes in the TPD vice unit. If she let him get started she would never get her desk clear before this afternoon's conference on the Cooper case, so she said, medium-friendly, "Sup?"

'I got this total dickhead in a cell over here,' he said. 'Calvin Inman, you know him?'

'Don't think so.'

'He thought you did. He's been hanging paper all over town.'

Sarah tsked. 'Didn't he get the memo about that going out of style?'

'This guy's retro in more ways than one, wait'll you see him.'

'Why do I need to? He kill somebody who wouldn't cash his check, or—'

'No, he asked me to call you to make you an offer. Because he saw the story in the paper about your box of bones.'

'Shee, my in-box is full of messages about those bones. Why's everybody so hot for bones? I just happened to take the call, Ed.'

'Yeah, well, congratulations, anyway – you got the case that's going to get all the ink. A box of bones is sexy, kid, and it never hurts to get your name in the paper.'

'OK, from now on I'll watch out for bones. What's your paperhanger want?'

'Well, he gets these brilliant ideas, see? Last week his brilliant idea was to plead not guilty and make us take him to court. Because he's sure we can't identify his handwriting—'

'Oh, that's ridiculous.'

'Well, everything he says is ridiculous, but it still takes

up time. But now, today, my little fraudster reads about your box of bones and gets a new brilliant idea. He wants to plead guilty to the check charge and get the sentence suspended in exchange for telling you who's in the box.'

'He just happens to know that?'

'So he says.'

'Maybe you're holding him on the wrong charge, huh?'

'He seems confident he won't incriminate himself if he tells us what he knows. But he won't talk at all till he hears about the quid pro quo.'

'Oh, now I'm excited. I hardly ever get a suspect who speaks Latin. He really said quid pro quo?'

'No, what he really said was "tell me which hole everybody wants fucked and I'll bet I can make 'em all glow."'

'I had to ask. Have you talked to the chief?'

'Out of town. I thought Delaney might be interested in clearing a case faster.'

'What's the quid pro quo for you?'

'I get this tiresome sociopath his reduced sentence, I can move him along to Safford and get him out of my sight.'

'He's not an amusing bandit?'

'Calvin Inman,' Ed said with a windy sigh, 'could get the Pope to campaign for abortion rights.'

'I'll ask Delaney. We do have enough going on here without that box of bones.'

'Yeah, the Coopers and what else?' Ed liked to know the skinny.

'Stash house last week on Camino Seco.'

'Oh, yeah, that was a big one, wasn't it? What was the body count?'

'Two men and three dogs.'

'*Shee*. I bet those dogs are going to be hard to ID.'

'Hang up now, Cokely.'

There was, for sure, plenty to do around the homicide division without wasting any time in a booth with a paper-hanger. But Sarah had promised Cokely, so she went looking for Delaney. He was not in his office and the steno said he had walked out five minutes ago, talking, no surprise, on the phone.

'When is he ever not?' Sarah said, and stood in the hall

a minute, dithering, before she realized she knew what Delaney would have said.

She went back to her desk, called Cokely, and told him that Delaney said the hell with making deals. 'He says we'll get DNA off the bones in that box soon enough, and when we do he's betting the victim has a record as long as your arm right here in the state. He wants me to concentrate on the two double murders we're already working, especially the Cooper case. He says that's the one everybody cares about.'

She was surprised how easy it was to channel Delaney, especially when he was supposedly saying what she wanted to hear.

Cokely said, 'OK, if Delaney doesn't care about the ink.'

'Trust me,' Sarah said, 'Delaney does not care about the ink.' That might have been stretching the truth just a little. Delaney knew as well as anybody that law enforcement lived or died at the pleasure of the public. But he had told her when she started in Homicide, 'Focus on clearing cases and let the publicity take care of itself.' When she heard him say the same thing to Jason Peete later, she realized it was one of his favorite bits of Old Cop Wisdom. So why not use it now to get Cokely off her back? She really did have plenty to do without Ed's bad-check bozo.

She was a little testy today anyway, sleep-deprived, seeing jumpy haloes around the items on her desk and fighting off a headache. She'd stayed at the hospital with Aggie till well past midnight, leaving Denny at home with the door locked. Denny had been a champ, dished up her own dinner and cleaned up after it, had herself ready for bed by the time Sarah called at nine thirty.

Sarah gave her the news that Aggie had had a slight stroke but was resting comfortably now. It helped that they got her to the hospital fast and the ER doc got her on the right blood thinner in a hurry. She was scheduled for more tests and appointments with a couple of specialists in the morning.

Before Sarah went home Aggie had moved both arms and wiggled her toes a little. Sarah left her sleeping and apparently out of danger.

By seven the next morning she was awake, sitting up and talking to Sarah on the phone, her speech only slightly slurred.

'What really makes me feel sick,' she said, 'is the fix this leaves you in.'

'Will you quit worrying about that?' Sarah said. 'You'll make your blood pressure worse. We've got everything covered, we'll be fine.'

Thanks to Will Dietz that was almost true. He'd called just before Aggie, on his way home from his night's work.

'I'll grab some sleep now and be at your house when Denny gets home,' he said. 'I checked this out with Denny last night and she's OK with it.'

'She told me that too. Thanks, Will. Get some sleep now.' They were talking softly, she realized, as if they were actually in the sickroom. Despite her assurances to Aggie about having everything covered, she felt as if she were holding her breath, waiting for the next blow to fall. Seeing unsinkable Aggie collapse had made all the other arrangements of her life seem fragile as spiderwebs.

And Will . . . *how will I ever thank him?* Then she knew very well how she would thank him, wished she could be thanking him right now, and went back to work feeling warm.

An hour later Ed Cokely was back on the phone saying, 'Crafty Calvin's just determined to make a deal with you.'

'Oh? What now?'

'He wants to raise the ante. He says now that he's thought about it, he realizes he not only knows who's in the box, he can also tell you why he was killed. Chapter and verse, with back-up evidence and leads to several other big cases that he knows you have still open. You hear me, Sarah? I'm offering you another crack at the winner's circle!'

'You really want to get rid of this guy, don't you? Hold on.' She put him on hold and thought a few seconds. What if he really had something and she turned it down without asking anybody? She went back on his line and said, 'I'll try Delaney one more time but if he throws rocks at me, I'm holding a grudge.'

Delaney was still not in his office and the steno said he'd left for a meeting with the chief and didn't expect to be back until three this afternoon. After that, she knew, he would not want to talk about anything but the Cooper case.

She dithered again, back at her desk, which by now was

marginally less loaded than usual. Her reports for Delaney's meeting were done, and she'd answered most of the emails. Ed Cokely had helped her get through the soul-eating grind of auto theft division, and she liked returning favors, maybe with a little bit over so you always had some markers out there you could call in.

She called Cokely back and agreed to meet him in half an hour at the Pima County Jail on West Silverlake. By the time she got there he already had Calvin Inman in the interview room.

Inman was a little more colorful than Cokely's description had led her to expect: a small, pot-bellied man with a carefully tended head of dark wavy hair and an ornate Van Dyke mustache and beard. The mustache was especially flamboyant, full and bushy, with the ends carefully curled up. From the shoulders up he looked like a Rembrandt portrait. From there down he was a pear-shaped loser in an orange jailhouse jumpsuit and flip-flops.

He rang some distant bell in Sarah's mind, but she couldn't place it until he turned his bright, urgently searching gaze on Cokely and demanded, 'Now, is Sarah authorized to deal? Because I'm not giving out any free samples, y'know.' He followed that ridiculous burst of arrogance with a nervous little grooming motion on his soul patch, and abruptly she remembered where she had seen him last.

'Calvin Inman.' She sat back with a satisfied smile. 'Of course. How could I forget you?'

'Well, you've certainly changed since I saw you last.' He peered at her badge. 'Detective Burke, is it now?'

'Yes. It's been a while, I was Officer Decker when we met before.' She told Cokely, 'I pulled him out of a bar on East Speedway one night about ten years ago. The bartender called 911 and said his customers were about to kill a guy and he was damned if he'd lift a finger to stop them.'

'Calvin did something naughty?'

'He moved in with a group that had a lot to drink and started picking up their change. The one who wasn't as drunk as the rest noticed and blew the whistle. His buddies picked up this little dandy by his too-tight three-piece suit and pinned him to the wall with kitchen knives.'

She remembered how pasty-faced scared he had looked hanging on the wall. Other details came back to her: the thread that dangled from the lost button on his right sleeve, the way he kicked his badly scuffed wing-tips at three feet of empty air. 'By the time I got there they were using him for target practice. They'd started with bar glasses but the man at the end of the line had a heavy glass ashtray in his hand.' She told Calvin, 'You had a couple more teeth then. Your hair's still nice, though.'

He patted it and said, 'So now I'm supposed to thank you? You had to call for back-up the way I remember it.'

'You were too heavy for me to get off the wall by myself. What have you done this time, Calvin?'

'I haven't done a thing. It's all a mistake.'

'OK,' Sarah said, getting up. 'In that case I'm wasting my time.'

'Well wait, wait, wait.' He twirled the curly ends of his mustache. 'Rather than go to all that trouble and expense in court . . . I have a better idea.'

'Tell me about it.'

'As soon as you promise me immunity.'

'From what?'

'From any of the serious crimes I'm going to tell you about.'

'You have to make that kind of a deal with a prosecuting attorney. I'm just a homicide detective.'

'You're the homicide detective that found that box of bones in the alley, aren't you?' He asked Cokely, 'Is this the right Sarah Burke?'

'Yup,' Cokely said. 'This is the famous Sarah Burke who found the bones.'

'OK, famous Sarah Burke,' Inman said. 'And when I tell you who's in that box I can also tell you who killed him and why, and I bet you can connect that crime with the two dead guys in a stash house on Camino Seco.'

'One thing about you, Calvin,' Sarah said, 'you do keep up with the news, don't you?'

'I make it my business to, yes.' He preened.

'Let's get specific. The crime you want to tell me about is not directly connected to the two dead guys in the stash house, but is involved in the drug trade?'

'Sure. What else is going on in this quaint western village?'

'Large quantities?'

'More than enough to kill for. Obviously.'

Oh don't I wish I could show you how obvious it was, Inman. She sat still and held her breath for a few seconds, surprised by how much she wanted to rub Calvin Inman's smirking face in that dreadful scene, make him acknowledge for once what the carefree self-indulgence of marijuana scofflaws cost this city. The once-attractive bodies of young men and dogs had been sprawled in pools of blood in several devastated rooms of the house on Camino Seco. Trails of their blood showed where bales of weed had been dragged across them and out the door. And just as Sarah was thinking there was nothing more pathetic than a dead animal, Oscar Cifuentes turned over one of the dogs and found something worse – a child's doll, the sequins in its blood-soaked ruffles winking forlornly on the morning light. The whole crew wasted a stomach-clinching hour after that, searching under beds and in all the closets, in the crawl spaces and under a weed-choked porch. They never found a child and finally decided that some lucky girlfriend must have taken her daughter home just in time.

Most of the scene work at the stash house was blood and fingerprints, so once the crime scene units and the narcotics detectives got busy, Delaney's crew was free to canvass the neighborhood. Identification of the victims turned out to be easy – several neighbors knew them well, or had thought they did. Affable young men with big shiny vehicles and high-end sports equipment, what was not to like? Everybody was shocked – such nice young men, who knew? God, right here in the neighborhood, what was this town coming to?

Identification of the guilty parties was going to be tougher. The killers had worn gloves and picked up all their casings.

'Pros,' Delaney said.

All his detectives gave him their 'well duh' look.

'But plenty of people know who did this,' he said. 'Greenaway, it's your case. Keep turning over rocks. Find their family members and girlfriends. Find their car dealers and doctors and lawyers and bank accounts.'

'Sure.' Ollie waved a paid bill he'd pulled out of a drawer. 'Hey, I already found their vet. Case is practically solved.'

The stash house job needled them all into flip remarks like that. It was gross and disgusting and pushed the waste and loss of the drug business right into their faces. There was no satisfaction to be had out of gathering evidence – they could not 'solve' cases like the stash house. The border was where it was; the appetite for drugs was bottomless; other well-built houses would soon be smeared with the blood of clever young men and their blameless, beautiful dogs.

But now here was Calvin Inman, a liar for all seasons, wanting to finger the Camino Seco assassins to bargain his way out of jail. She watched his face as she asked him, 'And you, who did nothing wrong, know about this how?'

Calvin rubbed two fingers of his right hand against his thumb. 'Got to pay to play, Sarah.'

'Detective to you. I've got another meeting to go to in five minutes, Calvin, and I'm trying to decide between coming back here tomorrow with some serious heat to hear your statement, and not coming back ever. So before I walk out that door in four minutes and thirty-six seconds your task is to convince me you're not just blowing smoke.'

Calvin switched his little butt around on the hard round seat, looked imploringly at Cokely. 'Damn, a hard woman's enough to make you cry, ain't she?'

'You think Sarah's hard,' Cokely said, 'wait till you see what I'm going to do to you if you don't convince her.'

'All right.' Calvin Inman puffed up his cheeks and blew a blast of air out, to relieve the intolerable stress of speaking one whole true sentence. 'I'll tell you the name of the person in the box, and that's absolutely all you get till you come back with a signed statement that holds me harmless for the rest of what I have to tell you.'

'Like what?' Sarah kept her eyes on her watch.

'Like how you can prove it.' He leaned close to her face and hissed, '*Like fucking whodunit.*'

'Three minutes and ten seconds,' Sarah said. 'Who's in the box?'

'Chuy Maldonado,' Inman said. Sarah's head came up abruptly. Inman met her eyes and smiled.

'You serious? The Chuy Maldonado who's a close associate of Huicho Valdez and Rafi Soltero?'

'Not as close as he used to be,' Calvin said. 'Does that get me an extra minute?'

'Maybe. Be careful, now, Calvin, I get really cranky when somebody tries to jerk me around.'

'No bullshit, Detective.'

'You're really talking about Chuy Maldonado, the well-known drug smuggler whose family claims he's been missing for quite a while and they have no idea where he is, so we all figured he had voluntarily deported himself?'

'That's the fella.'

'Uh-*huh*.' Sarah met Ed Cokely's eyes and sighed. 'Why do I answer my phone all the time? From now on I'm just going to let it ring.' Her headache was gone, though. She leaned across the small table toward the improbable little poser in the orange suit. 'I really do have to go to a meeting, now, Calvin. I'm going to try to persuade a guy I know at DEA to come back with me tomorrow and see what he thinks. If you've got what you say you've got, it's worth a deal, no question. Be ready to tell him some very convincing details.'

'I promise you, Detective, you won't be sorry.'

'I'm already sorry. I wish I never had to see you again. The only question is, are you going to make me look bad to my friends in the federal agency?' She stood up, patted her Glock a couple of times and told him, 'I never forgive a guy who does that.'

Calvin shook his head sadly. 'Jesus, Sarah, your job's turning you into a regular Nazi, you know that?'

'Remember that,' she said. 'Keep it firmly in mind.'

As she walked out with Ed Cokely she said, 'I really do have a meeting. I'll call you as soon as I see who's interested. I think Delaney's going to be glad to offload the box of bones. If DEA will take the case there'll probably be some kind of a deal in there for Inman.'

'Thanks for coming over, Sarah. Ain't he a piece of work?'

'Here's a mystery for you: why do people cash his checks?'

'I guess they like his facial hair.'

'It is pretty special.' She stood looking out at the sunshine, wishing so many beautiful days didn't have to be hurried through. After a thoughtful minute she said, 'You don't often see the non-violent ones cross over, though, do you? How do you suppose Calvin the fraudster got into the big-time drug trade?'

'With fear and trembling, I would guess,' Cokely said. 'Somebody had him by the short and curlies and made him do an errand.'

From the terrible moment when her grandmother's voice went deep and creepy and she toppled into Aunt Sarah's arms, Denny Lynch had been getting ready to see her own life get stuck out in the weeds again.

It was a little over four months since her mother went postal in a grocery store parking lot, and she'd come to live with Aunt Sarah. Less than half a year of getting used to clean clothes and regular meals, homework done on time and grades going up.

She knew it came at a price. Right from the get-go she could see that the three of them – Aunt Sarah, Grandma Aggie and her – if they made lists, left plenty of notes, always told the truth quickly and did exactly what they'd promised to do right on time, they could just about make it through the days. The two grown-ups didn't talk about it in front of her, but Denny had been practically on her own the last year in her mother's house, so she knew what food cost and how much work went into keeping clean. Lately she'd noticed that Grandma's answers got sharper when she was getting tired. And she understood why a nerve twitched in Aunt Sarah's jaw when she arrived home still thinking about the work left on her desk.

Denny tried not to be a pest, did chores and homework without being told, got ready for bed on time. Even so, she knew that taking her in without notice had caused Aunt Sarah major overload. Her mother had complained plenty about how hard it was to be a single mom, and homicide detectives worked some crazy hours. Aggie never complained but Denny knew coming in from the 'burbs to help every day had disrupted her grandmother's retirement, big time.

But there was only one other place for her to go: to the ranch where Mom and Aunt Sarah grew up. She liked the animals and there was plenty of room in the house, unlike here where she was crammed into one end of her aunt's bedroom. Uncle Howard tried to be kind. But lying upstairs in the ranch house, twisting in shame, she had more than once heard his wife tell him how much she resented having his sister dumping her kid on them 'like I'm some free babysitting service.' Aunt Barbara gloomed up just watching Denny walk in the door, sighed over the extra laundry, talked about family plans that did not include her. Her daughters, who had known from their cradles where Denny stood in the pecking order, gleefully whispered private jokes and left her out of their games.

So even though life in a single hard-up detective's house was crowded, subject to jolting phone calls at weird hours, and scheduled to the tooth-gritting minute on school mornings, Denny was glad to be there and wanted to stay. It was worth doing a lot of chores to live with Aunt Sarah, who was smart and thought she was a cool kid, and with Grandma Aggie, who adored her and was often quite funny.

What she hadn't realized at first, as she stowed her socks and underwear in shoe boxes under the cot behind the curtain, was that Aunt Sarah had the one thing Denny despised most in the world, a boyfriend. Not that her aunt ever called him that; she referred to Will Dietz as 'my friend', and never flirted and giggled with him the way Mom did with men she brought home. And Denny had to admit, he didn't come with beer and pot like her mother's leering boyfriends, to sprawl all over the kitchen getting wasted and scaring you half to death.

Will Dietz was just kind of a spooky cop, smallish, with a very quiet voice and odd scars. Aggie told her he'd been caught in a gun fight between thieves and almost died. Denny thought he hadn't quite recovered yet. Some days he seemed to have nothing to say, just came in and read the paper, hung out for an hour or two before his night shift. Good days he peeled potatoes or repaired something, or went out for milk – he was Aggie's main man for grocery runs. At first Denny wondered whose boyfriend he was, actually – Aggie was the one who was always saying how clever he was, so handy with tools.

But before long Denny noticed how he looked at Aunt Sarah, as if he thought she was some wonderful gift that just dropped from the sky. That was the one truly comical thing about him, Denny thought, since Aunt Sarah had her feet on the ground if anybody did; she always knew where she was and what time it was. You would never catch Aunt Sarah looking into the refrigerator, as Aggie sometimes did, asking, 'What am I looking for in here?'

On the terrible night when Grandma Aggie fell down, even Denny was grateful Will was there. He helped catch Aggie, called the ambulance right away, and had been helping everybody in the house ever since. Trying to take Aggie's place, Denny thought. *As if.* She was almost over being scared of him, but that didn't mean she was crazy about having him around all the time, and he would certainly never take Grandma's place. But at least he got Aunt Sarah to quit fretting about Denny being alone in the house after school, and it was handy when he picked her up after soccer practice. Denny couldn't figure out when he slept.

He had just left to go to work Tuesday night when Aggie called from the hospital to tell them that her doctors said her stroke had been very slight. 'Just a little wake-up call to get me to lay off the butter.' She'd be out in a day or two, she said, and they could all get back to normal. Aunt Sarah closed the phone and repeated the message, smiling. Denny smiled back, not saying what she thought, that it would be a while before Aggie got back to the overworked life they had all been choosing to call normal.

The next morning Dietz stopped in after his shift to ask if Denny had everything she needed for school, and should he make a grocery run this afternoon? This strange quiet man had worked all night but he still had enough juice to think about dinner – he asked Aunt Sarah, 'I could boil these potatoes and we could have them tonight with eggs, what do you think?'

'Sounds good,' Aunt Sarah said. 'There's bacon, too.'

'And lettuce,' Denny said. 'I'll make a salad.'

We're all trying to be perfect, Denny thought as she climbed on the bus. Like Mom when she first got out of detox. She remembered her mother's sing-song voice calling, 'Today is the first day of the rest of our lives!' as she waved her off to the bus after a nice breakfast. *And we all remember how long that lasted.*

That was the most discouraging thought she'd had in the whole scary week. She opened her social studies workbook to find something easier to think about, like global warming or AIDS.

SIX

The wall looked taller at night. It had an aura of crazy menace about it too, the bent-toward-Mexico section at the top gleaming in the fierce light from the other side. Below the flanged top, the section they were looking at was made of close-set metal strips painted dirty brown, eighteen feet high and discouragingly smooth. A cleared strip of sand at the foot of the wall was littered with climbers' rubble: plastic bottles, torn backpacks, greasy fast-food cartons and a cracked shoe. A starved-looking cat slunk through the trash, making a meager picnic from the remnants of many lives. Vicky and Jaime and the men he called his *amigos* watched him from the shadows across the clearing. The cat crossed the wall easily whenever he pleased, through small gaps in the foundation.

They had planned in secret for months, working extra jobs when they could find them, saving every peso. When they realized they could never save enough on what they could earn, they began asking friends and family for loans. That was slow-going too – everybody they knew was poor. Finally Vicky, afraid but desperate, persuaded Jaime they should confide in her mother.

They got the expected explosion of protests and warnings at first, but before long Marisol, somewhat to their surprise, agreed to help. She had resigned herself to the fact that Vicky would never be happy in Ajijic. 'Even getting a cute boyfriend like Jaime hasn't made her contented,' she told her sisters. 'Vicky was in Tucson too long. I am afraid she will never feel at home here.'

There was something else, never acknowledged but understood by both mother and daughter. Marisol had begun walking out in the evening with a widower, a skilled potter who had a small interest in one of the shops around the square. She knew he was attracted to her but was afraid Victoria, who already had a local reputation as a cheeky pest, would wreck the peace of his home.

Marisol made one of her rare phone calls to Luz. Usually she cried for a minute or so when she first heard her younger daughter's voice, but this time she was brisker than usual. She told Luz she must ask *La Cruz Rosa* to find Pablo, pleading a family emergency.

'And when you find him,' Marisol said, 'tell him I said it is time for him to carry Victoria to Tucson again.'

Luz didn't want any part of it. 'Please don't make me, *Mamacita*,' she pleaded. 'She will just make trouble for me here, you know she will.'

'No, Vicky has changed,' Marisol said. 'You will be surprised. Anyway you don't always have to have your way about everything, do this for me now.'

Pablo's first inclination was to run and hide when the social worker from the Red Cross found him on the job site and gave him Luz's number. But he had been cut off from family long enough to realize that his freedom carried a high price in loneliness. And while Vicky had always been his favorite daughter he knew that Luz was the one least inclined to rock the boat. If Luz wanted to talk to him, maybe it was serious. He was a little flattered that she would turn to him, and besides, his current girlfriend was beginning to cool toward him. He could sense a separation coming, he might need to seek shelter with cousins himself soon. For these reasons and perhaps simple curiosity, he called the number the social worker gave him.

Tía Luisa answered the phone and told him what she thought of *mujeriegos* who neglect their own children. When she finished her rant she handed the phone to Luz, who heard his voice and began to weep. For a time things were complicated as only families can make them, but by the time the storm of guilt and grief ended Pablo had reluctantly agreed to send money to Marisol in Ajijic, and to stay in touch with Luz so he would be available to help if Vicky made it across the border. Privately, neither Luz nor Pablo thought she had a chance of making it, and after doing what they had promised, they both decided not to worry about it till she showed up.

Vicky never doubted for an instant that she could make the trip. Hadn't her dumb-as-dirt parents done it years ago, without a word of English between them? Well, then. Her assurances gave Jaime the courage to keep asking questions, and collecting used gear for the trip.

They never got enough together to afford a *coyote*. Jaime hooked up with two men named Carlos and Paulo. Friends of cousins, they had made the trip before, insisted they knew enough to make it on their own now, and planned to leave soon.

'Those guides all lie and cheat,' Carlos said. 'You are better off without them.'

Vicky thought that could not be entirely true but she had heard so many different stories by then that she decided you had to pick one set of lies and stick with it.

'Find a good backpack for food and water,' Paulo said, 'and only take one change of clothes. Good walking shoes and a hat. Sew your money into pockets inside your clothes.' They debated every purchase, wanting to save all their money for the trip but afraid not to have the right supplies. Vicky bought a shirt with sleeves that would roll down, to prevent sunburn, and took her sturdiest jeans from the US. Jaime got new sandals and, at the last minute, a small, cheap cigarette lighter shaped like a bobble-headed doll. 'In case we need to light a fire,' he told Vicky when she protested.

'Is the girl strong enough?' Carlos asked Jaime. He would not condescend to talk to Vicky. 'She looks pretty small.'

'I am plenty strong,' Vicky said, giving him the flat-eyed stare she had perfected in the offices of the principals of Tucson schools. 'Don't worry about me.'

She was strong enough to keep up with them – just barely – but Carlos took a dislike to her anyway, and was always looking for an excuse to leave her behind. They rode buses part of the way, so after only three days they were all crouched in the shadows of buildings, facing this terrible wall. It was made out of metal posts set deep into cement, too close together to squeeze through, too strong to cut, and much too high for any sane person to try to climb over. What would be the use, anyway? Towering above it, on the other side, were huge lights that lit the immense clearing beneath them as bright as day. It was patrolled by border agents driving SUVs equipped with sirens and light bars and booming PA systems that roared out warnings to anyone who foolishly put up a ladder and risked his body in a terrible eighteen-foot drop to the other side. While he dropped, waiting for the painful landing he hoped would not break his legs, his picture would be taken by the video cameras on the other ominous towers.

This was not the border crossing she had been led to expect. All during the journey, while they waited for and rode the crowded buses from Guadalajara, she had listened to Carlos and Paulo boast about the many crossings they had made, how they had fooled the border patrol.

'We hire a team of helpers in Agua Prieta,' Carlos told them. Jaime had been listening to him with rapt attention the whole trip, and Carlos was enjoying the admiration, embroidering his tales a little more each day. 'They are very well organized, they have been doing this for years.'

He described how the teams would bring two ladders to the wall. When they reached it the headman would send two men west with a ladder, but keep the crossers with him, in the shadows, watching the wall. When his cell phone vibrated in his pocket, the headman would run and put his ladder against the wall. When he had set the feet firmly, he would motion for Carlos and his team to come up.

The decoy team that had placed the phone call would already be scrambling up a ladder a quarter of a mile west. In a few seconds, the leader of that team would make a great show of getting stuck in the overhang at the top. The man behind him would make a lot of noise trying to get him unstuck. That charade would continue for a minute or two, depending on how long it took the border patrol vehicle to reach them with all its lights flashing. When it got close enough to threaten them, they would climb quickly back down on the Mexican side and carry their ladder home. By then Carlos and his group must be over the wall and running toward the bushes of Douglas, Arizona.

That was the way it was supposed to go. As soon as they got to Agua Prieta and looked at the 'fence', they knew it was not going to happen that way.

Vicky and Jaime napped in the one room they rented, while Carlos and Paulo walked the streets of Agua Prieta, asking people there to explain all the changes that had been made since they crossed a few years ago.

'It is not a fence any more; now it is a wall,' Carlos reported. 'Much stronger than before, taller, set in cement. It used to be mostly just poles and wire. People could cut holes, break it down in spots, you could slip through. No more.'

'We could go through that stinky sewage plant they call The Rose Plant,' Paulo said, 'and jump the fence there, but then we would need a bath and a complete change of clothes before we could talk to anyone or get a ride. Also, sometimes they even patrol the sewer yard and pick up people as they jump the fence. We would have to be lucky.'

'I do not believe in luck,' Vicky said.

Carlos and Paulo looked at her with raised eyebrows, and Carlos said, 'Ah, Señorita Uppity speaks her mind.'

'Well, what then?' Jaime said, trying to keep the peace.

'We walk,' Paulo said. He pointed east, toward New Mexico. 'About ten miles, that way.'

'Over there it *is* a fence, easily crossed,' Carlos said. 'They patrol it, but we start from here in the morning, walk until sundown, rest a while and watch a couple of border patrol vehicles go by. When the stars come out, right after a patrol car goes by we jump the fence, cross the gravel road and run into the desert. We can be out of sight before the next patrol arrives.'

'How do we know which way to run?'

'Follow the trails.' Carlos smiled, bitterly. 'There are many trails, all headed north. Follow the ones that smell like Mexican blood and sweat.'

'All sweat smells the same to me,' Vicky said. She nudged Jaime. 'Let's go eat.' Carlos, she thought, had kind of an itch for drama.

It worked the way he said it would, though. They loaded their backpacks with sandwiches, granola bars and water, and hiked through the desert along the fence. As long as they stayed on the Mexican side they were safe from the border patrol. The only Mexicans around were *coyotes* offering to help them for a fee. If you refused them they might try to rob you, Carlos said, so they tried to hide or run away when they saw small groups of men coming. When one group pursued them aggressively, they each pulled a knife – they all carried knives of some sort – waved it and showed their teeth. Vicky thought they probably looked more ridiculous than dangerous, but it worked – or something did; the group walked away.

She was very tired by the time the sun blazed red above the western hills, and Carlos agreed they had gone far enough. The fence was nearby, on their left – a real fence now, crossed wooden posts strung with wire. All along it, as far as the eye could see, lay the cast-offs of border crossers: worn-out shoes, backpacks with broken straps, water bottles.

They rested in a nearby gully. Vicky ate half a sandwich quickly, lay flat and fell asleep. She was dreaming about being chased by an angry dog when Jaime touched her shoulder and said, '*Vámonos.*' They all walked silently to the fence, crouched in some bushes while a patrol vehicle went by, and then scrambled over. It was astoundingly easy. Vicky's heart beat fast. Back to Tucson at last!

She thought she had never seen so many stars. She was thirsty but drank sparingly, having no idea how long her water must last. Douglas lay just over the western hills but they had agreed they would not go into town. Many crossers caught taxis there, or phoned family or friends for help – but there was always the danger of being picked up. Vicky had worn the American clothes she had saved for the trip – jeans and a shirt. But the men had Mexican haircuts and mustaches, and wore Mexican sandals on their feet; they would be easy to spot.

They agreed they would walk till they passed the border patrol station. It was miles ahead, somewhere up there along the highway. When they were safely past it, Vicky would use Paulo's cell phone to call Tía Luisa's number, and beg whoever answered to send a ride for them.

Maybe Pablo would come. She had a daydream, never shared with anyone, about a happy reunion with her father. What jokes they would tell! If Pablo had a car by now or could borrow one . . . her new friends would be glad they had brought her along. In fact if her father came with a car, the balance of power would shift at once. She would be the one in charge, and the men would be asking favors from her. That daydream supported her as she walked, very footsore now, north west through the scrubby desert.

It was not an easy, level trail, either – there were hills, and mysterious buildings that could be anybody's, so they had to walk around them. When big vehicles came crashing through the unmarked desert, the four of them sank beside the biggest cactus they could find and tried to stay out of the lights. Dogs barked at them often now, and once there was a snuffling rush through the cactus, some animal that they couldn't see.

Thank you God for making him afraid too. Vicky had never been religious but she had been talking to God, asking for small favors, ever since they ran across the graveled road that paralleled the fence on the US side. They were headed north, she hoped, keeping the car lights on the highway a vague mile or so to their left. She knew she had never been so tired in her life and she was beginning to be very afraid of what would happen to her if she became too exhausted to walk any further. She knew Carlos and Paulo would leave her behind without a thought, and she wished she was certain Jaime would not. She had been sure of him when they left Ajijic, but he admired these new friends now, especially Carlos. Perhaps he would murmur some easy assurance about sending help, and go on without her. She remembered her mother saying, 'Men always just please themselves.' Vicky had forgotten that it was she who had manipulated Jaime into making this journey.

Just when she thought they were seeing the lights of the border patrol station ahead, her worst worries came true. Unknowingly, they had walked across a smooth patch of ground that a border patrol vehicle had made by dragging old tires back and forth. When another vehicle came by a few minutes later and shone its lights on the clearing, their footprints showed up clearly in the denuded earth. Trained eyes followed their track.

When the lights hit the four hikers, they ran, as they had agreed, in four directions. Vicky could barely walk by then, so her gimpy run was pitiful and she was quickly captured. She had to wait, wearing plastic cuffs, with one of the patrolmen while they caught the other three. He insisted she

sit by his feet. She had never been so glad to comply with
an order. The hard part was when the van came bouncing
back over the cactus and she had to get up and climb in.
The patrolmen took them to the temporary border patrol
station by the highway, seated them on a bench under an
awning and fastened their legs to the bench with plastic cuffs.

It was a busy night in the desert. Three more vans brought
loads of prisoners to the shelter. Two groups of men, seven or
eight in each, were crowded in around Vicky and her friends,
filling all the space on the cement slab. A larger group that
came pouring out of two vans had to squat in the dirt outside
the awning, their handcuffs connected by a chain.

Vicky slept through most of the night, sitting up handcuffed, leaning sometimes against Jaime, sometimes against
the half-wall next to the bench. She had made a firm decision in the van, when she saw one of the guards looking at
her, that she must remain alert and look out for herself, but
the night was long on the bench, and she was simply too
tired to stay awake.

When she woke she saw at once how lucky she had been
to be able to sleep. Daybreak made the human misery in the
station clearer. The baby that had been fussing at midnight was
screaming now, and its very young mother, who was out of
formula, looked as if any minute she might scream too. Two
of the women in the large group outside seemed to be debating
the tactics that had landed them here. Repeatedly, monoton-
ously, they threatened to kill each other.

The guards, who were young and impatient and felt badly
outnumbered because they were, began to yell, '*Silencio!*'
at irregular intervals. Their shouting didn't silence anybody
but it did make everybody more anxious, and the baby's
screams grew frantic.

When an almost-full bus taking deportees to the border
stopped at the station, one of the overstressed guards looked
at four empty seats in the back and muttered to his buddy,
'Whaddya say we clear a few of these bodies out of here?'

'Hell yes,' the other guard said, 'Those first four we got
in tonight, they're just crossers, right? Didn't turn up on any
list. Go ahead, put 'em on the bus.'

So in a blurry minute, with hardly a word spoken – the

guards didn't want to start any of the other arrestees yelling to go first – Vicky and her three companions found themselves headed back to Agua Prieta. With no idea what would happen next, Vicky took another nice nap, this time on a fairly comfortable seat.

They were dumped off an hour later and herded into an imposing cinder-block building with a sign that read United States Border Patrol. An enormous American flag snapped in the breeze at the top of a tall flagpole. The parking lot where they unloaded had rows and rows of big, shiny four-wheel-drive vehicles, most of them with cages in the back. Inside, they were led into a vast open space filled with prisoners like themselves, who were milling around a glass-enclosed central core. Men in uniform looked out at them through the glass, and stared into computer screens. They had bored, indifferent faces and expressionless eyes. Uniformed men and women walked among the prisoners, telling them to move here, sit there. Vicky and her friends were separated. On the women's side she was fingerprinted, waited a long time, got some water and two tasteless cookies, and waited another long time.

In early afternoon they were put together again and loaded onto another bus, with a new selection of prisoners. They rode through the town of Douglas, crossed at the border, and were dropped off on a crowded street. Across the road, a steady flow of vehicles crept toward the US, passports at the ready. Documents were destiny here. Paperless, Vicky and her little band stood in wobbly disarray on the sidewalk, blinking.

'Buenos Días,' a voice said, quite nearby. *'Tienes sed? Quieres café? Venga aquí!'* A sweet-faced young woman and a friendly looking man, both gringos, stood a few feet away. Repeatedly they asked, 'Are you thirsty, do you want coffee?'

Suspecting a trap, the undocumented desert rats panicked. Carlos and Paulo stepped into the street, looking for the best escape route. Vicky, who by this time had developed a low regard for the moxie of Jaime's friends, forgot her Spanish entirely, grabbed Jaime's hand and yelled, 'Come on!'

Jaime, perilously close to collapse by now, hung back, croaking, *'Que pasa?'*

The smiling coffee-offering young man, hearing Vicky speak English, met her eyes and said, 'Don't be afraid, it's

not a trap. We're from Frontera de Cristo – right there, see?'
He pointed to a sign. Behind it, on a shaded patio, sat several
tired-looking Mexicans, drinking coffee. A couple of them
ventured small waves.

Carefully, looking all around and still ready to bolt, Vicky
and Jaime went inside. In a small room lined with shelves full
of cotton socks and T-shirts, they drank sweet cold water out
of a cooler, got a cup of great-smelling coffee and a cookie,
and found seats among the other deportees on the patio.

It was a gathering of storytellers. The narratives were
similar, with small variations. A trusted friend told me . . . I
got a ride with a truck-driver delivering . . . family gave me
all the money they had saved for . . . There is a job waiting
for me in Ohio if I could only . . . The quiet voices went on
and on. Finally Jaime asked the man next to him, 'What are
you all waiting for now?'

'We're going to rest here a day,' one said, 'and then try a
different way.'

'You won't go home?'

'I can't go home. There are no jobs there and they gave
me all the money they had. I have to get to Arizona so I can
get a job and pay them back.'

One after another, they all said the same thing: there is
nothing to go back to. And I think I see now where I made
my mistake . . . Next time I'll succeed.

Vicky noticed that Jaime, increasingly silent and with-
drawn ever since they were picked up in the desert, looked
more and more discouraged as he listened. He would not
meet her eyes any more. After half an hour of stories, she
nudged his elbow and nodded her head, outside. He followed
her to the sidewalk and stood looking at his shoes.

Vicky said, 'Tell me what you are thinking.'

'That I wish I was home.'

'Are you serious? You would really go back?'

'I would give anything to be back in Ajijic right now. If
I could get there I would never leave again.' He glared at
her, expecting a fight.

But the desert had humbled her. She understood, now, that
the road north was an all-or-nothing struggle for survival.
Just to stay alive would take all her strength. She no longer

wanted to be responsible for what Jaime decided. 'You got bus fare home?'

'Just about. Close enough.' His eyes were getting brighter. 'You coming?'

'No.'

For a moment, he became her lover again. 'I cannot leave you here alone.'

She almost laughed. She thought she stopped in time, but she saw how his face changed when he saw the contempt in her eyes. As she watched, it set him free.

'I will be fine,' she said. 'Let's go inside and find somebody who knows where you need to go to catch the *camión*.'

While Jaime talked to the men on the patio, Vicky went to the bathroom. She got another glass of water and stood in the small front office drinking it, feeling scared and elated at the same time. Jaime had afforded protection on the trip so far, she would not take that away from him. But she thought she would be freer to explore all the options if she did the rest of this trip alone.

The sweet-faced girl who had stood on the sidewalk offering water was sitting at a desk now, entering information into a computer. They began to talk, idly. She said her name was Dee.

'What is this place?' Vicky asked her. 'Why is it here?'

'Frontera de Cristo is a mission supported by the Presbyterian Church,' Dee said. 'It is just here to help. Having risked everything to cross, the people who get brought back and dumped here are worse off than when they started.'

Vicky shrugged ironically. '*Por segura.*' And then quickly, 'For sure.' She was beginning to understand what the school psychologist in Tucson had meant by 'sudden mood swings'. Listening to the Mexican deportees on the patio, she had felt like an American girl dropped by mistake in the wrong place. But talking to this fresh-faced gringo girl, she found she had cycled back into a Mexican.

'So we give them water and coffee,' Dee said, 'a little food when we have it. Some have worn out their shoes and socks, so we try to keep some of those on hand. Mostly we give them a safe place to rest and decide what to do next.'

'You work here full time?'

'I'm a volunteer, I don't get paid. In another month I'll
go back to school at the University of New Mexico.'

'Ah. Lucky.' Vicky had always rebelled against the discipline of school and never spent a minute dreaming of
college. But now, looking at Dee's clear-eyed self-assurance,
she felt the nibble of a little worm of envy. I could do that
in Tucson, she thought, why not?

She poured another glass of water from the cooler – her
body was still demanding water, after that grueling desert
walk and the long dry wait in the shelter that followed it.
She carried the glass out to the sidewalk in front of Frontera
de Cristo, thinking that as soon as she had said goodbye to
Jaime she would find a chair on the patio and listen a while.
When she decided which ones sounded most experienced
she would start to ask them, *What's next for you? You got a
plan, anybody to call?* She would listen until she heard the
idea that sounded like something she could do. Then she
would rent a room and sleep for many hours. Tomorrow, she
would start over.

She saw Dee moving quietly inside, passing a cup of coffee,
handing out a clean pair of socks and some sneakers to a
man with rags on his feet. I'll need to get a map, she thought.
A crazy line of dialogue came back to her from her months
of movie-watching in her father's chair. *We don't need no
stinkin' maps.* Something like that. The cruel little *bandido*
in *The Treasure of the Sierra Madre*. She looked up, smiling
a little in spite of her dry lips, and saw a slender, handsome
black man standing a few feet away on the sidewalk, smiling
back at her.

'Hey,' he said. 'How you doin', lady?'

Vicky got her face straight in a hurry, and said, '*No hablo
Ingles.*'

'You must understand some. I saw you talking to the girl
in the mission in there.'

Vicky gave him a level, measuring look. 'What do you
want, *Señor?*'

'Now ain't that funny? I's just gonna ask you that same
thing, what do you want? Cause if you had enough of that
fine water and coffee they handin' out inside there, maybe
you'd like to come along with me and my friends and get

some, you know, *treats*?' He pointed across the street at a
long green convertible with tail fins and fancy rims. Vicky
knew very little about cars but thought it looked like something Chaco would call a pimpmobile. Two young women
in big sunglasses smiled and waved from the back seat. Vicky
thought their faces looked Mexican, but their big hairdos
were platinum blond.

'My cousins, they fun-loving girls,' the man said.

'I see that,' Vicky said.

'So you want to hop in, go for a spin?'

'No, gracias.' She turned away. *Do I look like I was born
yesterday?*

'And then a little later today,' he said behind her back, 'I'll
give you a ride to Tucson. Isn't that where you want to go?'

Vicky turned back and regarded him seriously. He smiled.
She said, 'Alas, I have no passport.'

'Oh, girl, you mustn't let people vex you about old pieces
of paper. Why, Stella over there –' he indicated one of the
girls – 'she probably got one she can lend you till we get
through the gate.'

'Then what would Stella use?'

'Be a lot easier to show you how all this works,' the handsome young man said, 'if you just go ahead and get in the *car*.'

Vicky said, 'Give me a minute,' and ran inside the patio
to tell Jaime. 'I have been invited to ride to Tucson with that
man out there, see him? And I am going to go.' She hugged
him for a short, fierce moment, suddenly fonder of him than
ever before.

He held onto her, saying, 'Are you sure? I do not like that
man's face.'

'I agree, I think he is evil. But he will take me to Arizona
so I can kiss the ground.'

Jaime looked downcast. 'I am so sorry I failed you in that.'

'Hey, you got me halfway!' They were suddenly buddies.
All the small angers of their anxious crossing were forgotten
and they loved each other.

'I hate to see you go alone,' Jaime said anxiously, 'what
will you do when you get there?'

'Don't worry. I will go to Tía Luisa's house, where my sister
is. I remember exactly where it is,' she lied. 'I will be fine.'

'I want to give you something,' Jaime said. He fished out
the silly cigarette lighter with the bobble head and pressed
it into her hand.

'What's that for?'

'To remember me by,' he said, and added with an ironic
shrug, 'and you never know when you might need to light
a fire.' He kissed her. 'Here, take my sharp nail, too, I won't
need it in Ajijic.' He did a little carefree dance, as if he was
already home.

Vicky laughed. 'You so crazy. Good luck on your trip
back.' Over Jaime's shoulder as she hugged him one last
time, she saw Dee pointing behind her own hand at the handsome stranger and shaking her head. In back of Jaime's
shoulder, Vicky made a quick circle with her thumb and fore-
finger. She smiled at Dee, kissed Jaime's warm cheek again
and ran across the street to the open car.

The black man said, 'OK, let's get acquainted.' He gave
her his card. His name was printed on it: Freddy O., with a
Tucson phone number and the message 'For fun and games.'

'And these are my faithful travelling companions,' he said,
'Bernice and Stella.' Up close, she could see they were definitely wearing wigs. Vicky told them her name and gave
them all a small, discreet smile. Freddy O. said, to the two
blonds in the back, 'Our new friend still kind of shy of us,
so let's be nice to her now, make her feel at home.'

Vicky never felt at home in the green convertible, but when
Freddy O. told her it was a fully restored 1962 Lincoln
Continental, she said it was pretty and he looked pleased.
They spun around Agua Prieta finding one treat after another
– she gobbled up fish tacos at one roadside stand, rice and
beans at another, an ice-cream bar at a third. Her hunger,
which had been stifled by fear and fatigue, was awakened
by the first taste of food, and after that for an hour she ate
everything they offered her. They smiled good-naturedly, like
fond cousins, when Vicky exclaimed how good it all tasted.

After several treats Vicky asked if they could go to a place
that had a ladies' room. Freddy said, 'Of course, why didn't
I think of that?' He asked Bernice and Stella where they
wanted to go and went where they suggested, to a hotel that
looked old but had nice tile floors and a fountain with several

tables around it. The ladies' room was very small so although
Bernice came with her to the door they could only go in one
at a time, and when she came out and Bernice went in Stella
was right there to lead her back to the table, 'So you don't
get lost in this great big place,' she said, laughing.

When they came back to the table Vicky took a sip of her
water and thought it tasted a little odd, so she told the waiter
she had seen a fly in it and asked for a fresh glass. Freddy
smiled as he watched her drink. He said, 'You careful, huh?
Smart girl.' Vicky smiled at him sweetly and said nothing.

Back out on the street Freddy said, 'OK, time for some
serious fun now,' and Stella said, 'All *right*!' Freddy drove
a few blocks, parked, and reached a hand across the back
seat to Stella, saying, 'Here we go.' She put a zippered black
bag, short but fat, into his hand and he got out and bopped
into a bar where, he said, the girls didn't want to go. When
he came back out he handed the bag, flat now, back to Stella,
reached into his inside pocket and pulled out a roach. He
said, 'Ta da! *La mejor hierba mala en todo el mundo!*'

Stella said, 'Oh, you clever man,' with a warm chuckle.
She lit up and passed it to Bernice. The three of them, making
small noises of contentment, began passing it around. When
it came to her, Vicky just passed it along.

'C'mon, we might as well smoke this weed right up,' Bernice
said, 'can't take this stuff across the border, right?'

'Oh, no, indeedy,' Freddy O. said. 'Don't need that kind of
trouble.' For some reason, this remark made them all chuckle
happily.

Vicky kept smiling and passing the smoke. Hemp was as
available as toothpaste on the street where she grew up, so
she was not surprised to see that smoking it right up made
the threesome even jollier than before. They rolled along the
crowded streets of Agua Prieta in the open car, enjoying
treats and telling jokes until the two blond girls were holding
their sides.

Besides not being naturally blond, now that she'd listened
to them for a while Vicky thought Bernice and Stella didn't
seem Mexican, either. Their accents were hip American with
inflections that made her think of the TV show, *Queer Eye
For the Straight Guy*. Stella was a little darker than Vicky

but looked as if she might have a grandmother with Aztec cheekbones. Bernice had lighter skin but her features looked more like Freddy's – maybe she really was Freddy's cousin.

Vicky wanted to keep watching all the members of this group until she figured out what they had in mind for her, so she sat sideways on the front seat, looking from one to another and wearing a clueless expression like a brain-dead rabbit. She did not laugh at any of their jokes even when – especially when – she could tell what was supposed to be funny.

She had her own joke to enjoy, which was that if this arrangement worked as well as Freddy O. seemed to think it would, she would make her third entry into Arizona riding in plain sight in a fully restored Lincoln Continental convertible.

SEVEN

Delaney walked off the elevator on the second floor with Leo Tobin, just as Sarah reached the top of the stairs.

'Ah, here comes the Iron Woman, climbing again,' Leo said. 'You heard about Burke's Law for elevators, boss?'

'No, what is it?' Delaney hated puzzles.

'Do Not Enter. Burke has decided elevators are evil.'

'I don't have time to go to the gym any more,' Sarah said, 'so I climb stairs to fight the flab. What's wrong with that?'

'Not a thing' Leo said. 'Why don't you get rid of your washing machine too? Take your clothes down to the river and beat them on a rock, that's good exercise.'

Sarah said, 'What river?' A couple of winter rains had sent a trickle down the middle of the Santa Cruz channel, but it had disappeared in a day.

Delaney made shushing motions at both of them. 'Come on, let's get to work.' He waved his arm at the rest of the crew in their workspaces. 'Guys, bring your notes. I set up a table back here by the . . . oh, now, who put these sketches all over it?'

'They're mine, from the Cooper crime scene,' Jason said, walking over. 'They're not in any particular order yet, just pile 'em up.'

They all brought their own chairs, plus one extra Delaney said they were going to need. Another five minutes passed while they trotted around, fetching coffee and water and notes. Delaney sat watching them with a muscle twitching in his jaw.

'What's this in the paper about bones?' Oscar Cifuentes asked, sitting down. 'My date last night got all excited about something besides sex for once.'

Jason said, 'Poor, poor Oscar, his ladies won't leave him alone.' All the other detectives made barfing noises.

'This one sure did,' Oscar said. 'She wanted to hear all the details, and when I told her I didn't know anything about it she told me I was a poor excuse for a cop. Why aren't we all briefed on the hottest thing in the news?'

'Sarah is,' Ollie Greenaway said. 'The paper quoted her twice. How come Sarah has all the fun?'

'Give me a break,' Sarah said, and added, for the tenth time that day, 'I just happened to take the call.' She was doing her best to downplay her involvement with the bones, because the bones irritated Delaney. He hated flamboyant headlines about cases that didn't conform to standard police work. Next we'll be seeing overheated letters to the editor, he'd said, asking what this town's coming to. She hadn't told him yet that she'd responded to Cokely on her own and uncovered a new, hot lead on the bones.

'What have you got on it so far?' Delaney asked her.

'It's not a critter, it's a human being. Or parts of one,' she said. She wanted to be alone with Delaney when she told him about Inman's proposition. 'We're getting lots of tips about possible identity, of course.' Phone messages were piling up on her desk, her email in-box was full.

'I bet.' Delaney winced.

'I got dibs on the next vampire case,' Ollie said.

'I get the alien abduction then,' Jason said, patting the top of his head.

'OK, enough!' Delaney slapped a file down and opened it. 'Come on, guys, the Cooper case!' They all put their cups down, opened files, sat forward. 'I've read the autopsy report twice and there are several things that don't make sense to me.'

'Tell me about it,' Leo said. 'Lot of medical jargon in there. If you ask me it's just The Animal covering his ass.'

'Or maybe he's just stating the truth,' Delaney said, 'which we don't have the training to understand. You were there Monday afternoon, what did you think at the time? Did you find the data confusing?'

'Well, yeah,' Leo said. 'But then I always do. All those Latin words! I expect them to sort it out for the report and give us a *conclusion*.' He flapped a hand over his own notes. 'Hell, what he sent over this time, I'd be just as well off sticking with my own notes.'

'Well, that's not the way we do it here. So I called Dr Greenberg and asked if he could possibly spare time to come over and explain some things today.' Delaney gave Leo a cool stare and added, 'I asked him very politely and he said he didn't have time but after he thought about it he said he'd do it anyway. So now just stifle those Animal cracks, please, Leo, because this is a big favor the man is doing us, and I want to see him treated with every courtesy here.' He looked around the table while Leo Tobin, the wise old man of the section, shuffled papers and swallowed his anger.

'Sarah,' Delaney said, 'your interviews with the two employees seemed straightforward enough, but the Cooper son and daughter . . . not much there.'

'I know, and I had to really dig to get that. They were both closed up like clams. Of course it was the first day, they were in shock. Even so . . . I think I should talk to them again.'

'I agree. As soon as possible, please. And the sister, you haven't talked to her yet, have you?'

'Lois Cooper's sister? She's been very hard to catch, she's never home and she doesn't have an answering device on her phone. I finally asked Nicole for help, and wow, is that the right answer, guys. In ten minutes Lois's sister Fran called me, and I'm seeing her tomorrow morning.'

'Good. Now, Jason? I know you looked all day for the bullets that killed the Coopers, but you finally found them both, right?'

'Mrs Cooper's wasn't so tough, once they got the body out of there and I got permission from all the other criminalists to get in there and dig out the hole in the molding where I was sure it was. Frank's was under the last scraping of bloody tissue off that stupid flocked wallpaper,' Jason said. 'Time I found it I was getting to know every fragment of his cranium by name. The crime scene techs wouldn't let me touch anything till they took its photograph fifty times like it was running for president or something. Jeez, what a day.'

'OK, but once you did find the hole, did you have any trouble getting the slug out of the wall?'

'No, we just cut out the section of drywall and there it was, in the fiberglass insulation.'

'I haven't seen the slugs yet. Do they look right for a . . . what did he have there? A .357 Magnum?'

'Yeah, a Smith & Wesson Model 66 with a four-inch

barrel. Uncle Mike's combat grip. Nice shooting gun. He
kept it in a drawer in the den, with a box of shells and the
cleaning cloths and oil, all nicely organized . . . looked like
he knew what he was doing. And the slugs are both .38
Special plus P. Just right for competition shooting with that
weapon.'

'And for shooting your wife, huh? Does Andy think they're
in good enough shape for a match?'

'Lois's is, for sure. She was shot in the ear and the bullet
passed through mostly flesh, just chipped a bone and lodged
in that fake molding that isn't even wood. So hers should
be a lock. Frank's . . . well, it's pretty flattened from going
through his skull and then drywall, but Andy says he sees
lands and grooves. He should be able to confirm it was fired
by that gun.'

'Good. How soon?'

'Uh . . . I didn't think it was right to try to put a rush on it
because the lab crew's processing all that ammo from the stash
house, and you know how much . . . I mean, there are two
casings right there in the chambers, anybody can see this
is the right ammo for that gun and two bullets were fired,
so . . .' Jason watched Delaney stare at him, blinking. After
a few seconds he said, 'I'll ask him to expedite.'

'Good. Now . . .' Delaney leaned back, rubbed his face
thoughtfully, rocked forward again. 'I want you all to put yourselves back in the crime scene. You remember that as we arrived
– let's see, I think it was Ollie and Oscar first?' They nodded.
'Ray was right behind them and then Leo and Jason, who were
still talking to me when Sarah arrived.' All his detectives nodded,
right, right, right, with their faces saying, so what? 'OK. Now
remember how, one after another, you all went to look at the
bodies and came back to me and said what?'

'That it looked like murder/suicide,' Ollie said. 'The way
the bodies lay, not side by side and the wounds not consistent. Looked like he shot her and maybe stood around and
thought awhile the way they do, and then stood at the other
end of the hall and ate his gun.'

'Exactly,' Leo said. 'Two bullets out of the same gun, the
wounds look right, the weapon is right there – all the signs
were right. For once we all agreed on something.'

'And when I looked at the photos later,' Ray said, 'I thought, bingo, we were right the first time.'

'Me too,' Jason said.

'And all done with only two shots,' Delaney said. 'But still, two shots out of the .357 Magnum, that's two big noises.' He looked at Ollie and Ray. 'How could it be that nobody heard anything?'

'There were big sports events on all the channels,' Ollie said. 'Everybody was inside watching games. And those are big lots in Colonia Solana – Cooper's house sits on a full acre, the plants are full-grown, it's like a forest.'

'Also, the news that night was a big battle in Afghanistan, a couple of suicide bombings in Iraq. It was a noisy night on TV, and every single person I talked to said they watched TV and then went to bed.' Ray turned his liquid brown gaze on Delaney and shrugged. 'It's not a lively neighborhood.'

'All the more reason why somebody should have heard a shot.'

'Well, there was one guy who said come to think of it he might have heard the shots. But then he said, "Three shots, right? Two or three hours apart?" So I guess he heard something else.'

'Well . . .' Delaney laid the report on the table in front of him and lined it up with the table edge. A waste of time, he'd be grabbing it up and flipping through it again in a minute. He did fussy little things like that when he was trying to line up facts in his head. 'Let's go on to your interviews, Sarah. When you asked about the couple's relationship, what kind of answers did you get?'

He'd read her report, obviously, but he wanted it plainly restated now so everybody around this table followed the logic of the evidence together. Sarah said, 'Everybody except Tom mentioned that they argued a lot.'

'Tom never heard any arguments?'

'He just wasn't ready that day to admit they had any faults at all. Perfect parents, worked all the time and took care of everybody, we should all be ashamed to speak ill of the dead. But his sister says they disagreed about almost everything, especially lately, and she didn't hesitate to call it *fighting*.

According to Nicole they had the loudest fight of all during the last meal she shared with them, lunch on Friday.'

'Did she say what about?'

'Yeah, a new store he wanted to build in Phoenix.'

'And Mrs Cooper was against it?'

'For now. She said until the building trade recovered they should put it off.'

'OK. And that manager, Phyllis, agrees there were arguments?'

'Yes. And that they were worse lately on account of the new store.'

'Well, so everything lines up, doesn't it?' Ray said. 'The couple's been fighting. Sunday night they had it out. She wouldn't give in, he went berserk and shot her.'

'And the rest is boilerplate,' Ollie said. 'When he realized what he'd done he knew he couldn't get away with it, so he offed himself. Motive, weapons, opportunity – it's the same old same old, isn't it?'

'Except the housekeeper says they've been arguing about the same things for over twenty years,' Sarah said, 'so why would it turn violent now?'

'A lot of money at stake, though,' Ray said, 'sometimes that's a game changer.'

Around the table, heads were nodding.

'Maybe,' Delaney said. 'But the housekeeper's a long-time employee. And she claimed, didn't she, Sarah, that Mr and Mrs Cooper argued to sort out what they thought about the stores?'

'Yes. She says the one thing they got really mad about was Tom. He wanted him out of the company and she wanted to keep him at the store with her. But the son doesn't seem at all threatened, and he defends both his parents, so . . . it's a little confusing.'

Delaney's face went through several shades of dissatisfaction. 'Well, families are. Now, Leo, any doubts?'

'Maybe an issue about time of death,' Leo said. 'You remember, at the scene we all remarked that the missus – what was her name? – Lois. We all thought Lois hadn't been dead as long as Frank had.'

'When did we all think that?' Ray Menendez asked, looking around. 'I don't remember that.'

'You were outside, Raimundo,' Sarah said. When she got promoted to Homicide she had said his name phonetically, Rye Moon Dough, several times a day in order to remember it, and sometimes she still called him that. It was ironically retro on a guy as hip as Ray Menendez, but it suited his classically Latin-lover looks. 'You and Ollie were already canvassing the neighbors by the time Leo and I viewed the bodies.'

'And me,' Jason Peete said.

'That's right, you were with us,' Leo said. 'And didn't you agree she looked a little . . . fresher?'

'No, I said leave it to the docs.'

'Ah, and here he comes now,' Delaney said, and jumped up to greet Greenberg as he walked off the elevator. 'This is very kind of you,' he said as he led him back to the table, showed him to the extra chair. All the detectives nodded pleasantly or smiled, which Sarah thought must be quite a shock to the doctor. His tongue had lashed them all at one time or another, so they usually tried not to talk to him at all. But Delaney had said to play nice and this was plainly no day to cross Delaney.

'The thing we're hoping you'll explain,' Delaney told the doctor, 'is that our theory of the crime – that Frank killed his wife and then shot himself – matches the weapon that's there and the fact we know he was experienced with guns. But it doesn't seem to agree with everything in your autopsy report.'

'I kind of thought that's what Leo had in mind when he called me.' Greenberg's sneer added contempt one twitch at a time. 'Trying to get kindly old Doc Greenberg to admit to a typo or two and make the report fit the theory, hmmm?'

Leo flushed red and said, 'I don't believe I've ever described you as kindly.' So much for Delaney's admonitions, lost already in the fog of battle. But Leo had misjudged his target. Greenberg smiled, looking genuinely pleased for once.

'Good!' he said. 'Now that we understand each other, let's talk about the numbers, shall we? Which body do you want to start with?'

'Lois,' all the detectives said in unison. They looked at each other, surprised.

'Jesus, it's a chorus,' Greenberg said. 'OK then, Lois.' He scrabbled through his notes. 'Body temp, first. A fraction under ninety degrees when I took it at a few minutes after six. Do we have to go back to Forensics for Dummies, now? Bodies lose between one and two degrees an hour after death, depending on so many variables we hardly ever mention body temp as evidence. Still, we all faithfully take it, first thing, so here we go: average one and a half degrees an hour, you get six to eight hours since Lois expired.

'Take lividity next: the book says it becomes fixed at six to eight hours. Lois was nice and purple underneath – indicating she hadn't been moved, by the way – and when I pressed a finger I got slight blanching, which returned to dark red almost immediately. Nothing there to disagree with the other estimate.

'Rigor was just getting started in the jaw and advanced considerably before we got the body moved. It's different for everybody but I can fit that into the initial estimate of six to eight hours.

'Now let's do Frank. He was cold to the touch and getting stiff all over, not completely rigid yet but well along. Measured temp was just under eighty-two degrees. Lividity was fully fixed – although I hope you all noted that it was somewhat blotchy in his arms and shoulders. If I didn't know any better, and I don't, I'd say his arms might have been rearranged at some point.

'Autopsy results, now: the stomach contents. Her dinner was better digested than his. Of course they didn't eat together, did they? So he might have eaten later than she did. So many variables in this area it would hardly be worth discussing except that this finding agrees with all the others.

'So I guess it's time you asked yourselves: why are you so married to this theory that the husband was the shooter?'

'There was no evidence of forced entry,' Jason said. 'No tracks outside, no theft or vandalism we could see. Two people alone inside a locked house.'

'And his wound is consistent with a self-inflicted gunshot,' Sarah said, 'whereas hers would be difficult to do. And obviously she didn't shoot herself in the head and then trot the gun down the hall to incriminate Frank.'

'That *would* be kind of tricky.' Something seemed to galvanize Greenberg, and he turned the full bright beam of his attention on Sarah. 'Even for a female in a rage, you're right, by God, that might be tough to pull off.' The remark was so gratuitously sexist that all her fellow detectives held their breath for a second, half expecting Sarah to heave her water bottle at his head.

But Sarah's admiration of Delaney's non-response to Tom Cooper was still fresh in her memory. 'And even tougher,' she gave the doctor her blandest stare, 'to walk down the hall and back without dripping, and then lie down and bleed out.'

The doctor's mocking eyes betrayed a touch of approval. 'Right again.'

'OK, so there we are,' Delaney plowed on, 'two people alone in a locked house.'

The doctor shrugged, looking bored. 'So somebody else had a key.'

'Their children, who both can prove they were out of town.'

'Convenient,' Greenberg said. 'Isn't it bothering any of you how convenient the evidence is?'

'Yes, it will comfort you to know that we're all getting twitches and tics over the convenience,' Delaney said, 'plus my blood pressure has spiked. But the evidence is still what it is.'

'Yeah, well . . .' Greenberg stretched and yawned, reminding them that life wasn't easy for him, either. 'My evidence all suggests that she died a little later than he did, but hey – comes to an inquest, if this is all you got, I can argue that all these measurements are known to be highly variable.' He stuffed his file into a bursting briefcase and stood. 'Any other little bits of graft and collusion I can do for you?'

'No,' Delaney said. 'This'll do nicely. Thanks.' He walked the doctor to the elevator like an honored guest, while his detectives studied their hands.

As soon as the elevator door closed Ollie Greenaway said, 'I could run down the stairs right now and kneecap Dr Greenberg in the parking lot, Sarah, you want me to do that?'

Sarah lined up her pages just so inside the folder, closed the file quietly and said, 'Doctor who?'

Delaney came back, perched on the edge of his chair like a nervous raptor and said, 'Well, that went well, didn't it? Everybody ready to make a list?'

'*Sin duda*,' Ray Menendez said. Being a little clownish to wipe away the shame of not having punched out The Animal, Sarah thought.

'Here we go then: Leo, thanks to our enlightened Arizona legislature, we won't find any state records on Frank Cooper's guns, but see if you can find purchase records, will you? Or maybe if we're lucky they might be registered federally, if he bought them new at a licensed dealer. Anyway check on membership in gun clubs, talk to friends he hunted or competed with.'

'What are you looking for?'

'An accurate count on how many guns he owned, so we know we've got 'em all. Sarah, interview Lois's sister, get her to give you the names of other living relatives and get in touch with them, and talk to the children of the deceased again. We need more details about these people! Jason, go to the courthouse and get all the records of everything the couple owned: houses, boats, cars, land – anything. Look for liens, loans, partnerships. And Ray, get with Nicole and get the dead couple's personal computers, bank statements, tax records – let's see if we can find some funny business with the money. What else?'

Ray said, 'How about grudges, flirtations, nutty politics . . .'

'Any of those. Oscar and Ollie, better get back to the stash house murders. The drug evidence goes to the narcs but the homicides – we got pulled off them by the Cooper case, but they're still ours. So think back, what leads didn't you get to work before?'

'Couple of neighbors we never found. And a girlfriend,' Ollie said, 'and I want to talk to the fingerprint guys. I got some ideas about where to look for a match.'

'And I never got to their vehicles,' Oscar said. 'They're both impounded and I'd like to be there when they work them over.'

'Go to it. The tox screens aren't back yet on either of these crimes and it'll be a long time till we get any help from DNA, so bring me something to feed the media while we wait.'

All the detectives began gathering up the records they'd brought to the table, piled them on their chair seats and began pushing the chairs back to their workspaces. In the middle of the racket, Sarah leaned across the table and asked Delaney, 'See you a minute?'

He looked up from the records he was stacking, scanned her face for two seconds and said, 'In my office?' She nodded and he got up and walked into his corner without another word.

That's another thing he's good at, she thought as she followed him in and closed the door, that ability to read faces quickly. She was beginning to think of time spent with Delaney as a kind of leadership boot camp.

He hated long, complicated preambles. When he started to twitch and blink, his next words would be, 'What's your point?'

So before she even sat down in front of his desk she said, 'I think I found a guy who can help us hand off that box of bones to DEA.'

EIGHT

When the fat toke was finished Freddy O. looked at his watch, stretched lazily and said, 'Well, ladies, I guess we better be gettin' along up the road, whaddya say?'

Bernice said, 'Fine with me, baby.'

Stella, afloat on her smoky high, said, 'Sure, honey, whenever.'

Freddy said, 'Probably a little too breezy on the road with the top down, huh?' and put it up. When everything was clipped into place he looked straight across the seat at Vicky, serious for once, and asked her, 'You got all your stuff with you? You ready to go?'

Vicky said, 'Yes,' and waited for him to show her now how this was going to work. Was he some kind of a magician? But Freddy just smiled a small, contented smile, looking like a cat about to lick himself, and drove around the block to a gas station. 'OK, Stella,' he said, as he parked by a pump. 'Show time.'

'All righty then.' Stella opened the car door, stretched her long legs out onto the cement apron and stood up in one lithe move. 'Show time it is!' While Freddy gassed up, she walked into the station, carrying the large black patent shoulder bag Vicky had noticed on the back seat as they drove around.

Bernice stayed put, with her eyes on Vicky.

Vicky said, 'Guess I better do that too,' and moved to open her door. But Bernice put a restraining hand on Vicky's arm and said, 'Just wait till Stella gets back, honey.' Her voice was friendly enough, but somehow Vicky felt she had no choice.

She watched people dodging in and out of the gas station across the lanes of cars, but never saw Stella come back. Presently a slim young man in jeans and a black leather jacket walked up to Freddy at the pump and said something quietly. He had a brown Mexican face with broad cheek-bones, two small gold hoops in each ear, and black hair, slicked back and oiled till it was shiny as . . . the patent leather bag he was carrying? Freddy looked him over carefully and nodded, and the two of them came over to her door and opened it.

'Your turn, now, darlin',' Freddy said. 'Stella here done turned into Dick, as you see. So now Bernice gonna take this bag and go in the rest room with you, and she'll help you get all fixed up nice so you can be Stella at the Border. You won't need that,' he said as she climbed out carrying her backpack. He moved to help her take it off but she held onto it fiercely, shaking her head and making little protesting noises. Freddy glanced around, saw a couple of people watching his group curiously, and seemed to decide her back-pack was not worth a fuss in public.

Good, now I know. Freddy's game, whatever it was, evidently depended on looking cool. He kept his self-satisfied smile on his face but his eyes were very businesslike as he nodded to Bernice.

Bernice took her hand in an apparently friendly gesture but held onto it firmly as they walked into the crowded, noisy station together. There was only one ladies' room and they had to wait. Bernice continued to hold her hand as they stood in line behind a thin woman in very tight jeans. When the door opened and the thin lady went in, Bernice moved them close to the door to guard their place. Vicky was uncom-fortably aware that one of the clerks was watching them off and on, probably wondering about the mismatched pair holding hands. But Bernice just glanced around coolly and hummed a little tune. The instant the thin lady opened the door Bernice grabbed it and pulled Vicky inside.

'Now,' she said, 'you gonna have to take that backpack off so I can pat you down.'

Vicky slid the backpack off but held the strap tight in her left hand. She flinched when Bernice's strong hands took hold of her shoulders. Bernice said, 'Nothing personal, you dig? Just gotta make sure you ain't packin'.' The strong hands searched her torso, paused at her crotch and Bernice said, 'Oh, it's that time of the month, huh?' Vicky nodded, blushing.

'Hey, better to get it than not to get it, huh? Don't worry, honey, that's as personal as I'm gonna get.'

Vicky watched the top of Bernice's spun-sugar wig as she patted her way around the buttocks, down the thighs and past the knees. She grunted a little, getting down to Vicky's ankles, and when she spoke again her tone was not so friendly.

'Now this here has got to go, sugar.' She squinted up at Vicky. 'You gonna fight me when I take it off?'

Vicky hung her head, looking embarrassed, and said, 'No.'

'Good girl,' Bernice said. 'Where's the buckle? Oh, I see – Velcro. Hmm. That's a pretty nice little lash-up.' She held up the flat canvas holster with the narrow stiletto handle peeping out the top, pulled the blade out and admired it for a few seconds before she put it back and dropped the whole thing in her purse. 'OK.' She stood up in one lithe motion and yanked the backpack out of Vicky's left hand.

Vicky cried out, 'No!'

Quick as a snake, Bernice's long hand wrapped around her throat, so tight she couldn't breathe. She leaned close to Vicky's ear and hissed, 'You don't want to make a fuss and have people come in here askin' questions, do you?' Her big dark eyes watched Vicky shake her head an inch each way – all she could manage with her neck in a vice.

'Good,' Bernice whispered, 'because soon as I find out you ain't got any weapons in here I'll give this back to you and we'll be on our way, OK?' She watched a couple of seconds longer and asked again, 'OK?' and Vicky, for whom the room was going dark, nodded as much as she could and Bernice let her go.

Vicky stood wheezing quietly as Bernice went through the backpack, found the birth control pills and nodded approvingly, wrinkled her nose over three crumpled pesos and dropped them back in, rummaged through the energy bars and extra shoelaces, looking disgusted. When she found the bobble-headed figure in the bottom of the pack she held it up and asked, 'What's this?'

'A keepsake from my friend back there,' Vicky said, looking down and away from Bernice's pitying smile.

'He gave you a bobble-head toy?'

Vicky said, defiantly, 'It was all he had!' She put on her most sincere look, hoping Bernice wouldn't pull the head off and see the wheel and flint of the lighter.

'Gave you his last worthless gadget, huh? You got some taste in men, kid.' Bernice dropped it back in the bag. Still unsatisfied, she looked down at Vicky with her head cocked like a curious chicken. 'Why'd you make such a fuss about hanging onto this old backpack? Ain't nothing in it worth a damn.'

Vicky said, 'It's private, though.' She put on the stubborn-as-a-brick look that usually worked with principals.

'Your very own private junk, huh?' Bernice snorted derisively as she handed it back 'OK, let's get to work.'

She closed the toilet seat, pulled several items out of her patent leather bag and stacked them on the seat: hairspray, lotion, a make-up kit, soap and a washcloth, two towels and Stella's blond wig.

Stella's sexy top and shorts were much too big for Vicky. Bernice said, 'Sorry, kid, I don't have nothing along in your size.' Vicky silently thanked her luck. Bernice dusted and tugged, making Vicky's cotton shirt and jeans a little neater. Using the washcloth, she cleaned Vicky herself up a little, with rough efficiency the way you'd clean a balky child. Vicky didn't want to feel that hand around her throat again so she submitted, stone-faced. When Bernice finished cleaning she slapped the wig on Vicky's head and secured it with pins. When Vicky squeaked, she said, 'Which one?' Vicky pointed, and she reset the pin.

Opening the make-up kit, she handed Vicky a passport and said, 'Hold it open to the picture now, so I can get this right.' Glancing occasionally at Stella's passport photo, she made sure the curl over the forehead echoed the picture, applied lipstick and eye make-up, and ended with blush that emphasized the broad Mexican cheekbones Vicky shared with Stella/Dick.

'See there? You Stella now,' Bernice said, showing her in the mirror. Vicky's eyes got wide when she saw how much she was changed. Forgetting her growing fear, she flashed a big smile at the mirror. Bernice's lips twitched and she said, 'Yeah, you hot stuff now, huh?' Vicky thought Bernice took a certain amount of pride in her work as the designated jailer/hair stylist.

'Now, we ain't gonna have another chance for quite a while,' Bernice said, 'so I'll turn my back and you take a wiz, huh?' When Vicky was done she said, 'Face the door now and don't peek, hear? Got to have my privacy while I pee.' When the hard stream began, Vicky managed one quick glimpse under her arm, and saw that Bernice was standing up.

The big change had only taken fifteen minutes, but even so there were people knocking on the door before they came out. A woman with two small children muttered 'stupid whores' as they passed her, and all the women behind her gave them dirty looks as well. But the waiting women didn't have time to fight, they were intent on getting in to relieve their bladders. They didn't notice that the two who came out were not quite the same as the pair that went in, and the clerk who'd been watching them before was too busy now to see them at all.

When they got back to the car Dick was sitting in front with Freddy, so Vicky got in the back seat with Bernice. Freddy looked her over, nodded to Bernice and said, 'Nice job.'

Approaching the gate, Freddy said, 'You each need to be holding your passports now.' Bernice pulled them out of the black bag and handed them around. Vicky got the one that had been Stella's. Stella was now Dick and had a new passport.

They idled along in the long, slow-moving line of cars and trucks approaching the gate. It was mid-afternoon, the winter sun was sinking quickly toward the horizon and the urgent need to get through these gates and get on with life had begun to rise off the purring vehicles like mist from a swamp. In the windows, the attendants' voices grew sharper as the tension rose. Vicky thought she could hear, in her inner ear, the whispered prayers, *Don't let anybody blow a tire . . . go into labor . . . fire a gun.* And running under those prayers like smoke was the sweaty realization that even if they all behaved perfectly, this jam-up was going to take a while.

Vicky felt her heart beat hard against her ribs. She imitated her three companions, who sat quietly, models of good behavior. By the time they reached the gate, the line behind them stretched back out of sight. A well-groomed lady in a white shirt with patches took their passports, compared them to the people in the car and asked Freddy, 'Where were you born, sir?'

'New York.'

'And where are you going today?' looking at Dick.

'Back home to Tucson, ma'am.'

She glanced briefly into the back seat. Her face indicated she thought there was no accounting for tastes. 'Have a nice day,' she said, handing back the passports and waving them through. They were silent as they drove away, silent as they passed the small shops along the roadway north of the border. When they were out of Douglas, rolling along Highway 80 toward Bisbee, Freddy O. said, 'Well, peeps, that went well, don't you think?' and he and his two companions chuckled contentedly.

'See, Vicky,' Freddy O. said, switching his butt around, getting comfortable as he set the cruise control, stroking the satiny teak wheel of his fancy car with his big hands, 'a while back I figured out that the best place in the United States for a black man is on the Mexican border.'

'Ah, here we go,' Dick said. 'The story.'

'Yeah, well, why not? It's a good story. Patriotic.' He laughed happily. 'I's cruisin' my Twitter one day,' he said, 'and this fine girl whose tweets I follow sometimes, she comes on with this remark that she's at a border patrol check-point, and she says, "Just showed my passport. No ID check! Black beautiful here! Not Mexican!" So I think, Hey, check it out, and I run down to Nogales in my green machine. And I find out, that sweet-faced little tweeter is right! Black gets treated fine at the border! So now,' Freddy O. said, looking more and more as if he was licking up cream, 'I often visit our good neighbors to the south.'

His two faithful companions chuckled comfortably, endorsing the legend of Freddy O. The car she was riding in and the carefree way he spent money suggested that Freddy O's street smarts and unmistakably American face had already brought him plenty of luck. And Vicky could see that it was not all a happy accident, Freddy was careful about details. For instance, the back seat of this luxurious car was equipped with kiddie locks. Now that the top was up, there was no way out unless he let her out.

NINE

'Everybody always thought we were twins,' Fran Gerke said. 'Because we looked so much alike. But we were three years apart, and Lois was older, so she was the boss. I think that's why she's so good at running the store, she practiced on me growing up.'

'Yet you stayed friends all your lives,' Sarah said. 'So you didn't mind being bossed when you were little?'

'No, I complained to Mom and called her a pushy brat,' Fran said. 'We fought all the time. But I went away to college, married a man from Cleveland and stayed away till five years ago when my husband died. By the time I moved back to Tucson Lois had her hands full with her family and the stores. She needed a refuge by then, someplace to be peaceful. I didn't have any children and I guess I was glad to find somebody who needed me. We shared the church, Bingo nights . . . after a while I got her started quilting and we did that together on Sundays. It's funny, as grown-ups we were like two different people.' Fran's eyes overflowed suddenly. She pulled tissues out of a box and wiped her face. 'Sorry. I miss her more every day. I guess it's beginning to sink in that she's really gone.'

'I'm very sorry for your loss. I'll try not to take up too much more of your time.'

'Oh, no, take your time, I'm glad to have somebody to talk to about it. Murder's so grotesque, you know. My friends don't want to hear about it, they think it's creepy. Well, it is weird, Frank exploding like that after so many years.'

'Nicole says their relationship was pretty troubled.' Sarah expected a stream of invective against Frank Cooper. When it failed to flow she asked, 'Did you hear them argue a lot?'

'Didn't hear them argue. Didn't hear them agree. I saw Frank Cooper on Christmas and Easter, when I went to their house for a meal because Lois insisted. Otherwise, he didn't exist for me and vice versa.'

'You couldn't stand each other?'

'We never had a cross word. But by the time I moved back to Tucson, Frank and Lois had arranged their lives so they saw as little of each other as possible outside the stores. She came here in her own car, he never came with her.'

'Did she complain about him?'

'Never. Her pride was at stake, I think. She didn't want to acknowledge that her marriage had become a business arrangement. And what Lois wanted or didn't want, you know, always came first. That part hadn't changed since we were kids.'

'So you just didn't talk about her husband?'

'If something came up about the store, you know, she might say, "Frank thinks so-and-so, but I'm not sure." And then go right on, as if it was just a matter of two opinions that hadn't been sorted out yet. But from things Nicole would say I could tell it was total war when they didn't agree.'

'How about Tom, did he get in on the arguments?'

'I think he tried to, when he was younger. But Frank came down on him so hard, by the time he was out of high school he was afraid to open his mouth around his father.'

'Really?' Sarah looked up from her notes. 'I got the impression he was quite aggressive.'

'Yes, well . . . I suppose he tries to imitate his father. That was kind of a tragic situation. Tom could never please his father and his mother was always sure he was perfect. Pretty hard for the kid to figure out who he really was, I think. Maybe he'll be able to do that now.'

'Inman, is that his name? The detective?' Phil Cruz's nostrils flared as he looked around at the video monitors, the pushed-to-the-wall girlfriends carrying babies. The Pima County Adult Detention Center was not his kind of place – it smelled of dirty socks, hangover sweat, and bleach. The poor audio and static on the phone system meant there was always somebody who couldn't hear, yelling, 'What? What?'

'No, no,' Sarah said. 'Inman's the check-writer. The detective's name is Ed Cokely.' She understood Phil's distaste. DEA Special Agents did not ordinarily waste their time in the county lock-up, talking to orange-suited losers in flip-flops.

Cruz was accustomed to high-dollar arrests, cases that made headlines. Pima County was where the street vendors went, the young cowboys botching burglaries and staging gun battles in parking lots.

Nevertheless, she was hoping Cruz would show a little respect for Ed Cokely, a hard worker who just might have finally turned up a decent lead on the Soltero crew.

Smallish for a cartel but too big and dangerous to be called a gang, however you classified the secretive and tight-knit outfit headed by Rafi Soltero and Huicho Valdez, it was 'rumored' – some said, 'known' – to be moving big loads of cocaine through Tucson now. The pair had taken to riding in caravans of big new SUVs filled with attentive-faced thugs who jumped out first and scanned the street before they held the doors for Rafi and Huicho. They were 'strongly suspected' of half a dozen murders in the last three years, which was bureauspeak for 'guilty but not nailed'.

Cruz had been close to them a couple of times. He'd had clearance last year for a stake-out on a stash house, crews in place with night vision goggles and the whole nine yards, when the house exploded and burned to its foundation, leaving no trace in the ashes that it had ever held anything more incriminating than futons.

To get the goods on Rafi Soltero and Huicho Valdez, Sarah knew, Phil Cruz would sit around Pima County Jail chatting with assholes like Calvin Inman until they ran out of breath to say one more inane thing. But pride required that he show his disdain, be a little condescending when he assured Sarah there'd be a nice little cut of the proceeds for the TPD if this contact led to convictions. Meantime he had his nose in the air like a debutante at a mud-wrestling contest, making Sarah feel protective of law enforcement spear-carriers like Ed Cokely. *Like you weren't trying to get him off the phone yourself yesterday morning.*

Even so . . . a few more minutes in this grimly sanitized moral graveyard with Phil Cruz, Sarah thought, she'd be siding with the prisoners.

The CO walked them in through the sliding master-controlled metal doors, to where Cokely waited by an interview room. She introduced them and they shook hands, friendly smiles

fronting measuring eyes like two cops anywhere. Ed told the
story about this pile of bad checks he'd compiled to make it
a felony offense. Glancing sideways at Sarah, he recalled how
his prisoner saw the newspaper story about her 'discovery' of
the bones, and realized he knew whose they were.

'Or so he says.' Ed had a barely-there shrug, like his shoulder
muscles were being saved for finer things. 'Calvin Inman has
a very relaxed way with the truth. But he says he has verifi-
cation, so . . . you decide.'

'Mmm. I can't use a witness who's under indictment, of
course. He'd have to make restitution first . . . how much did
you say it all comes to?'

Ed named the dollar figure, just under two thousand. Phil's
face suggested he shouldn't have to waste his time like this.
They all knew the forfeiture from the Solteros, if they were
ever convicted, would be huge – piles of cash if you could
find it, houses, SUVs, jewelry and boats. Not that DEA
needed to worry about the dollar captures – the agency was
well funded, recession-proof. But drug seizures provided a
much-needed boost to the budgets of local police chiefs and
sheriffs who assisted in the arrests and claimed a share of
the loot. The DEA shared generously – it was the headlines
they needed, to keep justifying their budget. They liked a
big splashy arrest now and then, front page photos of guns
and drugs, presided over by proud men in uniform. Rafi
Soltero's surly head shot with the prison drape around his
neck, a sidebar detailing all his bad deeds, that was the catnip
a DEA Special Agent wanted to roll in.

Another corrections officer brought Inman into the room
and seated him at the scarred metal table. He looked smaller
and older than yesterday. His mustache ends had lost their
upward curl and he had a scrape on one cheek, as if he might
have been in a scuffle. Sarah found herself hoping Phil Cruz
liked his story.

They talked about the bad paper first, Phil rubbing Inman's
nose in it, curling his lip as he asked again for the total dollar
figure. 'Assuming I get the nod for funding,' he said, 'you'll
have to make the restitutions yourself.' Inman nodded, trying
to look matter-of-fact. Already with a little light in his eye,
Sarah saw, speculating about the chances of making side

deals with complainants, keeping some of the cash. Cruz put the light out with admonitions about an ankle bracelet, verifying phone calls. Then he was abruptly bored with the process and asked to hear Calvin's story about the bones, making it clear he was dubious. 'You've really been dealing for Rafi Soltero?'

'Never.' Calvin pulled back, as best he could in the small space. 'Never did any street dealing for anybody.' He looked away into the corner, till he decided how to buff up the next part. 'Just did a little job once for Chuy Maldonado.' Cruz raised his eyebrows, waiting. Calvin twisted on his plastic chair. 'Because I owed him a *favor.*'

It took him a while to spell it out. He'd cashed a check in Chuy's cousin's bar. 'In good faith, I'd been assured the funds were on the way.' But when he 'came up short' at the bank, 'you know, that whole family is just hard as nails'. Cousin Bebe started talking about broken knees.

But Chuy happened to be in the place. 'He listened to his cousin yelling all these threats at me, and after a while he asked me would I like to work it off.'

The discussion bogged down then in Calvin's concerns about the quid pro quo. 'So far I'm no better off than when we started to talk – when do I hear about the bennies?'

Cruz quickly grew a disgusted look, stood up and said, 'I can't waste my time on a guy blowing smoke.' He clicked off his recorder.

'I'll give you plenty of straight answers as soon as you get me out of here!' Calvin cried.

'I can't justify parole until you convince me you really know something.'

Calvin put his face in his hands for a minute, and sat with his shoulders shaking. When he raised his head he looked into Sarah's eyes and asked her, 'Will this guy do what he says he'll do?'

Surprised, Sarah searched the normally tricky face of Calvin Inman, impressed by how quickly it had been reduced to sincerity by this jailhouse full of brutal teenagers. 'Yes, Calvin,' she said, hoping Cruz was enjoying this blurb. 'Phil Cruz is the real deal. You better tell him what you've got.'

Calvin sighed, patting his hair, which had somehow

retained its elaborate waves. 'OK, Mr Real Deal, turn that thing back on.' He folded his hands on the cold metal table in front of him, deciding where to start.

'Chuy said, if I'd rather work off the debt than get my knees broken, I should meet him at the baggage claim area at the airport tomorrow morning early. He wouldn't say where I was going. Just said, "Don't tell nobody, *claro*?" Like I'd be likely to brag about getting up before sunrise to meet Chuy Maldonado. I asked him if we were going out of town and he said, "Why, you got a date with the mayor?" Every thing he said was like that, mean.

'He met me at the baggage area and we walked outside. He told me a hangar number and pointed, told me to walk down there, and disappeared. I walked a long way, down to the end where the private planes are kept. When I got there he was getting out of a car; he could have given me a ride, he just enjoyed making me walk.

'It was still dark but there was a plane out on the apron, a pilot walking around it. I don't know anything about airplanes,' he said, seeing Cruz with his mouth open and pen poised. 'Two propellers on a Beechcraft, that's all I can tell you.'

'You got in it without knowing where it was going?'

'I didn't have a lot of good options. The pilot seemed to be in a hurry. Nobody talked. I rode in the passenger seat in front. Chuy supervised the loading and then waved us off. The cargo space was filled with bricks of cocaine wrapped in plastic.'

'You're sure? What size?'

'Chuy told me when I got in, "Keep your hands off the product." So I never picked one up, but they looked like kilos to me. The guys on the other end who unloaded them didn't have any trouble moving them, no grunting or any of that.

'We stopped for fuel at a small airport someplace in Arkansas, otherwise we flew nine hours straight. Before we took off from Tucson, Chuy had told me what to do – carry the briefcase, count the money, keep my mouth shut.

'I said, "Gee, I was so hoping to make new friends." Chuy said, "See, now you running your mouth again," and hit me on the ear. He put some kind of a special snap into it, hurt like hell. I said, "Hit me again, punk, you can peddle your own junk." He started telling me how many ways he would kill me if I gave him any trouble, but then the pilot spoke up for the first time and said, "Chuy, you fuckhead, will you shut up and load this airplane so I can get out of here?" He was very nervous. Later, when Chuy disappeared, I realized why.

'The pilot alerted me when we were a few minutes out. I called the number Chuy gave me to call, told them to meet us. We were near the ocean in the Outer Banks of North Carolina, that's all I ever found out. I could see the pilot getting tense and I saw why: it was a very short runway. For a couple of minutes I was sure we were going right into the sand dune. Then the wings wobbled in the wind and we were down and I was surprised my pants were still dry.

'Three white guys with funny accents were waiting in a beat-up truck that said Al's Yard Service on the door. Slatted sides hung all over with gardening tools, sacks of mulch in the back, tarp over it. Perfect camo.

'Two of them pulled samples out of all the bricks, sniffed it, tasted it, got out their little tester kits and went to work. They didn't shoot up, they didn't look like users – no sniffy noses and they weren't jumpy. When the tester said OK the third one climbed in the plane with me and opened a brief-case. I counted the money and put it in Chuy's bag, three hundred beautiful thousands, banded in little tight stacks.'

'Bet that gave you a hard-on, huh?' Cruz asked him. 'Did you manage to palm a few bills?'

'I thought about it, who wouldn't? But the pilot had bragged to me how many weapons he had on him. And I figured Chuy would count it as soon as we landed and he did.'

'The Carolina people give you any trouble?'

'Nobody said anything friendly but nobody shot at us either.

'We slept in the plane that night, took off at first light. Stopped for fuel again, somewhere in Oklahoma, and went right on. We had snacks in the plane and we were more relaxed going back, we talked some. The pilot told me about José, the guy who usually went on these flights with him, said he was home in Mexico now because his mother was sick.

'That's what gave Chuy the idea for this extra trip they were making, that the real dealers, Rafi and Huicho, didn't know about. While they were in Florida and José in Mexico City, Chuy made this deal for an extra shipment, using his own supplier and their customers. "You and I can split the profit," Chuy told the pilot, "and they'll never know."

'We got back to Tucson by mid-afternoon. Chuy took the briefcase, counted it right there in front of both of us. I said, "Don't I have a little tip coming out of that?" Chuy said, "Your pay is, my cousin don't break your legs over that lousy check." I said, "At least give me a ride back to town," and he said, "Get lost, we gotta get this plane serviced before tomorrow morning." They were in a hurry, but he enjoyed treating me like dirt, too.

'I walked back to the main terminal and cleaned up in a rest room. When a big flight came in I climbed on the airport shuttle bus, told him the plane lost my luggage but I was going to the downtown Hilton. I rode to the hotel, went in the front and out the back and walked home from there. I was so tired, I slept all day and all night.'

'But not too tired, I hope,' Phil Cruz said, 'to write down the call numbers of that airplane and put them in a safe place.'

'And the hangar number. As well as the address on that gardening truck, Special Agent,' Calvin said.

'All of which you are willing to give me.'

'Just as soon as you get me out of here.'

Calvin Inman's natural high color, Sarah thought, was coming back.

Back at the station, Leo Tobin followed Sarah into her workspace saying, 'Don't sit down, OK? Come with me to Delaney's office.'

Ollie and Jason were waiting by the door. They stood around Delaney's desk in the cramped space while Leo said, 'I just found a copy of the check for the gun purchase in Frank Cooper's file. It was attached to a list – one thing you gotta love about Frank Cooper, he kept neat lists. This one has one more gun than we've ever found.'

Delaney asked him, 'Purchased at the same time as the others?'

'Uh . . . yeah.' He read off a five-year-old date and the

description of the piece: 'S&W model 60 LS, .357 Magnum Chiefs Special.'

'Aha,' Ollie said, smiling his prankster smile, 'the LadySmith. Now isn't that interesting?'

'Niiiice.' Jason lit up, dragged the word out while he wiggled his butt and patted the top of his head. 'Uses the same ammo as his gun. Hey . . . his and hers shooting excursions, whaddya think? Pretty Freudian.'

'I wouldn't know about *that*,' Delaney said, looking as if he didn't think Jason should either. He turned to his computer saying, 'Remind me, Sarah, what day did you file your interview reports?'

'You don't need to look them up,' Sarah said, 'I remember what everybody said.' She stared into a corner while she recalled. 'Nicole said her father gave her the same weapon her mother had, a Beretta Bobcat. We brought it in for testing. Just as she said, it hadn't been fired – or cleaned – in years. She hates guns, she put it in a drawer and forgot about it. Tom Cooper owns the same model gun as his father, shared some shooting excursions with him when they first got the weapons, but they didn't get along any better at the shooting range than anywhere else. Tom claims he quit shooting a couple of years ago. We tested his gun. It hadn't been fired in some time and hasn't been cleaned since the last time it was used. Andy said he thought it was dangerous now and should be destroyed. Lois's sister Fran said Lois never wanted the gun Frank gave her and never used it. Fran says she feels the same way her sister did, never owned or fired a gun. Everything about her lifestyle says she's telling the truth.'

'What do you mean?'

'Doilies on chair-arms. Quilts everywhere. Bingo at the church Wednesday nights and a china teacup collection in a hutch . . .'

'OK, OK, I got it. What about the manager at the second store?'

'Phyllis Waverly. I asked her. She said Frank offered her a gun but she didn't want it and said no.'

'Well,' Leo Tobin said, 'somewhere there's a lady with a LadySmith.'

'Or anyway a LadySmith. We need to dig deeper into

Frank Cooper's life,' Delaney said. 'Are you sure you've got all his computers? Look for an extra bank deposit box, or a numbered account – follow the money trail. Wasn't there something in those interviews about bankers not being happy with his bottom line? Maybe the LadySmith lady got more than shooting lessons. Sarah, give him a hand with this, will you? I've got everybody else working on the stash house.'

Walking back toward their workspaces, Leo Tobin's voice sounded as if it was coming from the bottom of a well. 'I'm not a damn CPA,' he rumbled. 'He could have a dozen accounts hidden around. Where the fuck do we start, even?'

'I think I should start with Nicole,' Sarah said, 'since I already know her, a little.'

'Doesn't she have a vested interest in covering up any funny business, though?'

'Of course. Which is why *you* have to start where you just said, with his CPA.'

'Whose name I suppose we get from Nicole, right?' They stopped and faced each other. Leo's eyebrows twitched. 'We keep running into feedback loops, don't we?'

Besides, Delaney pointed out when they asked him, there was no money in his budget for a CPA. 'You'll have to handle it in-house,' Delaney said. 'Get somebody on the support staff to help you add up the totals. Then we'll look at them and –' he waved a hand vaguely – 'see what we think.'

'Which will be *nada*,' Leo said, as they walked away again. 'What a crock. This is a job for a specialist.'

'Actually it isn't,' Sarah said. 'Happily enough, this is just exactly the right kind of a job for Genius Geek.'

'Who?'

'Tracy Scott. Part-timer on the support staff.'

'That flamboyant kid with the big mouth and acne? I always try to stay away from him.'

'Ah, but if I told you he was a genius at searching files . . .'

'In that case I love the little creep. Is he working today?'

'Ask Elsie.' Elsie Dobbs ran the support staff and like Delaney was constantly being asked to do more with less money.

'He's not coming in unless I call, these days,' Elsie said. Her look said she might not call any time soon. 'I'm on orders to cut back where I can, and Tracy's certainly one of those places.' Tracy's noisy wackiness annoyed her, and he compounded the offense by being better at all her jobs than she was.

'But if I sign a request form you could get him in here tomorrow, right?'

'Oh, yes.' Elsie sniffed. 'Whatever Homicide wants, Homicide gets.'

'Why didn't I know *that* before?' Leo said, walking away. 'You think we'll get the weird kid some time tomorrow?'

'Probably. We have to work around his class times, he goes to Pima College. But he's fast and wicked smart. Tell Tracy what you're looking for, he'll find it if it's there.'

Sarah heard his clatter and wild laugh in the hall the next morning. He came into her workspace making his own breeze, scattering papers as he bent over her hand.

'My savior! I was afraid I'd been frozen out of the halls of justice forever. Thank you for calling, dear lady!'

'No thanks necessary. We have urgent need of your smarts this week.'

'Genius Geek is yours to command.' He rose to his full height, which was about five feet nine on tiptoes, and made a sweeping bow. 'Unfortunately I left my cape at home but . . . what anomalies can I ferret out for you this time?'

'You're going to be working for my associate, to begin with. I want to warn you that he's pretty, um, straight arrow? So to succeed in this job I would urge you to be a little . . . circumspect.'

'Ah, circumspect.' He smiled widely, his braces gleaming in the sunshine. 'Is that Sarahspeak for "shut your big bazoo"?'

'How precisely you take my meaning.'

'Fear not, dear lady. I can do starchy decorum when I have to. From your expression I gather I have to.'

''Fraid so.'

Tracy sighed. 'The things I do for love. Where do I go for this torture?'

'Follow me.'

Leo was stiff and forbidding while she introduced them. When they were all sitting uncomfortably in his small workspace she began, 'We have this apparent murder-suicide of a couple with a spotless public record . . .' Sarah described the domineering father with the argumentative wife and icy children. Tracy said he'd read accounts of the crime online, then sat with eyes half-closed while Leo told him about the many guns found and the LadySmith not found, the successful business with the big cash flow and skinny bottom line. When Leo paused Tracy said, 'Are his computers all here?'

'On a table behind those two cold-case detectives over there.' Leo led the way to a table wedged into a dark, in-hospitable corner. Industrial-strength power cord snaked along the wall, duct-taped against a baseboard so Leo wouldn't get sworn at any more by people tripping over it. On the table, a big Dell Dimension sprouted external drives and USB memory sticks all over itself like spring shoots on a palo verde. Sarah saw Tracy's fingers curl with delight. 'Over here is the little desktop he kept at home. He kept his personal banking records on here, correspondence about gun clubs and such. Otherwise he seems to have used it mainly to explore for new ideas on the Internet. And then he had all these other gadgets,' Leo said, showing him an iPhone, a Kindle, and an iPad. 'I don't know how much time he spent on any of these, but have a look, huh?'

Aglow, Tracy asked him, 'Is there a chair?'

Leo Tobin, suddenly all charm, went around the section borrowing a chair, a clip-on desk light, a yellow legal pad and a couple of ballpoint pens. Before he even had the chair, Tracy began booting up, making small, happy sounds. When Leo pushed the chair behind his knees he put his skinny butt on it and never spoke another word. They left him typing at awesome speed.

Back in his workspace Leo said, 'Weird kid knows the wired world, huh?'

'Just wait,' Sarah said.

'I've got the night off,' Will Dietz said. 'So don't worry, I'll get Aggie home.'

'What would I do without you?' Sarah said, and kissed him so he never wanted to find out. She and Denny packed that night, duffels full of their clothes and gear to take to

Marana, to stay as long as Aggie needed them. She gave Will a grocery list and another list of things to do in Aggie's house so it would be comfortable when she got there. With each list she asked him, 'Are you sure this is all right with you? I do thank you for all this work,' she said.

'Sure,' Will said. 'My other phone's blinking, I'll talk to you later.' His other phone wasn't blinking, but sometimes when Sarah started trying to run the entire known world at once, he needed an excuse to seek refuge.

A wheelchair pusher brought Aggie to the front door. Her hand was a little shaky, but not bad, when she stood up and took his arm. She slid into the passenger seat and buckled up with no trouble. 'Ah, sunshine,' she said, as they pulled out of the parking lot, and started a rant about hospitals. 'I know I owe those people my life, but I do hope I never see any of them again.'

They stuck monitoring gadgets all over her, she told him, and watched her vital signs as she walked and stretched and flexed. 'I wasn't flexible before,' she said, 'why would I need to be now?' Will thought Aggie was probably not the easiest patient St. Joseph's ever helped through stroke recovery.

While she vented about the week just past, he thought hard about the weeks and months ahead.

He and Sarah had fallen in love the same week Denny's mother disappeared. Will had resigned himself to waiting for Sarah's life to get sorted out a little, before he asked for anything more formal than their occasional get-togethers in his bare-bones casita on the east side of town.

Now, though, Aggie's illness had changed everything. Aggie was going to need help, and her lifelong habits of independence would make that hard for her to accept. Denny needed a home she could count on. He knew he wanted to keep Sarah in his life, and he was sure she felt the same about him; they hadn't been shy about showing their feelings. But driving all over Pima County every day to school and work and doctor's appointments was going to get old in a hurry.

So all week, while he cooked and washed dishes, fetched things to the hospital and answered hurried emails, he had been thinking about what other arrangements might be possible. It helped that Denny, with her finely honed instincts for staying afloat, had put aside her earlier doubts about the reliability of boyfriends and jumped on board the good ship Will Dietz.

'Will said he could pick me up after soccer practice,' he overheard her telling Sarah. And once she said on the phone, with a laugh, 'Will's here, between the two of us we'll find *something* to' cook.' He wasn't the only one, he realized, trying to show he was a team player. Seeing how much she liked to learn things other kids didn't know, he began to teach her how to identify cars on the street, so they'd have something more to work on when they'd run through all the burrs on his Dremmel.

Friday afternoon, negotiating curb-to-curb traffic north east across Tucson with Aggie in the car, Will Dietz thought she had probably obsessed over the healthcare system long enough, and might be ready to calm down and have a conversation. When she did, he was going to ask her if she thought three generations of scrappy females and one beat-up cop could live happily ever after in the same house.

She liked him enough, he thought, to overlook how little money he had to contribute to such a scheme. If she bought into the basic idea he'd explain how he could make up the difference with sweat equity and a secure future. Get Aggie on board, Will thought, keep Denny willing to help the way she's been doing lately. Feeling like a juggler with two oranges, a glass of beer and a box-cutter, he worked his quiet way across Tucson, dreaming of the solution to this odd family's housing problem.

TEN

'Oh, look at all the trees,' Vicky said. She hadn't said a word since they left Douglas, so her voice startled the other three people in the car. They all looked around at the small town, the towering cottonwoods. There were fruit trees, and vines – the lush green foliage looked unreal after the desert they'd just come through. 'What is this place?' Vicky asked them. 'It looks like a . . . whaddya call it? . . . oasis.'

Bernice said, 'You never been to St David before?'

Vicky shook her head. She had hardly ever been any place by car. *Soon as I get a good job I'm going to start saving for a car.* She wasn't old enough to get a driver's license yet, but her practical side told her she'd be plenty old enough by the time she'd saved the money. *And in the meantime I can be shopping.* The thought of walking around a used car lot with a salesman, asking about gas mileage and terms, made her feel grown-up and powerful, and right now she needed all the powerful she could get.

'There's a nice little stream over there and a vineyard that's run by the . . . what's that place where monks live?' Bernice asked the two in the front seat.

'A monkery,' Dick said.

'Ah shee, a *monastery,* come *on,*' Freddy said.

'So I ain't religious, so bite me on the neck,' Dick said.

'Don't do it, Freddy, he'll be all over you like a cheap suit,' Bernice said, and they all snickered like fifth grade boys on the bus.

Vicky smiled vaguely and looked stupid, which wasn't hard because her mind was becoming too occupied with plans to leave much attention for them. Rolling along this smooth highway in a beautiful car, getting closer to Tucson every minute, had been very pleasant until now, and she longed to stay in the dream world they were trying to create for her.

But she was a second-generation border crosser, so from the

time she was old enough to start school she had known that she lived in a dangerous world. Also that people like Freddy O. did not give free rides to stranded Mexican girls and expect nothing in return. Her mother had not wasted breath on anything so mild as 'Don't talk to strangers.' From Marisol Nuñez the message had always been: 'Everybody hates us, nobody wants us here, the Anglos will send us back first chance they get.' And when Vicky entered fifth grade she added, 'And remember, all men are pigs with girls. Don't trust nobody.'

The rest of Vicky's survival tactics had been picked up within a couple of blocks of her house in south Tucson, from tough little gang-bangers trying to impress her by describing the tactics of gangs they hoped to join.

So she had agreed to go with Freddy O. assuming that rape was the obvious hazard. And thinking, even if she couldn't fend him off, how much different could it be from what she had been doing with Jaime? She had willingly traded her virginity for help with a trip to Arizona, why get picky about the details now?

But after Stella went in that rest room and came out neatly dressed as Dick, and more urgently after Bernice grabbed her by the throat, it became clear to Vicky that she was riding with a trio of planners who had come to Agua Prieta to find someone like her. Their confidence and the slick way they handled the necessary supplies indicated they had done all this before. Common sense suggested their plan involved sex. What else did she have that they could want?

She had heard tales about what men did to girls they were breaking in for use as prostitutes. She did not allow herself to even consider the more ominous possibility that perhaps they simply enjoyed torturing young girls. Bad enough to think about gang rape and beatings, drug addiction in windowless rooms. She felt herself begin to tremble. To stop, she forced all the bad thoughts into a cold place at the back of her brain, and began to plan.

She needed to wait until she was at least close to the south side of Tucson, where she would recognize some landmarks. So she pointed to the pretty trees in St David and the car became one soft green chat room, everybody commenting on the sights, the wine that was made here and the good fruit in the fall.

At Benson, Vicky saw fast-food signs and said, 'Ooh, I'm so thirsty. You think maybe we could get a soda at one of these drive-ins?'

Freddy said, 'I don't like to have those big drinks in the car, honey.'

Vicky said, 'Oh,' and sighed. 'Those tacos were so salty.'

Bernice said, 'Yeah, c'mon, Freddy, don't be a stick. We're all dyin' of thirst back here.'

'I don't want no messes in my fine green machine,' Freddy said.

'Well, you know,' Bernice said, stretching her long legs, kicking the back of Freddy's seat, 'even us peons that never got our GEDs, usually we can drink one whole soda without spilling anything.' She said it softly but there was suddenly a feeling in the car, like thunder from a distant storm.

Dick turned on the front seat and said, 'Dawg, now, stay cool, OK?'

Freddy sighed and muttered something to himself as he pulled off the highway toward the 7-Eleven sign. Vicky got the super-size coke-flavored Slurpee, rattling with ice. She said, 'Ahhh,' when Freddy handed it back to her, gave him a big grin and thanked him.

He said, 'How about this, the girl can smile.' He got extra napkins and handed them around, making sure everybody had at least two.

She made a big show of drinking it, but only took small sips, because she wanted it to last all the way to Tucson. She was careful with the napkins, keeping them away from the drink so they'd be dry.

They rolled past the railroad yards at the east edge of Tucson, and Bernice, who seemed to enjoy educating this little Mexican hick who had apparently never been anywhere, pointed out the long conveyor belts carrying coal up to the power plant. Vicky pretended to be interested so Bernice went on to explain the loading docks where the trains picked up products from the factories making solar panels and electronics. They passed the exits for the airport and for Highway 19 to Nogales. Vicky praised the bright-colored designs on the highway overpass, telling herself to get ready, she was close.

Freddy took Exit 261 and was soon rolling north on Sixth Avenue, past the familiar signs for pay day loans and Food City. At the stop light on Twenty-Ninth Street, Vicky saw her chance. The street was busy, full of cars. She thought about what would get all three of these people to look the same way. Pointing left toward the setting sun she said, 'I wonder what all those cops are doing over there?'

Bernice said, 'Where?' and they all looked. While Bernice was turned away Vicky pulled the lighter out of her pocket, where she'd been keeping it ever since Bernice made fun of it in the rest room. She snapped off the bobble head, lit both napkins, and dropped them into the shiny shopping bag at Bernice's feet. They blazed up and the whole bag caught fire. Vicky reached across the seat back and dumped her entire Big Slurpee down the front of Freddy O. He screamed and began to curse.

Vicky yelled, 'The car's on fire!' She dropped her wig into the sack to keep the flames going, and began pulling on the door handles. 'Let me out!'

Bernice turned as the back seat filled with smoke, screamed, 'Open the doors quick, Freddy!' and reached for Vicky.

When Vicky felt the strong hand clamp around her left arm, she raised her right hand gripping the sharpened nail she had palmed all the way across town. She shoved it hard into Bernice's ear and said, softly, 'Let go of my arm or you're dead.' When the grip didn't ease at once she pushed harder. Bernice screamed in pain and dropped Vicky's arm as the locks popped on the doors.

The lights changed just then, but as two female figures burst out of opposite sides of the car and a billow of smoke and flame followed them out, the vehicle in the lane to Vicky's right hesitated long enough for her to dart across the street to the sidewalk.

Running full tilt along the sidewalk and into the asphalt parking lot on her right, she heard Bernice yelling 'Forget the stupid soda, help me get the fire out!' Behind them down the street, car horns blared, and soon she heard sirens coming.

She never looked back, or slowed. She ran as fast as she

could, through the bank parking lot and around behind the building, out the back driveway and across the street, between two parked cars and down an alley. She reached Fourth Avenue and ran across it, into a side street where the spaces between buildings were smaller. She ran alternately north and east until she saw a place where she could stand between two leafy bushes, just off the sidewalk, and catch her breath. As she stopped panting and calmed down, she decided running was too obvious. She would be safer walking.

Dusk fell as she walked along quietly, feeling grateful to Carlos, the ugly braggart who had guided her across the fence and into the desert, then deserted her quickly in Agua Prieta. He had always treated her with contempt, but he had been right about one important thing. Around a fire two nights south of the border, he had boasted, 'I always carry two weapons. One is concealed but fairly easy to find. If bandits or border patrol search me, I look angry when they find it. Usually they will stop looking then and I get to keep the one I have better hidden.' Vicky's second weapon had been hidden in her sanitary pad, which she did not need to wear that day but had rightly guessed that even very curious men would not want to examine.

Thank you, Carlos. I hope you get your wish to never see me again.

When it was nearly dark, beside a jojoba bush under a street light on Twenty-third Street, Vicky found a spot she felt sure was free of cactus spines and dog shit. She looked around – it would be embarrassing to be seen doing this, but she had promised herself. When she was certain no one was watching, she knelt and kissed the earth.

She stood up quickly and walked on. At the end of the block she looked across the street and laughed out loud. On the porch of the stucco house on the corner, her sister Luz was sitting in a rocker. Vicky had found Tía Luisa's house.

ELEVEN

'I'm like that Johnny Cash song,' Phil Cruz told Sarah. 'I keep my eyes wide open all the time.'

A week after their initial contact in the jail, he'd asked for a meet. 'A situation report,' he called it, but after a couple of minutes Sarah decided he mostly just needed to vent. Supervising a witness as tricky as Calvin Inman, Phil Cruz wanted her to understand, was a total ratfuck. 'Do you realize if I take my eyes off him for one minute that piece of pondscum could wreck my career?'

'Aw, come on. How could Calvin do that? All the firepower's on your side.'

'I have to give him *cash*,' Phil said. His face got paler while he spoke and his freckles stood out. 'He has to make the restitutions himself, you understand. I can't use an informant with outstanding warrants, and I can't be involved in satisfying them, he has to do that himself. By the time I use what he knows, this miserable crook has to be squeaky clean.'

'I see what you mean. Squeaky clean is quite a stretch for Calvin,' Sarah said. 'Is he showing as many signs of stress as you are?'

'Physically he's looking better every day. He loves the regular meals at this safe house and he's even adapted fairly well to seeing the sun before noon – Calvin's not getting any younger, you know. He detoxed cold turkey while he was in the slammer, so his cravings for booze and hemp are minimal right now. But there's no getting around how much it hurts a lifelong scam artist to play it straight with money.'

'Mood swings?'

'Exactly – fits of despondency, alternating with that disgusting little gleam he gives off when he thinks he sees a way around me.'

'Has he made any of his dodges work so far?'

'Please. I've got an ankle bracelet on him and a second GPS so small it could fit in his soul patch.'

'Is that where you put it?'

'No. But if he was cooperative I could have; they make some amazing devices these days. Also, I'm getting terrific cooperation from the TPD, every patrol car in town has his picture and if I had to I could put a chopper up. We've been able to get the restitutions done pretty fast – two more paybacks and he'll be ready. Just in time to monitor the Solteros' next flight to North Carolina.'

'All your people there OK with this?'

'Very happy indeed. They don't think they'll make an arrest on this flight, though. They've been doing some wire-taps and they're convinced this shipment will be fairly small like the last one—'

'Three hundred K is small?'

'Oh, yeah. Twice as big would still be small in their terms – coke is not for amateurs. My contacts in North Carolina want to wait till they're sure there's at least a million in play. Then they'll jump.'

'And when they say they've got the goods,' Sarah said, 'we'll pick up Rafi and Huicho here, right? They're not making any of the flights, are they?'

'No, no. Solteros have paid help for that.'

'Good. Because we're hoping to have enough evidence by then to try them for Chuy Maldonado's murder. Or one of the other open cases that have their signatures.'

'Uh-huh.' Homicide, Phil Cruz had told Sarah, just didn't ring the bell for him any more. He had worked it for a while, while he was still on the Tucson PD, but now that he'd seen the big hauls the Feds got to work with it seemed so futile, all that painstaking compiling of evidence around one corpse. And if everything went right after two or three years you got to take it to a jury, where the decision might come down to whether one of the jurors liked the suspect's eyes. Phil looked out the window and asked idly, 'The Soltero killings have signatures?'

'You bet. Evidence of torture – fingernails pulled out, cigarette burns. And the end of the nose cut off. Also, Chuy Maldonado's not the first one of their victims to get dismembered.'

'Mad dogs, huh? That doesn't seem to fit with how

carefully they plan their drug operations.' Phil Cruz had done some training in profiling and he liked to slot people in terms of their predilections.

'I'm not saying they're crazy. It's a tactic with them. They keep people in line by terrorizing them.'

'Ah.' He studied her, amused. 'You really want to put these guys away, don't you?'

'No,' Sarah said. 'I really want to kill them. But the law's the law so I'll settle for putting them away.'

'Be a couple of weeks yet,' Phil said, 'I'll call you.'

That was fine with Sarah, who had plenty of other work on her desk and less time than usual to work on it. The department had declared half a dozen furlough days this fiscal year, to balance the budget cuts the city said were necessary. Sarah took Tuesday and Wednesday that week, glad of the chance to stay home with Aggie.

The reversal of roles took some getting used to. She was not accustomed to being tactful around her mother, but Aggie was hypersensitive now about needing a caregiver. They took walks, slowly around the block at first and then every day a little farther and a little faster. The doctors told her Aggie's recovery was proceeding normally. Aggie complained about how slow it was.

While they walked, arm in arm and looking anywhere but at each other, they began to talk cautiously about the big change Will was urging them to make.

He'd started on Sarah that first Friday afternoon, when she got out to her mother's house after work. She was standing in the kitchen taking off her gun and badge when Will came in from the yard and stood close to her. He touched her face and asked, 'How are you?'

'I'm good.' She kissed him quickly. 'We need to talk, don't we?'

'Yes.' As soon as she said it, things they had put off saying all week took on urgent life and clamored for attention.

'Maybe tomorrow,' Will said, 'we could get away for a while. You think?'

Sarah nodded, holding onto his arm. Then Denny came into the kitchen saying, 'How soon is dinner?'

'Half an hour,' Will said, 'if you'll set the table.'

'Sure,' Denny said, opening drawers. She'd visited her grandmother often, she knew where everything was in the kitchen.

Aggie's longtime boyfriend, Sam, kept offering to help, so now Will enlisted him, too. He came over Saturday after lunch, hugged Aggie hard and said, 'How's chances for a visit with my buddy? I can stay all afternoon,' he told Sarah and Will, 'in case you two need to run into town for anything.' He had even brought along a deck of cards, so he could teach Denny some cool variations on Five Card Stud while Aggie took a nap. Sarah could see they were all being manipulated but wanted time alone with Will so urgently she didn't ask any questions.

And Will didn't give her time to ask any for the first half hour in her house, either. The pleasure of finally making love was so intense it swept everything else away.

Afterwards, as they lay sated with arms and legs wound tight around each other, Sarah listened in mute astonishment as Will Dietz, usually the quiet man who kept most of his thoughts to himself, spoke persuasively about what he thought they ought to do.

'Your life is getting to be too damn much for one person. What if Aggie gets sick again? And Denny's growing up fast – she can't stay in one end of your bedroom forever.'

'I've been trying to save a little something for a deposit on a bigger place . . .'

'But something always comes up. I know. And I want to be some use financially but as long as I keep my own place I don't have much left to contribute. I could help you so much more if we were living together.'

'Well, I've been wanting to talk to you . . .' She pulled back to look at him, amazed. After months of stoic silence he seemed ready to talk about anything.

'But there's never any time to talk,' Will said. 'I know that too. And even when there is it seems like nobody knows what to say. Look at Aggie, now. She's all lathered up because she's never had to ask for help in her life, but she's beginning to suspect that she's going to need some now and it scares the hell out of her. She's so afraid of becoming a drag on you, she thinks you've got too much to do as it is.'

'How do you know – have you been talking to Mom about this?' She was pulling back more, getting ready to be offended about having her turf invaded.

But he didn't give her any time for anger either. Pressing her head firmly against his chest he said very softly into the side of her ear, 'And then there's me, that you took in and loved when I was more dead than alive. After you gave me a place to go where I could feel like a man again, instead of a ghost, do you think I'm ever going to let that go without a fight?' She lay as if mesmerized as he stroked her back and kissed her cheek. 'All four of us, for different reasons, we need to help each other right now. But for three such feisty women, I gotta say with all due respect, none of you's very good at saying what you need.' Then he said it for her. 'We all need to move in together, into a bigger house.'

No clap of thunder sounded and the sky didn't fall. In fact their bodies seemed to find small accommodations that allowed them to move closer, and for a while they lay silently entwined, breathing in unison. Finally Sarah raised the practical question, 'How, though? I don't have much equity in this duplex.'

'I don't have any in my casita. But at least the lease is easy to get out of.' He chuckled, shaking them both all over.

'Mom's house is paid for, but even if it was big enough, Marana's too far for us.'

'I know. But houses out there are moving pretty well now, and Aggie says . . .'

Holding each other so close they could barely breathe, talking softly, using every bit of audacity they possessed, and tactfully skirting around the fact that Dietz had very little besides himself and his paycheck, they figured out how to make it work.

Cruz didn't wait two weeks to call. A few days after his big lament about Calvin, he was back on the phone. Sarah was surprised but not alarmed.

'Hey, Phil,' she said, 'what's shakin'?'

'That miserable little *fuck* tried to run.' Cruz was almost too angry to talk. 'I was absolutely straight with him, Sarah,

I told him about all the odds that were stacked against him. But he tried it anyway, he couldn't resist. *Damn* him.'

'How could he run? I thought you said—'

'He found an old safe-cracking buddy to get him out of the ankle bracelet. Then he hitched a ride with the safe-cracker's buddy, who was hauling scrap iron to Phoenix in an old pickup. That part, I have to tell you, was so dumb it was ingenious – the impromptu maneuver nobody could possibly foresee. He was hidden in plain sight, rolling along the road like a hundred other losers going to work.'

'So how'd you find him?'

'I never really lost him, I was just one step behind for part of the day because I was in a meeting with the sound turned off and didn't notice my monitor blinking. When I did I just followed the GPS I'd installed in his belt buckle. He was so pleased to have a belt again after two months in that orange jumpsuit, I knew he'd never take it off.'

'Where've you got him now?'

'Right back in the county lock-up where I found him, and I told him he can rot in there for all I care. Cokely's treating him like a pariah too. I gave Cokely strict orders, don't even talk to him.'

'Oh, that was smart – Cokely so loves strict orders.' She could feel the request coming and knew it was folly to try to dodge it. But why make it easy for him? She said, 'Well, hey, it could have worked, huh? Let me know if you get another idea.' She hung up quickly and smiled at her desk clock for twelve seconds. She let the phone ring three times before she picked it up and said, 'Burke.'

'All right, Sarah,' Cruz said, 'what do you want?'

'Did I say I wanted anything? You're the one doing all the calling. What do *you* want?'

'He's got something else to trade. I could tell all along by the way he was behaving – he was never very scared of screwing up because he's got more to trade than he's used.'

'Wow, that's pretty subtle. I'm not sure I can follow such a rarefied train of thought.'

'Make fun of me if you want to, but I wouldn't say it if I wasn't sure it was true. That's why, after he ran, I told him

I never want to see him again. I give him two days before he starts to get anxious.'

'How will you know, if nobody's talking to him?'

'He'll call you. I'd bet on it. You want to bet me? Twenty bucks, how about it?'

'I don't have any money to squander on gambling,' Sarah said primly.

'Bullshit! You won't bet because you know I'm right. He'll make a big noise about having the right to another phone call and when they get sick of listening to him and give in, he'll call you.'

'And say what?'

'That he's just remembered he knows something else.'

'If you say so. But if he doesn't call me there's really nothing I can do, is there? You're not expecting me to try entrapment, I hope.' She knew she was having too much fun and should shut up while she was ahead. But it was already too late, Phil Cruz had picked up the Kool-Aid and was gulping it down.

'Well, if he doesn't call you, maybe you could just walk by his cell, say you're on the way to another prisoner and be ever so surprised to see him back in there. Huh? Ask him what happened, show a little sympathy?' Sarah let the silence build. Cruz had a little rattle in his breathing these days, she thought. He might be getting a touch of asthma; this valley was hell on any tendency toward allergies. He coughed and asked her, 'What do you think?'

'I think it sounds like a high school play. I think you're overwrought and you need to get out of that building. You should come up and have a coffee with me at, oh, maybe El Minuto, how does that sound?'

He hesitated just long enough to let her know he was thinking about whether he wanted to sweeten the deal. 'Half an hour?'

'Done.'

She got up and stood in Delaney's doorway, knocked on the frame so he'd look up from the paper he was quoting into the phone. He held up one finger, said 'Yeah,' and 'Mmm,' and 'Yes, four o'clock.'

When he put the phone down she said, 'Phil Cruz called.'

She brought him up to date quickly with the latest wrinkle in what he always called 'Sarah's box o' bones caper'. When she finished her story she asked him, 'Granted that we would never stoop to consider the value of any possible forfeiture when we decide which investigations take priority . . .'

'Granted.' Delaney's pale blue eyes were reading her face like a crime stat report.

'But if we assist the DEA twice on a case that might net out in the millions, it's not unreasonable to request that some consideration be given to the incomplete state of our recording equipment for the interview rooms, right? By the Special Agent I'm meeting in a few minutes to talk about Calvin Inman's shady secrets?'

'Not unreasonable at all. Better still, since you have so many other pressing responsibilities, you could tell him to stop by my office after his coffee and cut the deal with me. Since I can be trusted never to stoop.' He held up his right hand like a traffic cop and switched from strategy to tactics. 'You pretty certain you can deliver this Calvin's shady secrets?'

'Oh, sure. He's dying to talk about what he knows. But then he gets with Phil Cruz and some testosterone thing happens, he has to prove he can outwit the fuzz – and the starchier the fuzz, the more he needs to prove it.'

'How come you're exempt?'

'I'm a girl. Guys like Calvin never see me as a threat to their manhood even when I'm locking them up.'

'I guess. You're past getting mad about it though, aren't you?'

'I finally grew up and realized it works for me as often as it works against me. Like today.'

'OK, go meet your guy, get him up here so I can make the deal. We do need to upgrade the sound equipment, and the general fund is circling the bowl.'

The box o' bones caper did not seem so amusing two days later, when Calvin Inman finally called. The last day of the week was always Crazy Friday, when a dozen loose ends had to be tied up. Today felt a little crazier than usual because Dietz had found a house he wanted her to look at after work, 'So try to get away a few minutes early if you can.'

'Will, Mom's realtor says she's got quite a backlog of houses right now. Let's not get ahead of ourselves.'

'I won't. But we need to get a feel for the market, see what's available.'

'I'll do my best,' she said. But then Leo and Jason began walking through the section saying they needed to get the whole crew together to talk about some new evidence in the Cooper case. And naturally the first available time turned out to be four o'clock.

And now ahead of that she needed to fit in some time at Pima County with Calvin Inman. She called Phil Cruz and told him the play was starting, Calvin had called. Phil repeated his solemn promise that after the cocaine case was made they'd bring the Soltero gang back to Tucson for trial. 'Help me get me that cocaine bust, Sarah,' he kept saying, 'and I'll get your murderers back here.'

My murderers. Look how I'm coming up in the world.

She asked Ed Cokely for an interview room at two o'clock. When he called to tell her he had it, she asked him, 'Do you have time to sit in with me?'

'Are you sure?' Ed asked her. 'Cruz keeps saying I mustn't talk to him.'

'That was before' she said, 'just to soften him up. Now we want him to be a regular chatterbox.'

'Well, that's one of his talents,' Ed said. 'Two o'clock, then.'

She wanted Cokely with her in the box, not Cruz. Something about the Inman-Cruz combination had turned toxic and brought out Inman's worst instincts. But she liked to have an observer on the enforcement side. Recordings were all very well but there was nothing better than a second eye on the suspect. And Ed was good in the interview room, he didn't yield to the temptation to show off a little for the camera as she had seen some officers do.

Inman looked sleep-deprived, needed a shave and a haircut and his mustache wax. 'Orange was never my color, actually,' he said with a lopsided smile when he saw her reaction to his appearance.

'Calvin, Calvin, what were you thinking?' Sarah said. 'I had you all set up to prosper with the DEA, and now you've got yourself on Cruz's shit list and he says he never wants to see you again.'

'He's an awful snob, Sarah,' Calvin said. 'Is he a failed priest or something? Nobody's pure enough to satisfy him.'

'He's responsible for that money he's been giving you. You can never seem to understand how enraged people get when you tap into their pocketbooks.'

'Oh, please. You know perfectly well that was Fed money and if they want more they just print it.' He really didn't seem to take seriously how angry he made people. Calvin, Sarah began to realize, saw life as a game. If he won a round, why couldn't people be good sports about it?

'I bet Cruz could get over himself pretty fast, though –' Calvin propped his elbows on the table, getting ready to play his next card – 'if you told him I know how he can find out where the head is.'

Sometimes, Sarah thought, watching the pulse beat over Calvin's eye, I feel like he's making it up as he goes along. 'You talking about Chuy Maldonado's head?'

'Would I call you about the Easter Bunny's head? Of course Chuy's.'

'Why would Special Agent Cruz care about the head? He's DEA, he's not tasked with proving homicide cases.'

'Ah, but if he's got the Solteros for murder one,' Calvin said, 'they'll gladly cop to the coke shipments instead.'

'Maybe.' *So damn clever.* She was afraid her amusement might be showing. 'How would having the head make it any easier to hang the murder on the Solteros?'

'The way I heard it,' Calvin said, 'they did the nutcase savage thing with the end of his nose.'

'Mmm. Here in the Old Pueblo we all think we know a Soltero signature when we see one, but you know that's not evidence. Lawyers will just say anybody could imitate that.'

'But I bet when Phil Cruz finds the box,' Calvin Inman said, 'he'll find some other helpful stuff like fingerprints and that. There might even be a bullet in that head, what do you think?'

'Ah, Calvin,' Sarah said, 'you do know how to tell a story, don't you?'

He knew how to enjoy being the center of attention, too.

She felt an odd mixture of excitement and despair, thinking about how much of her future was probably going to be spent responding to Calvin Inman's big stories.

The one he was telling right now concerned José Ojeda, the regular courier he had replaced on that unsanctioned trip to North Carolina.

José had made all the Outer Banks trips the Solteros knew about, Calvin said, ever since they made the deal. And because Calvin knew José was making good money for that, and thought he might have the occasional odd job he could well afford to pay cash for, he found out which bars José favored, and hung out in them till they got acquainted. Bought José some drinks one night when he was already more than half full of tequila. Let him ramble on about all the land the Ojedas used to own in Mexico before the crooked politicians cheated them out of it. Finally got him to talk about the time he helped Huicho Valdez and Rafi Soltero cut up Chuy Maldonado and pack the pieces in two containers.

'Ol' José knows exactly where they buried the head, down by the Santa Cruz below the reclamation plant, where the ground is nice and soft. And when the Special Agents grab that load of coke in North Carolina, if Phil Cruz has me on his side telling him just what to ask, he'll find it's easy to make a deal with José. He's not in the gang, he's just working for pay, like the pilot.'

'I've been wondering about that pilot. Why didn't they kill him too, when they learned about the extra flight?'

'He owns the plane. A crooked pilot with his own twin-engine aircraft doesn't come along every day.'

'I suppose. Omigod, look at the time.' Sarah began punching numbers into her cell. 'Ed, can you keep this bad boy put away by himself somewhere till Cruz gets here? He must not talk to anybody before he talks to DEA!'

'OK, Agent Smart,' Ed said to a tired-looking Calvin Inman, 'back you go into the cone of silence.'

As soon as she got Cruz's assurance he was coming to check his once-more valuable prisoner out of County lock-up and into another safe house, Sarah hurried back to South Stone, where Delaney's homicide crew was gathering around a table.

Leo Tobin was in a rotten humor. 'Last week I thought we were just about ready to close this perfectly simple murder-suicide,' he said. 'Now, every day we get a whole new mess to clean up.' He glared at Jason Peete, who was patting his shaved head nervously. 'Tell them.'

Jason inclined his head ten degrees right, shrugged his skinny right shoulder upwards as if to comfort his ear, and said, 'Ballistics says the bullet I took out of the wall behind Frank Cooper wasn't fired by his gun.'

TWELVE

'Soon as I saw it,' Dietz said, 'I felt like this house was made to order for us.'

'It is, isn't it? Wow, if only.' They were on Bentley Street in the Blenman-Elm district, an area of older houses, big yards and mature trees.

'Just a couple of blocks from the school,' Dietz said. 'Denny could walk.'

'It's the guest house in back that really makes it. Look, it even has its own little galley.' Her mother could be so comfortable in that tidy two-room space. Homier than just a bedroom but a lot less trouble than a whole house, and only a few steps across the patio from the back door of the main house. 'Mom could have privacy and still be close enough to get help if she needs it.'

Back in the bigger house, she walked along the hall. 'Three bedrooms and two baths. La de dah, we could have a den.'

'It's even got a little workshop off the carport, see? I could set up my table saw.'

'Yeah, how's that for having everything you need? Oh, Will – I know we can't afford this one, but you're right, a house as much as possible like this would be perfect.'

'Well . . .' He looked over his shoulder. The realtor was waiting discreetly outside as she had promised. 'It's been on the market for a while. She says she's pretty sure they'd lease for a year with an option to buy.'

'Oh, you mean so Mom could take her time . . .'

'Wait for her price, yeah.'

'Well, but price . . . even with the money from Mom's house, we could never pay for all this.'

'I think we could get it for less than they're asking, Sarah, if we nailed the price down now while real estate's still slow. This house has some problems, let me show you.' There was a bad floor in the second bathroom, woodwork in the hall that would have to be replaced. 'But I can do that myself.'

'With your trusty table saw, hmmm? But that's not the biggest problem, is it? This kitchen –' she made a face – 'looks like it's been here since the house was built. Linoleum floor. And that dinky little stove. Back to the Fifties, shee.'

'Think of it as making the place affordable,' Will said.

'Is it? Three bedrooms and two baths, plus a guest house?'

'But sixty years old. Let's go talk to the lady.'

On the way back to Marana, they went over it again. 'OK,' Will said, 'even if she doesn't take our first offer and the money from your two places doesn't quite cover it all, we can make payments on the rest, can't we? It'll be less than we're paying now.'

'Oh, yes, it's a good deal for both of *us*. Good for Denny, too, even if she does have to change schools. It sure is a step down for Mom, though, from her nice new house in the 'burbs. I guess we better show her and let her decide.'

Luckily the guest house was in the best shape of anything on the lot – it had hardly been used. Aggie walked through it the next day, nodding. In the main house, she waved away Sarah's concern about the kitchen. 'Kitchens are easy to replace, you just go to Sears.' She loved the big trees in the yard. 'Denny could have a tree house.' She smiled at the two of them, standing close together watching her anxiously. 'Can we really swing this?'

'Yes,' Sarah said, 'if you're still willing to sell your house.'

'In a heartbeat. Speaking of which –' she put a hand on her chest – 'I need to sit down.' They both jumped to help her. 'Hey, no big emergency! I just can't stand up very long. Yet.' She held onto Sarah's hand. 'Soon, though, I'll be worth my salt again.' Impulsively, she put her cheek against the back of Sarah's hand. '*Some* salt, anyway. Thanks to you, my darling daughter, and this good man you were smart enough to hold onto.'

When she looked up, her eyes were bright. 'Why don't you go get Denny out of that library where you stashed her? I want to see her face when she sees her new home.'

Ever since the terrible moment when Aggie fainted and got hauled off to the hospital, Denny had been trying to fight off panic attacks – the seashore feeling. She had seen only one beach in her life, in San Diego when she was five. What she remembered about it was the way the tide came in and washed the sand out from under her feet, and how her tiny self stood whimpering in fear, as the solid earth slid away and became ocean. Her mother, seeing her alarm, took her hand laughing and said, 'Back up a step if it scares you.'

She remembered squealing in glee, back up on drier sand, delighted to find such an easy solution. They had stood together and watched a couple of breakers roll in and recede, till finally Denny was brave enough to step forward and feel that sand slide again.

That day at the shore was a vague, happy memory, of walking the tideline for an hour, picking up shells, watching the shorebirds scamper and feed. Her life had been mostly good like that, until her Mom started serious doping and drinking and the family began to come around, giving each other sidelong glances. There was a lot of very quiet talk, somehow always in a room she wasn't in.

The first seashore nightmares began during that time, when she knew something bad was going to happen but was somehow never allowed to ask what it was. In her dreams nobody took her hand, she forgot to back up, and the waves quickly became monstrous and swept her out to sea. She woke screaming and ran to her mother for comfort. Janine was snoring loudly, under the influence of the several empties adrift on her bedside table, but Denny clung to her back anyway and finally got to sleep.

The next day Grandma Aggie, Aunt Sarah and Uncle Howard all came to the house at an odd time, just after lunch on a weekday, and got Mom out of bed where she was taking a little nap. Grandma took Denny into her own room, found her some dolls and toys, and asked her to stay in there and play.

How could she play? She stood by the door, feeling sand slide out from under her feet as she listened to solemn talk in the next room. Mom argued in a loud voice until Sarah said something sharp and short that made her stop yelling and start to cry. After the crying stopped the serious bargaining started, all the family taking turns. Then there was silence and a scraping of chairs as they all stood up.

When the door opened the women spoke to her in cheerful, unreal voices. Their faces looked hot and sore. Howard stood stiffly in the yard, smoking a cigarette, while the women packed bags, made phone calls and wrote notes. When they were ready Mom hugged her hard and got in the car with Aunt Sarah. Denny went with Grandma and Uncle Howard to the ranch. On the ride, Grandma explained to Denny about detox, that Mom had a bad habit that she had to break. Denny asked why she couldn't break it at home. Grandma explained that breaking some habits took help, and said they should be glad Mom was getting the help she needed. Grandma didn't look glad, though. Denny thought she looked almost as sad as she had when Grandpa died.

After lunch the next day Grandma went home and Denny stayed at the ranch. Nobody wanted her there, but there was no place else for her to be, so she stayed all summer.

Eventually Aunt Sarah took her to town so she could start school. When Mom got out of detox she rented a house on the east side and got a job in an office. She promised Denny they were going to be very happy from now on, and they almost made it for a while, until Mom started drinking again. Then there were boyfriends and dope, hungry days and scary nights. During the chaotic craziness that got Denny rescued again by Aunt Sarah, Mom ran away rather than face detox again. Denny worried about her but couldn't help liking the life she had in Aunt Sarah's house, regular meals and clean clothes and staying caught up at school. She was glad when Aunt Sarah filed motions in court to get custody, aiming at adoption so Denny's life couldn't ever get torn up again.

But Grandma Aggie made it all possible, coming over every weekday afternoon, to be there in the house when Denny got home. Even if Aunt Sarah had to work late, which sometimes happened in Homicide, Grandma was there to help with homework and supper. Denny knew she'd been managing those things herself and could again, but the grown-ups in her life now wanted her afternoons supervised, and so did the judge and social workers in the court where her adoption was going to take place.

Watching Aggie talk funny and fall down, and then hearing about her hooked up to a lot of tubes and being asked to wiggle her toes, had made Denny realize how much depended on a functioning Grandma who could wiggle everything. Denny tried to keep her mind on wishing her Grandma well, but the thought kept surfacing: *What's going to happen to me now? What if Aunt Sarah can't keep me?*

Why was her world always built on sand? She thought she would do anything to find a place on solid rock. She did her best, after Grandma got sick, to show how little trouble she could be, her clothes always ready, lessons done. But by the middle of the week the seashore nightmare came back, and she woke up crying. She held her breath, afraid she might have wakened Aunt Sarah, but luckily her aunt, during that exhausting week, slept soundly when she got the chance.

For a couple of days Denny thought she was building an alliance with Will Dietz. She had just begun to trust the strangely silent boyfriend a little, and when she saw him trying to find a foothold in the new scheme of things, she tried to show him she would help. Just when she thought they were a team, though, Aunt Sarah moved them out to Marana to stay in Grandma's house, and then they both got very tense about keeping everything nice and helping Grandma. Denny could hardly taste her food, she got so anxious to wash the dish it was in.

When she found Aunt Sarah and Will Dietz whispering in the kitchen, she knew she'd stumbled into the middle of a conspiracy. When Aunt Sarah took Grandma for one of their 'little walks' and lingered a long time on the corner talking, Denny knew for sure something was up.

Then Dietz and Aunt Sarah disappeared in town for most of a Saturday. When they suggested a ride into town on Sunday, she could tell by their faces they were excited about something. *I bet they found her a rest home. And that means I go back to the ranch.*

They dropped Denny at Martha Cooper Library, where she'd never been before. Aunt Sarah said, 'Have a good read while we do a little shopping with Grandma.' She reached into a row of books, pulled one out and sat staring at it, too frightened to read with understanding. Was she really going to have to go back to the ranch, where nobody but Uncle Howard ever talked to her? Maybe I'll just get on a horse, she thought for one wild moment, and ride away from there. But where would she go? She was brave, but too experienced to be foolhardy. She knew all about chaos, it was order she craved.

When Aunt Sarah came back for her, Denny walked out to the car on legs that felt rubbery with dread. They stopped in front of a strange older house and Denny thought, This must be the place they found for Grandma. Aunt Sarah parked in the carport, and led her through the back of it to a brick patio behind the house. Her grandmother was sitting there, looking happy and relaxed, almost like her old self.

'Hello, my little bird,' she said. 'Welcome to your new home.'

Denny looked around at them, waiting for the other shoe to drop.

Sarah said, 'Will and I have been looking for a way we could all live together, and Will found this house.'

'It's got a little house here in back for me, see?' Aggie said.

'Got a workshop here,' Will said. 'I could make you a tree house, would you like that?'

'You're finally going to have a room of your own,' Sarah said. 'With a dresser. Put your socks in a drawer instead of shoeboxes.'

When Aunt Sarah said that about the socks, and she finally understood that this was not a joke, Denny uttered one strangled cry, put her hands in front of her eyes and wept. The grown-ups watched her heaving shoulders in astonishment, saying, 'What? What is it?'

Aunt Sarah figured it out first. 'I should have thought of this,' she said. 'But there's been so much to think about, I just didn't . . . she thought her life was coming unstuck again, that I wouldn't be able to keep her,' she told Will and Aggie. 'That's it, isn't it, Denny?' Denny nodded mutely, still leaking tears between her fingers. 'OK now,' Aunt Sarah gathered her into her arms, hugged, rocked a little and patted. 'I understand this time and I'll take all the blame, I should have told you what was going on. But this is the last time. You hear me, Denny? I want you to promise me you will never have doubts like that again. Look at me!'

Reluctantly, Denny pulled her hands down from her wet face and looked at her aunt. Aunt Sarah smiled into her red, swollen eyes and said, 'We're a family now. The four of us are going to live together in this house. We'll probably drive each other nuts soon enough, but right now, sweetheart, let's walk through it and enjoy ourselves.'

As soon as she let herself believe it, Denny loved it all. 'So . . . so . . . beyond wonderful,' she said, bestowing a blazing smile none of them had ever seen before. The plain little room she picked for a bedroom began to be adorned at once, in her imagination, with framed awards and gorgeous posters. She said the old kitchen faucets were 'cute', and when she saw Will's tool shed she said, 'Dremmel's got a home!'

There was a long wait in the realtor's office while the grown-ups did a lot of bargaining and signed a complicated three-way lease-with-option. It would have been very boring for Denny, but she tuned out most of it and imagined her room in different colors, moving the bed from wall to wall in her mind.

By the time they drove back to Marana, she was incandescent. She said, for the tenth time, 'I love it all,' and saw Aunt Sarah nudge Will's elbow. She recognized it now for what it was: not a conspiracy, just a simple nudge of pleasure.

'I don't know yet where the missing gun is,' Tracy said. Leo and Sarah leaned over his shoulder, watching filenames scroll down off the screen. 'Why don't you bring me his other computer, I'll see if there's something in about it?'

'What other computer?' Sarah said.

'You've got the desktop he had in his den,' Leo said. 'Plus Kindle, iPhone, iPad, monitors, speakers, modem – that's all we found.'

'It's not any of those gadgets,' Tracy said. 'It's not brand new, either. Look for a laptop or maybe a netbook, something small that he carried around for Internet fun.' He smirked. 'Naughty fun, mostly.'

'Frank Cooper?' Sarah frowned. 'You found something that says he's got this other—'

'Other computer. Yes. The modem's LAN status page lists

a second machine named "funbox". Explorer on this box shows an L Drive mapped to a share on another machine with a local 192.168.yaddayadda address. And I found old thumbs of nasty pictures on this machine that didn't get here through the browser.'

'Talk English,' Leo said.

'O Immortal Software Gods,' Tracy Scott said as he lay back in his chair and implored the ceiling, 'why hast thou abandoned thy faithful servant here in Neanderthal Country?' He lifted the coke-bottle glasses and pinched the bridge of his nose for a few seconds, emerged from his funk with a bright smile and lifted his right index finger like a baton. 'Think of it this way. You know how you always have your techies photograph a crime scene before you set to work on it? Why do you do that?'

'Because the laws of physics say that as soon as you start to measure and evaluate the scene you're going to change it.'

'Exactly!' Tracy crowed happily. 'So you need to be able to look back and see how it was before you touched it, don't you?' His smile kept growing brighter; he liked this mentor persona he was working up. 'So in the very same way, a person who's tasked with finding important things in a computer, *if he knows what he's doing,* will very carefully, and in the most deliberate way, start from the outside in, check what's hooked up to the box or has been, how the folders are organized, what's in them or has been, *etceter-aaahhh.* Because he knows, as soon as he starts to mess with this thing, he's going to start changing file dates and all that, isn't he?'

Sarah watched Leo examine his loafers and realize this brat knew he'd been mucking around in Frank Cooper's computer for days, without taking any of those precautions.

'OK, smart ass,' he said. 'You know so much, tell me where to find the LadySmith and the second computer.'

'Hey, you're the detectives. I'm just the geek. I don't know where that second machine is, I just know it exists. And I'm pretty sure that's the machine he was using to surf the web and download the naughty stuff. The browser history on this machine is clean as the driven snow. It hasn't been erased;

it's complete but full of harmless sites. Occasionally, though, he'd transfer pictures to this machine from the one he was using to download – maybe to see stuff on that big flat-screen monitor. That's what makes me think it might be a netbook – you could be looking for a real small box, fine for downloading but not so good for watching the juicy bits.

'He clearly tried to clean up after himself. I didn't find any actual pictures anywhere, but I found some leftover thumbnail image files, from a couple of years old to one updated last month. He must have thought that since *he* couldn't see the thumbnails any more they were gone. But of course I can see exactly what pictures used to be there with a free tool that takes about 2 minutes to download over the web.'

His derisive laughter echoed through the entire second floor. 'Why are people so brain-dead about this stuff?' His hilarity was infectious – people began coming out of their cubicles to see what was funny.

Sarah and Leo walked away from him, shaking their heads, trying to look disapproving. Tracy was a lot more amusing, Sarah realized, when all of his comedy was directed at some-body else.

'Please don't put her in my room,' Luz implored Tía Luisa. 'She will interfere with my studying and drive me crazy.'

'Stop whining, it gives me a headache,' Luisa said. 'I will talk to your mother before I decide what to do about Victoria. For now she will use the other bed in your room, what else would she use?'

As soon as Luisa was out of the room Vicky seized her sister's arm, stuck the shiv in her ear and whispered, 'Complain about me again I will make you deaf in one ear.' She pushed on the point and Luz squeaked in fear. 'I am going to stay here and you are going to help me, you hear? Nod your head!' Luz bobbed a tiny nod. When the point hurt her ear she panicked and put her hands together in sup-plication. 'Very good. When Luisa asks you how we are getting along you will say fine, fine.' She took the sharpened nail out of her sister's ear and smiled. 'And we will. Get along. Just fine.'

'You are a devil,' Luz whispered.

'Exactly.' Vicky smiled. 'Remember that.'

Tía Luisa had a long talk with Marisol, put the phone down, sighed, and seated Vicky on a stool by her feet. 'Very well, you can stay here for the present if you will do everything I say. Everything, you hear me? Now I will tell you the rules.'

She said Vicky could work on one of the cleaning crews if she kept her mouth shut and caused no trouble. 'Marisol says you are done with school. That's good. One scholar in the family is enough.' *Ah, someone else is tired of Santa Luz of Tucson.* 'You must pay cash for everything. No checking accounts, no charge accounts or subscriptions, nothing to leave a paper trail to this house, you understand?

'Be careful what you say to gringos. You talk like one yourself, that helps. Get rid of those sandals, anyone can see they are Mexican. If you get caught I will not help you, don't call me. Say you have been living on the street, don't carry anything with this address on it.'

The American child she had once been would have felt cruelly treated. But Vicky, fresh from Ajijic where she had shared a cot in a room crammed full of many cots, looked at plentiful food on a table where the dishes matched, saw several pairs of shoes in each closet under rows of clean clothing, and felt her heart swell with pride.

She had made it, she was home. Tucson was her city whether it wanted her or not. *I got here on my own, surely I am clever enough to find a way to stay.* And the last weeks with her mother and aunts in Mexico had taught her how to ingratiate herself quickly with hard-working older women. *Take something off her back.*

'If you give me a job,' she said, showing Tía Luisa her most sincere face, 'I will show you I am worth my keep.'

She took all the hardest jobs without complaint, worked extra hours if somebody failed to show. She took separated days off instead of two together, and often worked one or both of those to replace a worker who was sick. The other women on the crews, mistaking her willingness for hick stupidity, whispered behind their hands that she '*no sabe ni como canta el gallo*', and maneuvered her into the dirtiest houses, the ones with small children and a couple of dogs. She saw what they were doing but said nothing. Tía Luisa would hear no complaints from her.

She knew that Tía Luisa paid her lower wages than the rest of the crew and took out a generous cut for board and room. One advantage of being paid under the table, though, was that she did not get a pay stub showing payroll tax deducted for social security she would never collect. She remembered how her father used to rage about the money he suspected his employer of pocketing.

For the present, she put all of that out of her mind. Her task was to survive in a society that both did and did not want her. This town would keep her as long as she was useful and discard her when she was in the way, because there were ten more behind her trying to take her place.

She had very little spending money, but she no longer felt poor, as she had when she was growing up in this neighborhood. Ajijic had taught her what real poverty was all about – hard labor with no hope for improvement. She was in Tucson now, where better times were always just around the corner.

'I just got a call from my guy in North Carolina,' Phil Cruz said. 'Lucky we made this deal with Inman when we did, Sarah. Those dealers called Rafi Soltero yesterday and said, "Enough foreplay, let's fuck."'

'So a big load's going soon?'

'Later this week. If everybody does his job right the whole outfit will be in custody by the end of the week.'

'And just as soon as they tell you they've got that end secured, we're going to pick up Huicho and Rafi here, right?'

'That's the next step, sure. You got your warrants ready? You got enough people?'

'You bet. Judge Galsworthy says she'll sign warrants any time, day or night, whenever I'm ready to go. Bless her, she holds a grudge the same way I do, she's been wanting to get that crew off the streets for years. Depending on what else is going on, I might need some help for our uniforms – you got some bodies?'

'Say the word, Sarah, we'll come running.'

But the next day he was in her workspace, speaking very softly as he explained that a team of DEA agents would be coming down from Phoenix to help Phil arrest the Soltero gang and transport them to North Carolina. It was felt, Phil told her, that it would 'make more sense', and 'play better for a Grand Jury' to have them charged there for the cocaine smuggling – there where the load was going to be seized. They wanted to have the story run in all the big East Coast papers, with photos of the drugs seized, the weapons laid out on a table, a row of uniforms smiling behind.

'How come they get what they want instead of us?'

'Three big metro units involved. Lotta clout. And they *are* making the arrests there.'

'What about the head, though? Chuy's head in the river-bank? Are they going to come and take the big river walk with José?'

'No, but they promise, soon as they've got him indicted on the coke charge, we can get him back here to help us find the head.'

'And if we find it, we get to try Rafi and Huicho here for the murder?'

'We'll see. They're mainly interested in seeing them go away for a long time on the drug charge, you know. I mean, there's so much money involved in that.' Phil Cruz kept his eyes fixed on the ceiling light over Sarah's desk. 'They're thinking if we prove the homicide they might want to fold that into the drug case, make it a federal crime so it's got a little more weight.'

'I could make it plenty heavy right here in Tucson. I could make it Murder One.'

'I know how you feel, Sarah. I'd rather have the whole case come back here where we did all the work. Unfortunately at my pay grade I don't make those decisions.'

And if you ever want to reach that pay grade you don't make waves about jurisdiction.

'I understand,' she said, and booted up her screen. She held her breath to keep from saying any more.

'So,' he said, turned sideways in the door of her cubicle, examining his shoes, 'you want me to call you when it's time for the river walk?'

'Sure,' she said, 'I'll bring my binocs, make it a birding day.'

'I got my lease cancelled at the end of the month,' Will said. '*This* month. Did you hear me, Sarah? Five days from now. So I'm going to take as many furlough days as I can next week and move my stuff into the Bentley Street house.'

'Fine,' Sarah said. She had just come in the door after still another futile search of Frank Cooper's office, and her head wasn't really in the game. 'You don't have much to move, do you?

'Going to get the rest of my tools and stuff out of that storage space where I've been keeping them. And I hope you're going to approve of the trade I made yesterday,' Will said. 'Come and look.'

A somewhat dented but solid-looking pickup sat behind her car in the driveway. 'You rented a pickup?'

'I traded my car for it. What do you think?'

'But you loved your almost-new car that you finally got.'

'This is more what we need now. Ford F-150, a very serviceable vehicle. We've got all these houses to move out of and I think I can do most of it myself. I can start taking some of your stuff next week too. Make it easier to get your house cleaned up for sale if it wasn't so crowded.'

'Sounds like a plan. Next week's looking kind of like gangbusters at work, though. I doubt if I'll have much time for house-cleaning.' Besides the two homicide cases heating up, the extra drive times every day to get to work and school from Marana were wiping out what used to be her time off. She had all she could do to keep Aggie's house clean. And they certainly didn't want to make any work for Grandma, she kept reminding Denny, who was beginning to roll her eyes sideways at her aunt every time she put down a spoon or a cup.

'And the week after that isn't going to be any easier,' Will said, 'so you shouldn't even be thinking about cleaning, you've got too much to do as it is. But I called a couple of house-cleaning services today and checked out their prices. It's not as much as you'd think, Sarah, I can pay for it out of what I save on the storage space.' Will Dietz seemed to have discovered his inner cock-eyed optimist, he had all kinds of fuzzy math like that going on.

He didn't want money anxieties to spoil the fun of the new house, Sarah thought, but what she kept noticing was that neither of them had much cash in hand. She suspected Aggie of giving Will's wallet a boost now and then, and she was determined they must have a more detailed conversation about how this three-way split was going to work. But she wanted to do it when they were all calm and there was time to get it right – and chances for that occasion dissolved as she approached them.

'What I really need,' she told Will Dietz later that night, when she walked him to his pickup, 'is a twin.'

'No you don't,' he said. 'You've got me.'

Frank Cooper's corporate office occupied half the space in an office suite on North Campbell Avenue. Nicole's accounting offices took up the other half. Frank's side had been sequestered, and the connecting door between the two sides was locked. But Sarah wasn't very impressed with the soundproofing in the connecting wall – she could plainly hear all Nicole's office machines and phone calls.

The décor in Frank's office was even more nondescript than the Cooper house: gray carpet, laminated desks, serviceable chairs. It was strictly for work: good lights, plenty of power outlets, no extras. Frank's muscular computer with its several exterior hard drives and sexy flat-screen monitor had been the only impressive item in the room, and it was gone to South Stone. One of Tucson's most successful businesses had been run from here, but plainly, Frank Cooper didn't need a lot of shiny toys or even much comfort while he worked.

Which made it all the more interesting that he had felt the need for a second small computer to carry around and – what? Play games, amuse himself? Nothing in this office suggested he was a playful man.

'It's not here,' Leo Tobin said.

'Nicole said it wouldn't be. I'm convinced,' Sarah said, softly, mindful of the bad acoustics, 'that Nicole is telling the truth when she says she never saw him use a laptop. She told me he used to shake his head when he saw college students curled up with their laptops, muttering about kids taking a brilliant machine and turning it into a toy.'

'They do a lot of learning curled up like that.'

'I know. Everything Nicole and Tom say about their father makes him seem crusty and old-fashioned. If Tracy's right about what's on that spare computer, it's going to come as quite a surprise to his children.'

'Unless it isn't. You think there's any chance Nicole's hiding it so nobody can find out about the old man's hobbies?'

'I don't think so. I told you before that I think Nicole is hiding something, but I'm pretty sure it's not her father's extra computer. I questioned her closely about that machine, and she seemed genuinely puzzled by my questions.'

Leo didn't question her conclusion. They knew each others' interrogation methods well and trusted them. He threw his hands in the air and said, 'Well then, let's go take another look in his house.'

'Didn't we toss that pretty thoroughly before?'

'That little den where he had a home office, yes. I'm ready to swear there's nothing in there I haven't looked at. His bedroom, though . . . when we were looking there before, I wasn't even thinking about a second computer. Seems to me we were all looking for money, jewelry, or letters, something they might have been fighting about before he killed her.'

'OK,' Sarah said. 'Back to the house with no soul.'

It still had the crime scene lock on the door. The bodies were gone but the smell of death lingered faintly. It was a big handsome house, designed for pleasure, but the crippled marriage that occupied it had sucked out all the comfort and ease. The rooms looked like showrooms in a store run by people with no particular taste.

Frank's bedroom shared a bath with the bedroom on the other side, which he'd converted into a den. It was a nifty set-up, Sarah thought – and it could have been charming, if the rooms had been filled with family pictures, books being read, a hobby or two. But Frank's rooms looked as cold and impersonal as his wife's.

The closets were filled with suits of good quality but no elegance, predictable shoes, ties that said nothing. Like his wife, he kept everything neat. The walk-in closet, Sarah thought, was the most attractive thing she'd seen in the house. It was full of drawers and cupboards well-planned and built by a skillful carpenter. To give herself more time to enjoy it, she told Leo, 'I'll take the closet if you'll do the bedroom.'

The shorter drawers on the left, full of socks and under-wear, were the hardest, so she did them first. She took the many small pieces out systematically, left to right, so she could be sure when she'd looked through everything. The long drawers on the right would be shirts and sweaters, sports clothes – big pieces, easy to inspect. This little row of drawers in the middle, not much point in opening them, they were all too small – well, but in the interest of being thorough, just a quick look. A jewelry drawer, lined in velvet, the man actu-ally had cufflinks and studs. The next held handkerchiefs, not as many as you'd think . . . she pulled them out, moved back a step and closed the drawer, measured the front with her thumb and index finger, pulled it open again and said, 'Leo?'

He came in, squinted, measured the same way she had, saying, 'Hmmm' and 'Ahh.' It took him a couple of minutes to figure out how to cheat the catch so they could lift out the drawer. From the back, they could see there was a slot, but the false bottom was so cleverly fitted Leo couldn't slide it out.

'Not enough space here for a computer.' Sarah had never noticed before how Leo poked his tongue out of the corner of his mouth when he concentrated. 'But maybe a LadySmith?' He found a tiny button at one end of the slot, pressed, and the bottom popped out half an inch. 'There we go,' he said, and then looked down, puzzled, at a silvery surface. 'What is it?'

'A netbook.' Sarah pulled it out, popped it open. 'Neat little PC.'

'So small . . . what's it good for?'

'Email. Facebook, Twitter. And web surfing to your heart's content.'

'Ah. So let's see what made his heart content.' He carried it into the den, set it on the desk. 'Jeez, hard to work this little keyboard with gloves on. But oh, yeah, here we go.'

'Just what Tracy said we'd find.'

'Yeah. Wow, he liked it kind of rough, didn't he?'

'Sure did. Ewww.' She'd had enough of Frank's dirty secrets in about a minute. 'Let's look at the emails. Maybe we'll find out who's got the LadySmith.' The count at the top of the list said 3685. 'Most of them are from the same person. Cheeks@aol.com? Open a couple, let's see what Cheeks had to say.'

Leo opened the last message, dated the day of Frank Cooper's death, just before noon. He read it aloud, '"C U @ 5." Hmmm. Cryptic. Let's try the one before. "No must C U today – MAKE TIME!" Argument about a meeting – no fun there. Let's go back a few, see if we find anything livelier. Yeah, here we go.' He read, '"Told U it could be like old times, now do you luv your Cheeks?" Looks like there's been a little trouble in the luv nest, huh?'

'Look back a couple of pages. Still mostly from Cheeks. Let's see how they were doing in January.'

Leo opened one and read, '"Too much fun last nite Big One – Cheeks has bruises! (LOL) More soon?"' Leo made a face. 'She called him Big One?'

'Worth a LadySmith any day,' Sarah said.

'I suppose. What about this other messenger? LJH20.'

'Look at the "sent" list, see if he was sending . . . yeah, there's one.'

Leo opened it and read, '"How's my Tasty Toes this morning? I'm thinking about you and wishing we were . . ." Hoo-ah.' Leo read on in silence. His glasses steamed up and he polished them on his tie.

'Still staying in touch with Cheeks though,' Sarah said. 'I wonder how long the second one's been in the picture.'

Leo flipped back through a couple of pages. 'Look, here's one near the end of November, to Laura Hughes, LJH20. "Laura, As I told you, I was very impressed yesterday by your beauty and charm. All I ask is a little of your time, a chance to tell you how I can make your life better. I promise you will not be sorry. Yours, Francis." Wow, formal.'

'Yeah. Let's see how long the formality lasted.' Sarah watched as he scrolled through the December messages, and opened one from a few days before Christmas. "My crazy crazy lover, I absolutely love mink! But you know, you don't ever have to give me any more than the thrill I get when I feel your big thing in my . . ."'

'Let's find out which vitamins Frankie was taking,' Leo said. 'I'll order a case.'

'You can do that,' Sarah said. 'But first let's take this pretty little toy back to Genius Geek and see if he can find out if either one of these ladies has the LadySmith.'

'You want me to turn all these red-hot messages over to a teenage boy? Sarah, isn't that reckless endangerment? I could get arrested.'

'Not to mention how noisy it's going to get on the second floor. But a guy's gotta do what he's gotta do. We need to find that gun.'

'For sure.'

'And I think we better ask him to figure out a timeline for when the second romance heated up and the first one began to go sour.'

'Yeah. You know, Frank and Lois had a lot more than a new store to fight about. Think about this guy's life.'

'I am thinking about it. And the more I think the more interesting it gets. Cheeks may have just figured out why things weren't going so well with her Big One.'

'Yeah, we need a timeline for everybody, don't we?'

'Genius Geek can do that for us. Because you and I need to interview Nicole and find what's her name, Tasty Toes? Laura Hughes. We can't spend all our days slavering over Frank Cooper's secret emails.'

'Sarah, you may be too busy to slaver,' Leo said, looking pious, 'but I can make time for it, if I must.'

THIRTEEN

'Got a crew coming to clean your house this afternoon,' Will said, 'because the realtor wants to show it tomorrow. She says the duplex market is kind of brisk right now.'

'That's good,' Sarah said, not paying very close attention. Will Dietz had turned into some unlikely combination of Dudley Do-Right and The Little Engine That Could. Besides having one more day off every week than she did, he seemed to have altered his circadian rhythms somehow – on the four days when he worked all night he was getting along fine on three or four hours of sleep plus an occasional nap. He was moving three sets of household goods into the Blenman-Elm neighborhood without much assistance from her.

Denny was similarly energized. Besides helping Will figure out the odd couplings that held her old iron bed together, she had conquered the mysteries of the gas stove in the Bentley Street kitchen and was cooking up a storm. 'A pinch, what's a pinch?' Sarah heard her ask Aggie, who was perched on a kitchen stool, talking her through a recipe in an ancient family cookbook that had surfaced in the move.

This family dwelling has lit everybody's fire, Sarah thought. And that was very lucky, because she had hardly any time to think about it at all this week. The intel gods had evidently opened a gusher somewhere. Information was pouring onto her desk from all points of the compass.

The Tucson crime lab had found one perfect thumb print that didn't match any of the Coopers, or their housekeeper, or Lois's sister.

Ollie Greenaway, following a rumor he only half-believed, had discovered a small-time dope dealer languishing in Yuma prison who claimed to know the two stash house victims well. Imprisoned before the murders, he could not be a suspect, so he felt secure enough to trade everything he knew about the drug business for a little time off his sentence. Ollie's long emails were streaming in from Yuma.

Phil Cruz called and said José Ojeda was on a plane with a US Marshall, would be landing in Tucson in a couple of hours and could take their river walk tomorrow. And now here came Tracy Scott, saying, 'You are going to love what I have for you today.'

'You too? I think every question I ever asked in my life is being answered this week,' Sarah said. 'It's getting so I'm afraid to pick up the phone.'

'Then don't,' Tracy Scott said. 'Turn on your answering machine and listen to me. Because I've got some nice juicy stuff.'

'Let's get Leo.'

'He's coming. I told him.'

He took her seat without asking. She brought in an extra chair and she and Leo huddled knee-to-knee on the visitors' side of her desk, reading the printouts as they slid across from Tracy – Mr Lucky, Leo had started calling him, since he gave him the job of reading all Frank Cooper's emails.

'Oh pooh, those emails, I made quick work of them,' Tracy said, 'they're all that same crud, it gets boring in a hurry. The really juicy stuff is in the Accounts Payable.'

'Isn't that just like a geek?' Leo said. 'He thinks math is sexier than sex.'

'Maybe not sexier, but a lot more actionable. Remember you told me, Sarah, that you were convinced Nicole was hiding something?'

'You found it?'

'Pretty sure.' He nodded happily, his coke-bottle glasses throwing off light beams in all directions. 'Look here.' Rows of numbers marched down the page, under headings that read: 1st Q, 08, 2nd Q 08, four quarters to a year for the last three years.

Leo said, 'These notes at the bottom of the page in code?'

'Only till you know what they mean. 1st Birm means the check on the first Friday of every month was written to Birmingham Mills. 2nd Kens means the one on the second Friday goes to Kensington Paper Products. 3rd Wall is for Waller Chemical, and 4th Hed is for Hedley Paints.'

'All electronic payments?' Sarah asked him.

'Sure. Why?'

She shrugged. 'Fraud is easier to track on paper. That's all.' Next to her, she felt Leo nodding vigorously.

Tracy rolled his eyes up and muttered, 'Easier on paper, gag me with a spoon.' He sat up straight, took a deep breath and went on. 'Anyway! The thing that started me looking was that all four of these companies get paid strikingly similar amounts. You see? A few bucks north or south of five hundred dollars, and they always get paid on the same Friday of the month. Which seems odd for a wholesale supplier of retail products, doesn't it?'

'Damn right.' Leo looked at Tracy Scott with new interest. 'And you haven't found any bills that back these up?'

'None in the electronic files. They could all four be dinosaurs, still billing on paper, but to prove *that* you need to go into the downtown accounting offices of Cooper's Home Stores and ask for a look at the paper files. Then I bet you find the bills to back up these payments have mysteriously gone missing.'

'You seem pretty sure,' Leo said.

'I am. Because I Googled all these firm names, in Phoenix where they're supposedly located, and got no match. So I tried the Chamber of Commerce up there, and the Better Business Bureau and a couple of phone companies. I got the same result every time – zippo, nada, none such.

'When you ask Nicole to show you some hard data to support these payments, I think the feces are going to hit the fan. I suppose you'd like to be there when that happens.' Tracy smiled benignly and slid a second sheet in front of Leo. 'This details how she was performing the exact same maneuver for Mommy Dearest, with four different companies in Albuquerque. All equally fictional as far as I can learn.'

'Isn't this fun?' Leo said. 'They're all stealing from each other.'

'Mostly from Uncle Sam, don't you think? And the two ladies must have been in it together, Nicole was doing all the bookkeeping.'

'But did Daddy know?' Sarah said. Then: 'Oh, wait. This all came off his computer, didn't it?'

'Bingo.' Tracy nodded, pleased. 'Even if he didn't know in advance he would certainly have spotted payments to dummy companies by now. And he's had plenty of time to blow the whistle if he wanted to. So – a better question might be, did they know what Papa Bear's been up to?'

'With the two girlfriends, you mean?' Leo said.

'In addition to. On top of, if you'll pardon the expression.' He had a spread sheet on Frank Cooper. Unfolded, it took up the whole desk top. They fastened the corners down with staple guns, a paper clip holder and a pencil mug. 'To begin with,' Tracy said, 'every Wednesday, this big honking draw, a thousand dollars in cash.'

'Wednesday,' Sara said, 'was Lois's bingo night at church. And she stayed over after with her sister.'

'So, play night for everybody,' Leo said.

'Looks like it,' Tracy said. 'And to judge by the Thursday morning emails, some of the Wednesday night fun got pretty lively. Here's one from about a year and a half ago – Frank sent this to Cheeks.'

They all read silently: 'Like new position we tried, do U want to try with dildo?'

Leo glanced at Tracy, guiltily, and told Sarah, 'See, I told you we shouldn't use the kid for this work.'

'Don't worry, Leo,' Tracy said, smiling tolerantly at the foibles of older folk. 'The Internet has worked its magic for us all.'

'I suppose.' Leo peered angrily out the door of Sarah's workspace as if searching for somebody to shoot. 'Great world we invented here.'

'Isn't it?' Sarah said, thinking of Denny.

'The Wednesday afternoon draw stopped a couple of months ago,' Tracy said, watching their faces curiously as he went on. He had brought new information, his expression said, so why wasn't everybody pleased? 'But Frank started a new, bigger one on Saturday. To pay for the new love nest he was setting up in Phoenix, I expect. Busy, busy Sundays in Phoenix. They were costing him a packet, so he really needed to get that third store going.'

Sarah said, 'You know what strikes me in all this?'

'No, Sarah,' Leo said, looking as if he might need his

blood pressure checked, 'please do tell me what strikes you in all this.'

'Well . . . Lois had plenty of reasons to kill Frank. Has had, for years. Tom did, too. And who knows? Maybe Nicole just discovered this big new leak in the cash flow – if so she'd have a good reason to want to get his hand out of the till. And now it looks as if Cheeks just got a reason. Motives for murdering Frank are thick on the ground. But the only reason we've found for anybody to kill Lois is the one we started out with, Frank in a rage.'

'And granted that guys always want to kill their wives sooner or later,' Leo said, 'why now? He seems to have been too busy lately to even notice her.'

'Except for the money fight.'

'Well, yeah. That.'

'But what I started to say was, I can think of many interesting adjectives to describe Frank Cooper, but suicidal isn't one of them.'

'Boy, you're right about that,' Leo said. 'This guy was having a high old time, wasn't he?' He added thoughtfully, 'Living every middle-aged guy's dream.'

Tracy twitched his nose in disgust. 'Please, somebody save me from maturity.'

Denny answered the doorbell at Sarah's nearly empty duplex. The cleaning crew stood there smiling: one youngish woman with a worn face, a gray-haired man missing a couple of fingers, and a pretty girl a few years older than herself. The woman and girl went to work at once, cleaning the bathroom and kitchen, while the man fetched things for them, carried out trash and ran the vacuum. A sharp-faced older woman who said she was Tía Luisa followed them in and sat at the round table under the light with Aggie, explaining the services she offered and the cost of each. Aggie chose a partial clean-up of the duplex now and a final one next week after it was empty, told her about the bigger house they were moving into, and said her daughter would help her decide how often they would need cleaning services there after they got everything moved. Aggie paid her in cash as she requested, gave her the address of the new house, and agreed to meet there in two days.

'Oh, but wait,' Aggie said, 'that's Saturday, isn't it?'

'It's OK,' the sharp-faced woman said, 'we work Saturday.' She shrugged. 'Any day we get work. Now I must go and check on my other crews,' she said. 'Then I come back for these darling girls before you fall in love with them.' When she was not talking about money she adopted this strange jocular tone that was meant, Denny thought, to make people like her. Tía Luisa and the man drove away then in the white van with a sign on the side saying, 'Tía Luisa's Home Cleaners.'

The sage green Lincoln Continental was parked down the street from Sarah's duplex with the top up. With its tail fins and hood ornament, the car was more noticeable than the three men inside. They all wore black T-shirts, baseball caps and dark glasses, and were lithe and quiet.

'You're sure?' Dick said. 'There could be lots of Tía Luisas in this town.'

'That's her,' Rod said. That wasn't his real name either, names were fluid with this group, but he was definitely not Bernice today. 'Apron or not, I'd know her little butt anywhere.'

'Thought I heard her say "Tía Luisa" that day,' Freddy said, 'to her boyfriend the fancy lighter boy.' He'd been rubbing Rod's nose in the mistake of overlooking that lighter ever since Vicky got away, but he didn't dwell on it today because he was feeling pleased with himself for the first time in ages.

Besides the expense of having the car put right again after the fire, it was beyond humiliating to get out-maneuvered by a wetback kid – a girl, at that. Freddy made a point of always coming out ahead, he felt it was good for his mental health. He had insisted they could not enlist any help with the search for Vicky because he didn't want the story getting out. And he hadn't heard any jokes to suggest . . . but you never knew. Suppose she bragged to one of her friends on the cleaning crew? Good story like that could go viral overnight around the bars in south Tucson. Freddy O's business was built on cool.

'Not crazy about grabbing her here,' Dick said. 'All these roundabouts and speed-bumps, what if she starts to yell?'

'She yells we snuff her tight here,' Rod said.

'I don't want to do her in the car,' Freddy said. 'One restoration a season is enough to pay for.'

'Aw, shit, you and this Lincoln,' Dick said, 'sometimes you . . .' And then quickly: 'Make up your mind cause here they come.'

But it wasn't the whole crew, it was only the gimpy gray-haired man and the woman with a hawk's face. They came out with their hands full, not hurrying or talking. The man put his bag of trash into the back and went around to the driver's seat while the woman climbed into the passenger's side and began reading the lists on her clipboard and making calls on her cell.

'So, what now?' Dick said.

'I'm not going into that house after the chica,' Rod said. 'There's two or three Anglos in there, what if somebody makes a call before—'

He quit talking when Freddy O. put the car in gear. 'We'll hang with the van a while,' Freddy said. Spotting the van and confirming his memory about what the quiet little crosser said that day in Agua Prieta had cheered him up, he felt like he had his mojo back. 'Tía Luisa'll come back for the crew. We'll watch her routine for a while, get René to get us an address offa that plate.' René was his inside man at DMV.

'Not very likely she lives where her boss does,' Rod says.

'But she might. Let's find out,' Freddy said. 'Don't want to get in a hurry and mess up again. What she cost me, I want some fun out of killing this cunt.'

Denny made up one reason after another to hang out near the house-cleaning crew so she could see how they did their work. She was hoping to take over some of their jobs and save the family some money. She could tell by the hesitant way her grown-ups made decisions involving money lately, they were all worried about it.

The older crew member scrubbed bathroom tiles and ignored her, but the younger girl said, the second time Denny came in the kitchen where she was working, 'You afraid I'm going to steal the refrigerator?' It was the only thing left that was moveable – they had taken all the dishes and pans to the other house.

Denny said, 'What?'

'You keep watching me,' the girl said. 'Do you think I will take something that belongs to you?'

'I'm just trying to learn how to clean,' Denny said. Faced with the girl's incredulous stare, she added, 'I like to learn things.'

The girl laughed, not at all politely, muttered something and shook her head.

Denny said, 'I'm sorry if I bothered you,' and walked away, mortified. She found the book she had left by the front door, went out and sat by Aggie in the yard, and read until the van came back to collect the crew.

When they were gone Denny walked through Sarah's clean, almost empty duplex with her grandmother.

'It looks so small now,' Denny said. 'I can't believe we got so much stuff in here.'

'I think I can hear it groaning with relief,' Aggie said. 'Let's go home and put the meat loaf in that strange little oven. You really think you learned how to turn it on?'

'Will made me do it five times.' Denny laughed. 'Will gets very serious when he's teaching, doesn't he?'

'Especially when there's a chance of an explosion. He gave up on me pretty fast, though. Every time I leaned down far enough to see that little gas flame, I got dizzy and started to fall over.'

'It's too bad we can't afford to get you a new stove, Grandma. I bet you miss the one you had at your house, don't you?'

'I'm fine with this one as long as I have you for a helper,' Aggie said. 'And you're a little young to be worrying about what we can afford.'

She must have said something to Aunt Sarah about that conversation, because early Saturday morning they all sat down together for what Aunt Sarah said was a 'breakfast conference'. They did the breakfast part first, because Will's pancakes and sausages were so good Aggie said she wasn't thinking about anything serious until she finished the second pancake. Then while Denny cleared the table Aunt Sarah brought out tablets and pencils and passed around some printed lists.

'You take a set too, Denny,' she said. 'You're part of this outfit now, and I want to make sure we all clearly understand where we stand. No more worrying in secret.'

Denny took a tablet and pencil and went to work on her first budget. She could tell by the time they got past the 'rent' line that there was quite a bit more going on here than just keeping the kid up to date. She had to admire the way Aunt Sarah coaxed Grandma past her reluctance to figure out exactly how much money she had invested in her house in Marana.

When it came to divulging her monthly income, though, Grandma said, 'Well . . .' She dropped her pencil and blew her nose and finally said, 'Darling, do you really need to know that?' Ranchers were accustomed to a lot of privacy, she had once told Denny, it was a big adjustment when you moved to town.

'I don't see how else we'll figure this out,' Sarah said, 'if we don't start by saying what we've got. But we'll go first if it's easier for you. Go ahead, Will.'

'I'm kind of like your mother,' Will said, switching around in his chair as if his pants had suddenly grown too tight, 'I didn't expect to go public quite so soon.'

It was the first time Denny had ever seen Will Dietz embarrassed. The most self-possessed man she had ever known was blushing. He looked the way she felt sometimes about things boys said on the bus. Evidently money effected grownups the same way. Who knew?

'Honestly, you two. OK, I'll start.' And as usual, nothing stopped Aunt Sarah once she made up her mind. She spelled out fearlessly what her take-home was, and got hilariously specific about what the divorce fight with her ex had done to her savings. She had even figured out how much she'd save on her taxes when she officially got custody of Denny. Now Denny was blushing. She'd never thought of herself as a deduction before.

'You mean it saves money to have a kid around?' she asked her aunt.

'Oh, you bet,' Aunt Sarah said, and showed her how much. 'And here's how much I've got built up in deferred comp. I'm going to try not to spend any of that, though, I need to add it to my pension when I retire.'

'Aren't you too young to think about retiring?'

'Honey, no cop is ever too young to think about that.'

Knowing he was not the only impoverished law enforcement officer in the room seemed to make it easier for Will to describe what a drawn-out divorce and two near-death work incidents had left him, which was, essentially, a newly acquired eight-year-old Ford pickup and the clothes he stood up in. He made a respectable salary, though, he pointed out, and was eligible for a substantial pension whenever he wanted to take it.

'Twenty-two years, I've got in. I'd like to make it to thirty, but it's optional now. You get a bigger pension if you do the full thirty, but there's some merit to the idea of quitting while you're still young enough to start a second career.'

'Well now I never thought about that,' Aggie said, and suddenly the two tales of financial disarray she'd just heard opened a floodgate she'd kept closed all her life. She told them how her husband, when he was young, worried through drought years and bad markets about having all their eggs in one basket. '"Nothing but this ranch," he was always groaning, "it's a recipe for disaster." He tried for years to liberate some cash to put in the stock market. Now that Wall Street's gone south I'm so grateful he never succeeded. Everything's in land and cattle, and my faithful son pays the mortgage every month. Here, I'll show you.' She kept the deposit slips in her checkbook. 'And on top of that whenever I want a treat I've got my sweet little co-op account – look, here's the book.' Denny watched, enchanted, as her secretive granny flipped open her account and showed them the bottom line. 'All from that part-time job I took the last twenty years on the ranch. Jim would never let me spend a penny of it. He said if he couldn't support a wife he'd go drown himself.' Looking anxiously at Will, she added, 'No offense, darling, those were different times.'

Denny, forgotten behind her tablet, thought this family soap opera beat any Saturday morning entertainment she had ever found on TV. She was almost sorry when they settled down to business, agreeing on an amount they would each pay into a household account every month. The last item they agreed on was an allowance for Denny.

'You mean it, I get an allowance?' She knew how to steal money, from her mother and the boyfriends, had done it routinely to survive. But now they were each going to give her five dollars a week, money she was entitled to.

'And you get this,' Aunt Sarah said. She handed Denny a new cell phone. 'We've got a lot going on. We need to be able to find each other.' She told Denny which speed-dial numbers she'd programmed. 'I'm two, Will is three, Grandma is four. Keep it with you so I can reach you. Don't forget!'

'I won't.' Was her smile wide enough? 'Thank you!'

'You're welcome. We're getting more than full value out of you these days. I hope I'm not breaking any child labor laws.'

'Don't worry, I know how to look useless if the cops come around. Oh, wait, you are the cops.'

'OK, smarty pants. Are we done here?'

'Done for while we're renting,' Will said. 'Soon as we buy, we get to do this whole fun thing again.'

'And oh boy, that bill of sale is going to be bloody hell,' Aggie said.

'But in the meantime, we're all better off than we were before,' Sarah said. 'Pooling your resources with two other people is like making a lot of money fast.'

'Which is a definite first for me,' Will Dietz said. 'Thank you, ladies.'

'Now Will's going to drive Denny and me out to my house,' Aggie told Sarah. 'He'll move my living room furniture in here today, and Denny and I will stay out there while the cleaning crew starts getting my place cleaned up for sale.'

'And while I'm in town,' Will said, 'I'm going to meet the realtor and a potential buyer at your place. This is going to be quite a day.'

'Whereas all I'm going to do,' Sarah said, 'is walk the Santa Cruz river below the reclamation plant. That drug courier's in town today, the one who's supposed to help Phil Cruz and me find Chuy Maldonado's head.'

'Good grief,' Aggie said.

'You picked a poor day for it,' Will said. 'Paper says chance of rain.'

'Won't that be swell?' She got out her weapon and shield. 'Can't wait to hear what the Mexico City boy thinks of the drug trade after he walks through wet mesquite trees all day, handcuffed to a US Marshall.' She laughed. 'Remember that, Denny. Contrary to what you have probably heard in grade school in Tucson, crime does not always pay.'

It didn't take all day, it just seemed like it. By two thirty, having flushed the same flock of black-necked stilts out of the river three times, they were taking turns digging in a spot they'd been walking back and forth over, Cruz pointed out, ever since morning. And this was their fourth hole.

Sarah had brought her gardening gloves and was fine except for some lower back pain. Phil Cruz had disdained gloves and had blisters, and a growing contempt for careless hoodlums who couldn't quite remember where they buried body parts.

'Been quite a while, man,' José Ojeda said. 'And one part of this river looks a lot like any other.' He was comfortable, sitting on a rock. He had talked his keeper, whose name was Blake, into letting him smoke one more cigarette – 'my mid-afternoon smoke break, how about it?' – and was enjoying his Marlboro with the gusto reserved for people who know their lungs aren't going to be needed for marathon running anytime soon. Blake was very nervous about second-hand smoke, so the entire day had featured interminable arguments over José's smoke breaks. Sarah had begun to dream about braining José with her shovel if he said one more fucking word about needing a smoke.

In the beautiful silence after Blake lit the cigarette for his prisoner, while José sat contentedly sucking on it, Sarah drove her shovel into the hole and hit something hard.

'Probably another rock,' she said, not letting herself hope. Phil got excited, though – he came over and helped her dig, not even waiting for his turn. It better not be a rock, he said, because they needed to get out of this stinking ravine before that lightning flickering over Wasson Peak got down here.

Pondering the kind of mind that believed it could work hard enough to stay ahead of lightning, Sarah scooped up one more shovelful of gravelly sand and saw a corner. It looked soggy and gravel-colored but was definitely the unrocklike corner of a man-made object.

She was too happy to say anything but, 'Corner.'

They both began digging with silent ferocity. When the whole top was exposed Phil asked José, 'Well, is this the right box? Come over here and look, is this the way you remember it?'

José got up reluctantly from his comfortable seat, strolled over with his perpetual companion keeping step, looked in the hole and shrugged. 'Yeah, that looks about right.'

'It seems big for a head,' Sarah said.

'Got a lot of wrapping,' José said, and went back and sat down. He still had a few puffs of his cigarette left and he didn't want any of them wasted.

The box, they could see, was wrapped in burlap and clear plastic sheeting. It had been a long time in the ground alongside a river, though, and wrapped or not it had absorbed a lot of moisture.

'Heavy son of a bitch,' Phil said, trying his first lift. They dug and grunted, finally got both shovels under it and tried coordinated heaving. Blake didn't offer to help; he had told them he wouldn't.

'I guard the prisoner,' he said. 'I have to stay focused on that.'

Sarah was considering a suggestion about where Blake could put his precious focus when Phil remembered a pair of canvas straps he had in the car. He brought them over to the hole and snaked them underneath the box while Sarah raised it a couple of inches with the shovel. Phil was lying full-length along the edge of the hole by that time, long past caring how filthy he got. When he had four ends more or less even they each grabbed two ends and heaved, groaning, till some mud fell away and the box popped out of the hole with a sucking sound. Phil dropped on one knee and Sarah only just managed to stay out of a prickly pear cactus with nine gazillion spines.

'Look again,' Phil said, leaning on his shovel, panting. 'Is this the right box?'

'No, I don't think so,' José said, and then yelled, 'Wait, wait, I'm joking!' as Phil came at him swinging the shovel. After José raised his right hand and swore this was the right box (Sarah thinking, why would this man give a damn about what he swore to over a mud hole?), Phil brought the department SUV as close as he could. Using knees, shoulders, gritted teeth and groans, they manhandled the box into the back as thunder rumbled through the black cloud over Panther Peak. By the time they found all their dirt-encrusted tools and flung them in with the box, the first big drops of rain were plopping onto the windshield.

'All right!' Phil Cruz crowed, grinning all over his mud-streaked face. 'Let's get this puppy down to the lab.'

They drove through thunder and sprinkles, then a hard burst of rain that hit like hail, followed by a patch of bright windy sunshine – the 'occasional showers' weather predicted in the morning paper. Phil and Sarah gave each other a muddy high five that scattered sand liberally over the front seat. Exhaustion faded as they enjoyed their triumph – they had pulled it off, found the box and got the sucker out of the ground.

Ojeda and his keeper sat in back, Blake watching the rain, looking mildly annoyed. This was not his town, he couldn't know, didn't care, that rain in Tucson felt like a party any place else.

José was already thinking about dinner – where would they eat, he asked Blake, could they go some place that had good steaks?

'I'm not going in a restaurant with you, are you kidding? You're going back to the Pima County jail until time to catch our flight tomorrow.'

'Aw, come on, I want something good,' José said. 'I won't get many more chances.'

'Poor baby,' Blake said.

Phil, who had been paying close attention to traffic during the cloudburst, tuned into their conversation suddenly and said, 'Nobody's going anywhere until we get this box unwrapped and you ID Maldonado's head for me. And oh, Jesus Christ, it's Saturday, isn't it? Which means we're out of office hours at the lab – we may not even get anybody to open the damn door.' He pounded on the steering wheel in frustration, yelling, 'Shit! I forgot about this!'

'Let's give them a call,' Sarah said, pulling out her cell.

'They won't answer the phone,' Phil said. 'It's just doctors in there now, carving up bodies.'

'They won't answer the office phone,' Sarah said, punching in numbers, 'but a couple of the docs have given me their cell numbers for times like this.' She listened to a couple of rings, got an answer and said, 'Bernie?' They had a nice humorous chat during which she asked him if he had any rule against heads that had no bodies attached, and Bernie asked which species? She told him rumor said this head had once been on a man and Bernie assured her he was no stickler when it came to portions of homo sapiens. He opened the back door, smiling, when she knocked a few minutes later.

He wouldn't let them come in, though. Pulling his plastic wrappings closer around himself to avoid contact, he gave them a severe look and said, 'Do you people have any idea how filthy you are? And this box you're talking about –' he peered out through the rain – 'looks even dirtier.'

'We just dug it up,' Sarah said, 'how else would it look?'

'Well it can't come in here like that. And we can't get to it this weekend anyway. I'll get somebody to open one of the bins for you.' He turned and yelled into a long echoing hall, 'Juan?'

A janitorial type came with a ring of keys and an umbrella, splashed across the gravel yard to a free-standing row of storage spaces, unlocked one and stood aside while they slid the box in. He had a form Phil signed, leaning in under the umbrella to keep it dry. Phil took the numbered stub he tore off, slid it carefully inside his pants at the waist and hurried back to the car. Sarah blew a kiss to Bernie and called through the rain, 'You're a hero!' Bernie put his left index finger on his right bicep and flexed. She laughed and he waved her away.

'I can see why women like police work,' Phil said as they drove away. 'You all get special favors because of your sex, don't you?'

'Wash your mouth out with soap,' Sarah said. 'When did I ever get any special favors from you?' Her back was beginning to hurt a lot and now that she had her gloves off she could see she was getting a blister too. She looked in the glove compartment for band-aids, didn't find any, slammed the door shut and watched it fall open. 'Did I ask for any special favors down by that bloody river when we heaved

that stinking box out of that fucking hole? Did I? Well, then!'
She slammed the door again, harder, and it fell open again.
'Stupid door!'

José Ojeda crowed in delight. 'Hey, Mr Big Shot Cop,
you better watch it now, you said the wrong thing and you
gonna get it from her! Hee hee!'

'Hey, Sarah, come on, I'm sorry,' Phil said. He leaned
across and closed the compartment door quietly. 'I know that
was a helluva job you did down there, I didn't mean to
squeeze your shoes.'

'Aw, don't kiss and make up yet, what fun is that?' José
said. 'C'mon, lady, let him have it some more.'

'OK, José, just settle down now,' Blake said, obviously
mortified by this breakdown in procedure.

José, though, was enjoying himself for the first time in a
long time and he didn't want it to end. 'Look at that asshole
driver trying to drown his passengers,' he said, watching a
Sun-Tran bus stop at a flooded curb and disgorge passengers into two feet of fast-flowing muddy water. José squealed
with pleasure as men cursed the driver and one lady lost a
shoe. When the bus closed its doors and pulled away he
sighed and said, 'You know, I been thinking.'

'Now, there's a first,' Phil said, taking his blisters out on
José.

'Yeah, seems to me we had so much fun today, we oughta
get together again tomorrow.'

'Oh, for sure,' Phil said, 'that sounds as amusing as a
rubber crutch.' He rolled his eyes sideways at Sarah, trying
to get her back on his side.

'I mean, long as we gotta hang around this stupid town
tomorrow anyway,' José said, blissfully oblivious to the angry
discomfort of the other three people in the car, 'why don't
I show you the house where they capped ol' Chuy?'

Sarah swiveled inside her seat belt and fixed José with a
red-eyed stare. 'You saying you know the house where the
Solteros . . . Phil, you want to pull over someplace?'

'In a minute,' Phil said, 'we're in a flood here if you
haven't noticed.'

'A good place to pull over,' José said, 'would be right up
ahead there at that Wendy's drive-in, so you could buy me

a double bacon cheeseburger and a large frosty. I eat that, I bet I could remember exactly where that house is. And the Home Depot store,' he added quickly, to counteract the angry noises Blake was making as Phil turned in at the Wendy's sign, 'where Huicho made me drive him so he could buy the saw and cement and all that shit. What you bet they got that on videotape? And you could find it easy if I can just remember which day – get me some fries with that, will you?'

While Eduardo drove them home from cleaning the duplex in mid-town, Ynez asked Vicky if she had noticed the men watching the house from a green car.

'What?' Vicky looked all around. 'Where?'

'They are gone now. But I'm sure they were watching that house.' Vicky tried to ask her what kind of car but of course she didn't know, and then she got all agitated about the little Anglo girl in the house back there. What did she want, hanging around them like that? Ynez had no English yet and was afraid of everything all the time – rightly so, Vicky thought, because she never had a clue what was going on.

'*No sé*,' Vicky said. 'I don't know. Why would anyone want to watch while we clean? I cannot imagine.'

'I thought you asked her,' Ynez said.

'I? No.'

Luisa had warned them, 'Be very careful in that house. Do not speak to anyone.' So Vicky was not going to admit she had. Ynez seemed like a brain-dead robot half the time, but you never knew, she might be Luisa's spy. Vicky was sure that Luisa, like all despots, had spies everywhere.

'I heard your voice,' Ynez said.

'She asked me for something, and I said I do not speak English.'

'Ah. Good idea.' Ynez hugged herself, a characteristic gesture. She got goose-bumps from fear. '*Son policías*,' she said. *They are police*. More than rapists or mad dogs, Ynez feared the police. Rapists only took more of what had always been taken from her anyway, but the police would send her home. Before they did they would find out where her family was, and if she ever let that happen, her husband had promised, he would beat her. 'I wish,' Ynez told Vicky, 'that I did not have to work in their houses.'

'Ask Tía Luisa to send you someplace else.'

'No, no. I never ask for anything. She gets angry.'

'So? She is angry most of the time anyway, I think.' An idea came to her, a way to get this loser out of her life and still make her an ally. 'I will tell Tía Luisa you would be better working with Elena, who is from your home town and looks after you. Elena always does the public buildings and you would be better off there.'

'Would you do that?' It was startling to see how almost-pretty she was when she smiled. 'Tía Luisa likes you. Be careful not to make her angry, though.' Her husband would also beat her if she lost her job.

'I will be very careful.' Really, Vicky thought, it was impossible not to sound like an idiot when you were talking to Ynez. She turned her collar up and closed her eyes so Ynez would think she was asleep. Behind her eyelids, she considered the little girl again, the one who had been watching her in the kitchen. Vicky's reaction to her had come from a lifetime of training – 'Anglos always think Mexicans steal,' her mother had warned her, 'stay away from them if you can.'

Now, though, she thought, Maybe she just wanted to be friendly. Small and plain, a little . . . underfed looking, actually, for an American girl, she certainly seemed harmless. *Why was I so rude to her?* She had often wished she had some Anglo friends, but whenever the chance came along she grew defiant and turned away. *If I want to succeed here, I should get over that.*

On Saturday morning, riding north-west in Tía Luisa's van under an overcast sky, she decided, *If I see her again I will smile and say hello. After Tía Luisa leaves, of course.*

She had already managed to get Ynez transferred to Elena's crew.

When she first mentioned it Tía Luisa got, not exactly angry but . . . grumpy. She said, 'So, already you want to run the business, do you? Luz was right, you are the pushy one.'

'And Luz is the whiny one.' It popped out before she could stop herself. She waited, expecting a reprimand, but saw something that might be amusement in Tía Luisa's eyes. So she took a chance. 'Ynez could work better if she was not so afraid.'

'She will always be afraid, her husband is a beast.' Luisa banged some pots around on the stove and finally said, 'But you are right, she likes to work with Elena. You notice things, eh? Perhaps we will get along.'

So Vicky got to partner with Ana, who was noisy and profane but cleaned tile and glass like an angel from heaven. Vicky was going to watch *her* now and learn how she did it.

In the van on the way to the job she decided, *It might be good practice, being friendly with this Anglo girl. Start with a small one, maybe they are easier.*

The house in Marana was set in a street of houses that all looked exactly the same. *They must have to memorize their house numbers the first day.* But all the streets looked alike, too, you would need a map in your hand to live here.

Inside, the house was nice, though, with comfortable-looking furniture and clusters of family pictures on the walls. The weak-looking granny who was telling them what to do today was the same one they had met in the smaller house. She looked much younger in the ranch pictures, smiling across many animals. There was a handsome man, probably her husband, who looked at her as if he wanted a bite. Vicky thought resentfully, This lady never had to sneak across a border to make a living. Looking at her today, though, how carefully she moved, you had to guess things had not gone so well for her lately.

The little girl was here too, with a man who must be her father, except they seemed too polite. They carried out a chair that he loaded into the pickup in the driveway while she came back in for two kitchen stools. Vicky watched her covertly. She was being careful to keep her distance today.

Tía Luisa told Vicky to start in the kitchen, and got Ana going in the bathrooms. Eduardo brought in everything they would need from the van, and vacuumed the hall while Tía Luisa got final instructions from Granny and collected, as usual, in cash. She always asked for cash payments and usually got them. Vicky was amused to see that most Anglo homeowners, in spite of the angry signs they sometimes

carried and the stories they told reporters, gladly paid Mexican
day laborers in cash, assuming they had no bank accounts
and no social security cards. A long-time citizen like Tía
Luisa simply exploited this loophole to save on the taxes.

When the talk was over, Eduardo drove Tía Luisa to the
next job site. Getting this job in Marana had emboldened
her to slide brochures under the windshield wipers of cars
in several parking lots. Now she was going to talk to the
two homeowners who had called her. Vicky could see she
was proud to be getting new accounts in this suburb. It was
farther to drive but the houses were new and easy to clean.
She could earn more with fewer employees.

When they were gone the granny asked them to finish up
in her bedroom first so she could lie down. While she was
resting the little girl took a book to the shaded patio at the
back of the house, where she curled in a chair and read.
*Always reading, does she have no friends? When does she
play?* Carrying the kitchen trash can, Vicky stepped out the
back door and stopped a few feet from Denny's chair.

'Excuse me, I need to clean this trash can,' she said. 'May
I ask you, where is the hose?'

'Oh, it's . . . um . . . right around the corner, I think. I'll
show you.' She left her book on the chair seat and walked
around the corner of the house, where she stopped, embarrassed. 'Must be the other corner.' She trotted across the back
of the house. 'Yeah, here it is.' Screwed onto an outlet that
came out of the foundation, it was coiled in a terra cotta
bowl. 'You turn it on here, see?'

'You must not live here all the time,' Vicky said, spraying
the trash can inside and out. It had contained a plastic liner
and was not dirty at all when she started. But the water spray
kicked up a lot of dust and gravel, and soon the outside of
the trash can was quite dirty. 'Oh damn,' Vicky said, and
then, 'Sorry.' She could not seem to get the spray turned off.

'Here, let me help you,' Denny said, and turned off the
hose at the outlet. She laughed. 'You must not clean houses
all the time either.'

'No, I . . .' She looked around guiltily, afraid she heard
someone coming.

'Stay there, I'll get some paper towels.' She darted in

through the door and was back in an instant with a whole roll. 'Let's go back to the patio, it's kind of muddy out here.'

Up on the dry brick, they wiped down the plastic can. 'This is my grandmother's house,' the little girl said. She was friendly again, she seemed to enjoy helping people. 'She got sick, so now she's going to sell this house and live with us.'

'Ah. Too bad.' To Vicky, it sounded like crowding and hard times.

'Oh, no, it's going to be . . . it's a nice house. You'll see it next week, I guess. You seem to be cleaning all our places.'

'So many houses,' Vicky said. 'You must be very rich.'

'Hardly.' The little girl seemed to find that idea comical. 'But Aunt Sarah says we're better off now that we –' she thought, wiggling her skinny little butt – 'pooled our resources.' She grinned, wrinkling her nose. 'All the grown-ups did, anyway. I don't have any resources.'

Pooled our resources? Anglos talk such crazy shit. Vicky said, 'What's your name?'

'Denny. What's yours?'

'Victoria Nuñez.' Denny had trouble with the *nyuh* in the middle, so Vicky said it again a couple of times until she got it. When she was smiling, happy about learning something new, Vicky asked her, 'Want to make a trade?'

'Sure. What?'

'You tell me where you got that blouse, I'll show you how to clean an oven.'

FOURTEEN

'We're moving out of this house today,' Aggie told Sarah a few days later. 'Howard's coming in from the ranch with the stock truck to help Will move the big pieces. Howard and Will are turning into a team, can you imagine that?'

'Two silent men. I wonder what they talk about when we're not there?'

'Fishing, if Howard has anything to say about it. Anyway we'll be sleeping in Blenman-Elm tonight if all goes well. Check with me before you leave work.'

'OK. Is Will's cleaning crew doing the job to your satisfaction?'

'Boy, are they. Couple of them are at the new house right now, cleaning around everything as fast as we bring it in. Then they'll all come back out here tomorrow so we can leave my empty house looking brand new.'

'Terrific. You think the girl is old enough to be working?'

'Or here legally? Both good questions. Will says the woman who runs the crew came recommended by one of his men on the night shift. I'm paying cash and asking no questions. When we get done with this move and have time to catch a breath, Sarah, you can investigate all you like. But for now, since you've taken to working seven days a week, I strongly urge you to concentrate on your job and leave this end to us.'

'Point taken and I'm happy to comply. I hope we're not wearing you out, though. Will and I dreamed up this move so we'd be available to help you, and now you're saving my bacon once again. What's wrong with this picture?'

'Don't worry about that, I'm hardly lifting a finger. I sit and give orders like a queen to Will and these cleaners all day, and for evenings and weekends there's Denny, my good right arm. You want irony, consider the fact that you and I set out to help *her*. Now she's the chief cook and bottle washer.'

'I know. Let's think of it as adding life skills, shall we?

It sounds more respectable than just putting the kid to work.'

'In a way it is a life lesson. That girl on the cleaning crew has captured Denny's imagination – she's discovered a life more torn up than her own. She told me, "Vicky's mom's in Mexico and she can't find her dad."'

'Hmm. That argues for Undocumented, doesn't it?'

'You can't fix everything, Sarah. Go to work.'

'You do not want to hear about my weekend,' Sarah said, and then told the homicide crew all about it, with special emphasis on the effort to get the box out of the hole. 'And that was all on Saturday. Now, Sunday . . . I'm sorry about blowing the budget, boss.'

'Two crime scene techs and a detective on overtime? Don't mention it.' Delaney punished his gum, looking pained. 'I'm going to try for a refund from the Feds, but we better not have any more emergencies till I work something out.'

'And getting me a search warrant signed on a Sunday morning, that was above and beyond.' Sarah was spreading it on a little thick, because she wanted his okay for her trip today. The weekend had been all for the box-o'-bones caper, even less popular with Delaney now than it had been to start with. Today was serious business, a solid lead in the Cooper case. 'It's a good thing,' she told her crew-mates, who were looking increasingly cynical, 'that we've got a boss who knows an understanding judge.'

'Especially when he's losing big on the golf course,' Delaney said. 'He was glad to get in out of the sun, he settled right down in the bar after he signed our warrant.'

'The other big-budget item was that Ojeda guy's hollow leg,' Sarah said. 'So far he's into us for two pizzas and a cheesesteak with curly fries. Besides that Wendy's Super-Value meal he ate Saturday night while he sold us on the Sunday house hunt.'

'I must say,' Delaney said, 'it was worth a trip across town to see the way Coomassie Blue made those bloodstains bloom in the bathroom. Hard to believe all that blood came from one man.'

'Maybe it didn't,' Sarah said. 'I mean, all over the kitchen too? And the place was so clean when we went in. That's what made me sure he'd led us to the right address. That old, old house so spotless.'

'Apparently they never rent it out.'

'No. It's their safe house, Ojeda said. Safe meaning radically dangerous – they kept it for when they needed to kill somebody.'

'The lab crew's finding DNA in all the cracks, they say. We may solve some cold cases off of this. So, what's next? Let's go around,' Delaney said. 'Leo?'

'Got a date to talk about money with Nicole Cooper.'

'Ah. Are you going there or is she coming here?'

'I just made the appointment and said I'd let her know about the venue. I'm pretty sure we're looking at tax evasion, but do we want to look at it very hard? I mean, if we liked her a lot for the murders . . . but I've checked with the friends she told us she was with that night. Very substantial people. Her alibi looks pretty solid.'

'Which doesn't mean she wasn't in on it. But . . . OK, you just want to squeeze her about the money and see what pops out?'

'That was my thinking, yeah. And we've got more leverage, haven't we, if I don't have her on a CD confessing to tax fraud?'

'Leave her some wiggle room,' Delaney said. 'I agree. I mean, we could easily prove embezzlement too, but the way things have turned out she was just stealing from herself. So, a nice visit in her office and see if she cries on you?'

'For my sins, I get punished this way,' Leo said.

'Fine, who's next? Ollie, I read some of your transmits from Yuma, you got some good stuff, huh?'

'Think so. I need a couple of days to find corroboration here, can Oscar help me with that? Good, because if my Yuma stories prove out we can hang the stash house on the Solteros too.'

'Aren't we the best little helpers DEA ever had? And Sarah, I suppose you're going to be down there at the lab with Phil Cruz and the head all day, huh?'

'I did plan to do that, I told Phil I'd be there. But now

I'm wondering . . . is it OK if somebody else takes that? Jason said he's got some time.'

'And I haven't had enough experience staring at skulls,' Jason said, patting his head, trying to make it sound like a joke because he actually had quite limited experience with detached body parts, and he had puked at his first autopsy. He both wanted and dreaded this day.

'Why can't you go?' Delaney asked Sarah.

'My clever Genius Geek did a back-trace on Frank Cooper's phone,' Sarah said, 'and read the GPS chip in that snazzy red Porsche he's been driving to Phoenix every week, and I do believe he found me Laura Hughes.'

'Aw come on, Sarah,' Leo said. 'Not fair you get Tasty Toes and I'm stuck with the bookkeeper.'

'Well, see, I left a message on her phone that said, "If you are Tasty Toes I need to talk to you urgently." And she called me back just now, in the sweetest voice you could possibly imagine, and said, "I can make time today if you can come right away."'

'You two talking in code or what?' Delaney said.

'Will you tell him about the emails?' Sarah said. 'It's already nine o'clock and the radio says northbound on I-10 is backed up a mile at Picacho Peak.'

The apartment was on the third floor of a four-story building on Cave Creek Road, in a row of buildings just like it. Not a slum, but more workaday than upscale. Well-worn terrazzo in the hall, and a light out in the elevator. Frank Cooper didn't spend all of that big weekly draw on this place, Sarah thought as she rang the bell.

When the cover slid aside on the security viewer she held her shield up by her cheek. The deadbolt clicked and the door was opened by a late-thirties vanilla pudding of a woman who could not possibly be Tasty Toes. Round white arms and the beginnings of a double chin, a big ba-zoom busting out of a V-necked print dress in a harmless shade of blue. *In twenty years she's going to look just like Lois Cooper.* Sarah had been expecting a sizzling blond. This woman had light-brown hair in a short pageboy cut with a couple of light streaks in front.

'Sarah Burke,' Sarah said, putting her hand out.

'Laura Hughes.' She shook hands and opened the door wider, smiling. 'Come in.' Sarah walked into the kind of living space she thought of as Classic Blah-blah – a lot of beige, a lot of glass. Fat couches grouped around a flat-screen TV and a couple of large predictable prints, an R.C. Gorman and a collection of pots. In the background, a round glass table and four hunter-green painted ladder-back chairs under a light. It all looked recently assembled by a beginner taking no chances. The view through the big windows was roaring traffic in the foreground, desert in the distance.

Sarah put her shield back on her belt and settled her jacket with a shrug. Her service weapon was out of sight in an ankle holster and she'd left the taser at home. She said, 'Thank you for making time for me.'

'Cancelling lunch was no problem. I do have to go to work in two hours, though.' She indicated two facing chairs by a window and they sat.

'That should be plenty of time. Where do you work, by the way?'

'In the lingerie department at Macy's. The one in Biltmore Fashion Park. I'm only getting about thirty hours a week right now because things are slow in retail, as I'm sure you've heard.'

'In everything, I guess. Except law enforcement – we're busy.'

'I suppose. People have to live, don't they? Right now I'm working three to nine, five days a week, and split days off, how's that for a rotten schedule? But I took it because one of the days off is Sunday, and I wanted that day with Frank.' She smiled again, an easy smile that shaded a little toward smug. 'That's what you want to talk about, isn't it? My friendship with Frank?'

'Yes, please.' *What's the use having an interrogation technique if the persons of interest tell everything without being asked?* 'How long have you known him?'

'Since last December.'

So we found the first emails. 'How did you meet him?'

'Right there in the store. He came in to buy a gift for somebody. Men always find it hard to say what they want in lingerie, but it's no problem for us because they always want the same thing: something skimpy and very feminine, you know, the sexier the better.'

'I suppose that's true,' Sarah said. Her husband had been a restaurateur whose gifts had been mostly high-end cook-wear. On the rare occasions when Dietz got to see her underwear, all he seemed to care about was how fast he could get her out of it.

'I mean they're not going to buy the white cotton sports bras, are they? A man comes into my part of the store, he's looking for a gift that's going to please a woman first and him later on.' She rolled her shoulders and laughed a throaty laugh. 'Hopefully not too much later on.'

Oh, yes, this is Tasty Toes.

'Well, Frank was in his fifties and you never know, so I showed him a couple of nice nighties. I could tell by the way he looked at them that he wanted something racier. So I brought out some teddies, expensive little wisps of things in silk and satin with a lot of lace, and right away he got interested. He took some time deciding on the right size, asking me, in the very nicest way, very polite, if I would hold them up to myself so he could judge. I finally got him to settle on the pale rose silk one in my size but the long-torso option. I was putting it in the box, getting ready to wrap it up, when he started to look, you know . . . kind of thoughtful.

'I said, "Now you look as if there might be something else, what is it?" thinking, maybe some perfume. But he said, "I was just thinking how nice a garment like that would look on you."' Laura's voice broke on the last two words and big tears ran down her cheeks and onto her hands. She grabbed tissues out of a box beside her, wiped her face noisily and thoroughly, cleared her throat and said, 'Sorry.'

'I know this is hard,' Sarah said. The usual police formula – 'I'm sorry for your loss' – didn't seem quite appropriate, although now that she saw this surprising woman's obvi-ously genuine sorrow, she thought, Why not? Grief is grief. 'I'm sorry for your loss.'

'Thank you. And thank you for not being a, you know, *prude*. One of the hardest things, when you're just the girlfriend, is you don't get any sympathy. Hardly anybody knew I was involved with Frank, he asked me to be discreet and I was. But even the ones who knew I was dating him, my girlfriend and my sister and like that, they just figured I was in it for the extra money and good times, so except for the inconvenience what's to be sad about? But really, it wasn't . . . well.' She recrossed her legs, blew her nose. 'OK, maybe it did start out like that. I got propositioned in an underwear store by a man who was obviously buying a present for his girlfriend, not his wife, so yes, in the beginning it was maybe a little crass.'

'His girlfriend. Would that be the one he called Cheeks, do you know?' Sarah thought the nickname might evoke scorn or jealousy, but Laura didn't bat an eye.

'Hey, it beats me what he called her. Seems like we never got around to talking about that.' That sensuous little chuckle again – this woman liked to stick it right in your face. 'When he asked me to dinner I knew it wasn't just to talk about the retail climate in Phoenix –' she wound a curl around her finger – 'although I thought it was pretty sweet of him to put a little gloss on it like that.' She blew her nose again and asked, 'Would you like a soda or something? I feel kind of thirsty.'

'Glass of water would be nice.' While Laura was fetching the drinks Sarah took a quick look at her checklist, where none of the items had as yet been crossed off. 'Money,' she read, 'LadySmith, Anger, Suicide?' *Better move this along.*

Laura came back, put down two coasters and then two glasses of water with plenty of ice. Sarah took the big paper napkin she offered and said, 'OK, so it started out as standard sexual high-jinks but grew into real affection, is that fair to say?' Laura nodded emphatically, looking grateful.

'It's such a relief that you're understanding. Some people still get pretty puritanical about extramarital sex. Which is pretty dumb, isn't it? If it's such a bad thing how come there's so much of it going on all the time?'

'That's a very good question,' Sarah said.

'Isn't it? Frank and I were just incredibly well-matched. From the very first time, we hit it off in bed like gangbusters, we liked all the same things.' She chuckled, remembering.

'Most guys are a little too . . . reticent for my taste. I mean, you're there to have fun, why hold anything back? Frank felt the same way, so we got totally nuts about each other in a short time, couldn't get enough. And after all we weren't hurting anybody. I never expected him to give up his wife and family. I understood he had obligations in Tucson and I had no intention of interfering with any of that. I didn't even care about the other girlfriend. He started, once, to make promises about giving her up and I said, "You do as you please about that. All I care is if we do plenty of *this*," and I put my hand on him and right there, standing up, we did it again.'

She wiped her eyes again and said, 'I'm just going to have a dickens of a time getting over missing him. My old Poops.'

Sarah said, 'Did you know he wanted to kill his wife?'

'What? I certainly did not. And I don't believe he did. Frank had great respect for his wife, he said she was a real partner. She just didn't, you know, *put out* for him any more. And he wasn't the type to go without.'

'Was he the type to commit suicide?'

'Are you kidding? I don't know who dreamed up that scenario, but it's way, way off the mark. Why would Frank kill himself? He had everything he wanted, and I'm here to tell you he knew how to enjoy it.'

'I hear you.' *You're too banal not to believe.* 'And how long had you known him when he gave you the gun?'

Laura looked puzzled. 'What gun?'

'The Smith & Wessen LadySmith, model 60 LS.' *Batter them with information, make them think you know all their secrets.*

But Laura Hughes just stared at her and said, 'Honey, Frank never gave me a gun. Whatever gave you that idea?'

Mostly the fact that I know he gave it to somebody and I was hoping it was you. But looking into Laura's astonished blue eyes, Sarah could see she didn't have it. 'He never offered you a gun?'

'Actually, except for some Sunday afternoons I'm going to remember for the rest of my life, Frank never gave me a whole lot,' Laura said. 'I know everybody's going to think I got tons of loot, but I didn't. Well, a mink jacket, last

Christmas. Craziest, most impractical – the mink season in Phoenix is maybe two weeks in January. But he was trying to impress me then, show me what a big man he was.' She shook her head, ruminating fondly about Frank's foibles. 'Like I didn't know who he was. Clarice there in the store told me that first day, "That's Frank Cooper from Cooper's Home Stores. They say he's building a new store up here. Be nice to him, maybe he'll hire you to manage it." She snickered in that mean way she has, like that was the most unlikely thing she could possibly imagine. I have so been looking forward to telling her that's exactly what I'm going to do.'

'Manage the new store, you mean?'

'That's right.' She sighed. 'I mean, it *was* right. I guess it's never going to happen now. Even if the family went ahead with the plans they wouldn't hire *me*.'

'Do you think it was a firm offer?'

'Oh, you bet. Not that I'll, you know, sue or anything. But I could make plenty of trouble for the Coopers if I wanted to. I mean, I've got a signed contract.' She winked. 'Everybody thinks I'm such a bimbo. But I've got a good head for business and I know how to take care of myself.'

'I see that. Was Frank paying for this apartment?'

'Heck, no. I was living here when I met him. I have some money from the divorce settlement from my second husband. Frank helped me with some upgrades from the store – this carpet, the bedroom furniture.'

'OK. But if Frank wasn't spending money on you, why was he drawing so much every weekend?'

'Oh, well . . .' Laura did some evasive head-tosses and considered her fingernails briefly. 'I didn't say he didn't spend it here. Frank liked to party. But he was a man with a lot of responsibilities, so mostly he liked the kind of a party where he could control everything.'

'And that costs more?'

'Of course . . . oh, well!' She jumped up. 'Come on, I'll show you.' She waved her plump arms toward the hall. Sarah followed the sway of Laura's round behind past a standard kitchen off the dining area. Down the hall, a bathroom where the only luxury items in sight were a large square tub and a great many fluffy white towels on racks. At the door to her bedroom she paused and said, 'I hope you're not easily shocked.'

'I'm a homicide detective, Laura.'

'Yes, well – OK, come on in.'

The Hugh Hefner school of design. Why did she think I'd be shocked? This is really a cliché. There were mirrors on the ceiling, of course. An honest-to-god round bed, with red velvet covers and draperies, and pink satin sheets. A closet full of lacy little nothings for her and silk bathrobes for him. The biggest flat-screen TV in the known world, mounted on the wall above a console stuffed full of pornographic movies. Sex toys in a cupboard. Laura showed it all off proudly, saying, 'Everything for pleasure.'

Sarah could almost hear Leo getting ready to slaver. 'I see the roach,' Sarah said. 'But no champagne?'

'Frank didn't like to drink much. He said it dulled the senses.' A quick little flick of the eyelids. 'He liked his ciggies, though. That's what he called dope, "my ciggies." I always had to keep a nice fresh supply of Mexican weed. I guess I can count on you not to get stuffy about *that*, can't I?'

Sarah gave her a noncommittal 'Mmm' and got ready to go. Just inside the door she turned and asked, 'By any chance, do you have a copy of that contract here? Could I see it?'

'What, you think I might be making it up?'

'No, I—'

'I never bluff,' Laura said. 'I never have to.' She pulled it out of a drawer and watched Sarah read it. 'You recognize the signature?'

'Yes.'

'I've got my scanner right here,' she said, with a smug little smile. 'Would you like a copy to take along?'

Watching her make the copy, Sarah said, 'It's pretty unusual, isn't it, signing a contract to manage a store that isn't built yet? How did you happen to do that?'

'Well, you know how men are,' Laura said, enlisting Sarah in her women's club. 'When he first started talking to me about the new store, Frank said he already had somebody to manage it. But after he knew me for a while he said he'd rather have me, and I said, "Let's get that in writing before you change your mind again."' She chuckled. 'Frank said, "You are one shrewd little cookie, you know that?" Besides the sex, he liked that I was smart.'

Shortly after lunch, Delaney looked out and saw Leo hunched in front of his computer, not typing. He walked out to the cubicle opening and said, 'Leo?'

Without turning his head, Leo said, 'Isn't it quitting time yet? I've had such a long, terrible day.'

'Leo, it's only a little after noon.'

'So?'

'Was Nicole difficult?'

'No,' Leo said, 'Nicole Cooper was not difficult. She was impossible. Beyond impossible, actually – somewhere in the realm of the perverse, with overtones of mulish intractable rage. I think it's safe to say –' his voice rose and cracked – 'that Nicole Cooper has not met with serious opposition or questions about her judgment in years and years.'

'Better come in my office and tell me about it.' When Leo stood up, Delaney saw that his shirt front was streaked in subtle tones of bronze, light umber and slate.

'You asked her about the fake payments?'

'Sure. And she denied everything, to begin with,' Leo said. 'Told me I was a disgrace to the department, going around accusing upright citizens of wrongdoing because I was too ignorant to read a profit-and-loss sheet. Offered to send me back to school at company expense.'

'My, my. How did you—'

'Fortunately I took Tracy along, and you know, he's pretty good at slinging big words around, too.'

'I have noticed that,' Delaney said. 'Is he too distracting, though?'

'No, no, he's a genius. I should have had a Tracy years ago, my whole career might have been different.'

'What did Tracy do?'

'Cornered her with plain and fancy math. When she saw she couldn't talk her way around him she went all passive-aggressive on us, said she really didn't control anything in this company and was only following orders from Daddy. Well, and occasionally Mommy, if I wanted to get picky about that other weekly draw. I'm just the bookkeeper, remember, she said. They said this is the way we want you to handle it, so that's what I did. And by the way do you have any idea what a huge percentage of police salaries and pensions are paid by our taxes every month?' Leo took a big pull off his water bottle and blew hair out of his eyes.

'We went around that maypole a couple of times and then she had a temper tantrum that she must have been saving since she was four years old. Turned blue in the face and almost passed out, and *then* she hurled herself on my fatherly shirt-front and wept bitter tears. My wife's got another good sturdy rag for her hooked rug basket.'

'But I don't seem to hear you saying you found the LadySmith.'

'No,' Leo said. 'Nicole's into money, not guns. Let's hope Sarah found the right Laura Hughes and *she* likes to shoot.'

'I don't know about that,' Delaney said. 'She called a half-hour ago. All she said was, she was on her way home but she had a stop to make.'

A few shoppers browsed the aisles of the North Oracle store, but the morning rush of contractors was long past, and the after-work crowd hadn't hit yet. Good time to talk, Sarah thought, and asked the clerk at the first checkout counter inside the door to page the manager.

'Anything I can help you with?' the concerned retiree in the Cooper's Home Stores apron asked her. 'Something you can't find?'

'No, thanks, I just need to talk to Phyllis a minute.' Sarah gave him the friendly-but-firm smile, trying not to show her badge. He got on the horn, and in less than a minute Phyllis walked out from behind a rack of drip irrigation parts and waved. When they met halfway Sarah said, 'Sorry to drop in without notice but I was going by and decided to see if . . . I just have a couple of things about the case we can clear up fast if you can spare me a minute.'

'Let's go in my office,' Phyllis said. She moved a couple of thick sample books off the chair in front of the desk. 'Always have so much *stuff*,' she said. 'Have a seat.'

'I'll get right to it,' Sarah said. 'First thing, I want to review the new store controversy. Nicole said her mother was against it but she agreed with her father that it was a good idea. Were you in favor of it too?'

'Well, sure. I mean, if it was what he . . . what they decided to do, then I'd be for it, of course. But I told you, I'm just a hired hand.'

'But a key employee,' Sarah said. 'And slated to be more important soon.'

'Well, yes.'

'And you had every reason to care about the success of the project, didn't you? Since you expected to manage it.'

'Yes. That's kind of irrelevant now.'

'OK. But I'm asking what your feeling was at the time. Did you think this was a good time to open a new store?'

Phyllis held her right hand up and rocked it. 'I thought it was very risky but if Frank wanted it badly enough, he had a track record that indicated he could make it happen.'

'So you didn't argue against it the way Lois did? It didn't affect your relationship with Frank?'

Phyllis sat back, cleared her throat, and said, 'Why would it? I keep telling you, I just work here.'

'Oh, but you had a little something going on the side, didn't you?' She pulled out a page of notes and read, '"Too much fun last nite Big One – Cheeks had bruises!"'

Phyllis's mouth and eyes formed three round circles in her flaming face for a long couple of seconds. 'How do you know . . . ?' Her eyes darted everywhere. 'How did you find out . . . ?' By the time she got herself back in control, she realized she'd confirmed that she was Cheeks.

She tried for indignation. 'You read our personal emails?'

'Afraid so,' Sarah said cheerfully. 'When there's a homicide, you know, we dig through everything!' She did her best to make it sound like a booster message from the Police Benevolent Association.

'That is so . . . utterly filthy.' Phyllis said. She leaned across her desk and whispered furiously, 'People have a right to their own personal lives!'

'Ordinarily, yes. And let me say right off, Phyllis, we have zero interest in your sex life except as it relates to this crime.

I understand how you feel and it's just a shame when inno-
cent bystanders get caught in the crossfire like this. Believe
me, we'll do the best we can to protect your privacy. But
until a homicide investigation is closed, everything's fair
game, nobody gets to hide anything.

'So here's my next question. You told me earlier you didn't
want to carry a gun. You said Frank offered you one but you
turned it down. But a little over a year ago he sent you this
message: "Great session at the range yesterday. Proud of
you, hitting the kill zone so many times – my sexy Deadeye."'

Phyllis turned the full force of her remarkable eyes on
Sarah's face and looked as if she might be deciding where
on the jugular to sink fangs. Sarah plowed right along, as if
reading to her book club. 'Then there's this: "Don't forget
I'm almost out of ammo, so bring me some of yours if you
want to 'shoot first and screw later' on Sunday, my naughty
one."' She put the paper in her lap. 'So he gave you the
LadySmith. Why lie about it?'

Phyllis raised her tense, beautiful hands alongside her
face with the fingers spread. 'Oh, you know the answer to
that perfectly well, Detective. Frank and Lois were dead
and nobody knew Frank and I had a relationship outside
the store – we were careful. I had no idea he was going to
go off half-cocked and kill his wife. When he did, I thought,
why not leave the gun and our love affair out of it? Easier
for everybody. After all, what we did – it might not meet
with everybody's approval, but it had nothing to do with
the crime, either.'

She rested her head against the back of her leather chair
and closed her eyes for a moment. When she spoke again
she was calmer. 'I never wanted that damn gun anyway. But
Frank could be so . . . insistent. He liked the his-and-hers
aspect of those guns, it turned him on. And, as I guess you
know if you've read all those messages, I always tried to
please him.'

'Except there was some kind of a lover's quarrel right at
the end, wasn't there?'

Sarah lifted her notes again and read, '"Told U it could
be like old times, now do you luv your Cheeks?" You'd been
apart for a little while there, right? And a little later: "No

must C U today – MAKE TIME!" That was on the day of
the murders, Phyllis. Did you see him that day?'

'You bet I did. As the saying goes I was mad as hell and
not going to take it any more! But it was all about my job.
There I was, working my butt off at the store, all four Coopers
off doing as they pleased and they hadn't done any of the
things they'd promised to do on Friday before they left!
Nicole forgot to transfer a slew of inventory, left me short
to fill orders at both stores. Lois was supposed to call in a
replacement for a sick checkout clerk and didn't, east side
was swamped at ten thirty when churches got out – I mean,
I suppose it was because of that fight they were having Friday
at lunch, but I said to Frank, Is this any way to run a great
organization?'

'That does sound difficult,' Sarah said. She let a little
silence build before she said, 'I thought it might have been
about this.' She slid the copy of Laura's contract across the
desk.

It was only two pages long. Phyllis read it once quickly
and again a little slower. By the end of the second read she
was beginning to wheeze. When she slammed the paper onto
her desk her whisper came through her rattling throat like a
message from the lowest reaches of hell. 'I should have shot
that lying bastard in the nuts first and watched him suffer a
while.'

Sarah waited a long minute to see if Phyllis was going to
choke on her rage. When her breathing had calmed a little,
she said, 'I understand about Frank. Why did you kill Lois?'

'I don't think we're going to talk any more,' Phyllis said.
'I think I need to speak to an attorney now.'

FIFTEEN

'I thought out here in the 'burbs'd be perfect.' Dick said. 'But there's always somebody going in and out.'

'Folks moving *furniture*,' Rod said. 'Ever see anybody so slow? And neighbors with farewell gifts, shee-it. Stand in the door and hug.'

'And I'm starting to feel too conspicuous out here in this car. Lotta these old guys really eyeballing it, reminds them of when they were young.'

'You two ever listen to yourselves?' Freddy said. 'Sound like Whiners Anonymous.'

'Well, we can't spend the rest of our lives waiting to cap one stupid little piece of cooz. Gotta get *on* with it,' Dick said. 'Got things to *do*.'

'You don't have to get high every day,' Freddy said. He turned sideways on the seat and gave Dick a searching look. 'Or do you now?'

'No, of course not,' Dick said. But he looked away. He sniffed a couple of times, then jumped and said, 'What?' when Freddy touched his arm.

'Tía Luisa's van following that last load,' Freddy said. 'Let's go get set up on Bentley.'

Denny tried not to get in the way, but she couldn't resist trotting from room to room to see how Grandma Aggie's furniture fit in this house. The sweet little three-drawer dresser from the spare room in Marana made her old iron bed look like a real antique, she told her grandmother.

'Well, it is an antique, sweetheart,' Aggie said. 'I slept in it myself when I was your age. Figure it out.' Her neighbors had brought her picnic food for moving day, so she didn't need to worry about cooking as she toured the rooms with Denny. Howard and Will were on the way back to Marana for the last load, and Howard had agreed he could stay for supper. 'Because Sarah just called and said she'd be home by six,' Aggie told him. 'It'll be a chance for you to visit for once.' Howard was friendlier when his wife wasn't around.

The cleaning crew was working its way out the door. 'You are better than elves,' Aggie told them, as they loaded their gear in the van. 'I'll see you back here next Tuesday, will I? We'll have made a mess of ourselves all over again, unpacking.'

'We will be here,' Tía Luisa said. 'And you will recommend us to your neighbors out there? We always looking for more work.'

'Absolutely,' Aggie said. 'Tell them to call me.' They were all out on the sidewalk, feeling good in the sunshine, smiling like neighbors saying goodbye. Aggie said, looking across the street, 'Isn't that an attractive car? You hardly ever see those anymore, do you?' Then she gave a little yelp of alarm because Vicky, whose face was suddenly a mask of terror, dropped her work basket with a clatter and ran full speed toward the corner.

The green Lincoln with the tail fins laid rubber on the street as it screeched past them, following Vicky. It caught up with her at the end of the block, and ran up on the sidewalk to block her path. Two slender men in baseball caps jumped out to grab her. Vicky looked back once, hopelessly, as they threw her in the car.

For two precious seconds, Denny stood by the cleaning van with her mouth open, frozen in shock. Then all her good survival instincts, so tuned up six months ago, came alive again and added themselves to Will Dietz's lessons and her aunt's recent advice. She stepped into the street, where she had a good view of the Lincoln, opened her phone and punched the number two. Waiting through two rings, she memorized the vanity license plate.

Sarah was clearing her desk, getting ready to check out when her phone rang. She almost let it go to message waiting, but glanced quickly and saw it was Denny's new number calling. *Probably too proud of her new phone to resist.* She answered, thinking she'd have to remind Denny she'd said never to call her at work except for emergencies.

Denny said, with a quiver in her voice, 'Aunt Sarah, my friend has an emergency and I don't know what to do.'

'Which friend?'

'Vicky. The girl who cleans our houses. They were just leaving—'

'Is Mom there with you?'

'Yes, she's here.' Her voice got stronger. 'Will you just listen?'

Wow. Spoken like a cop's kid. 'Go ahead.'

Denny described, in a rush, the three men who had just grabbed Vicky and put her in a car. 'She looked very scared, and they're too far away for us to do anything, so I called you because I thought you—'

'You did right,' Sarah said. 'Can you describe the car?'

'Four-door convertible. Greyish green? It looks new but also old – what's that word?'

'Restored?'

'Yes. Tail fins? Oh, and I saw the word Lincoln.'

'You pretty sure?'

'Vanity plate,' Denny said, ignoring the question as the car roared away. 'FRDOFUN.'

'Good! You did good, Denny. Is Mom OK?'

'Yes.'

'Stick with her. Talk to you later.' She hung up and put out the BOLO.

They ate a mostly silent supper, since Aggie decreed they were not to talk about whatever was happening to Vicky. Tía Luisa had loaded up the rest of her crew and left without a word, and Aggie had not asked for explanations. Denny sat mouse-quiet during dinner and went early to bed.

After Howard left, Will sat out in the gathering dusk until Sarah pulled into the carport. He got into the front seat beside her and said, 'I hear you had quite a day.'

'Indeed. And that was *before* Denny called.' She told him a little about the rest of her day – not much, because exhaustion was reaching out for her, and she still hadn't eaten. 'What an end to moving day for my poor mother. But damn, Will, that kid did one helluva job, calling me as fast as she did with those bang-on descriptions. And the license plate, are you proud?'

'I have to say I am.'

'Our guys have already got that snake, he's being booked. Along with his two helpers, who have extremely interesting rap sheets of their own. Menendez knew who it was as soon as he heard the plate, he went right to his house. Artie's been trying to nail Freddy O. for some time.'

'Abducting a child, that ought to cook his goose.'

'He's a pimp and a dealer and most of his girls are undocumented and quite a few are underage and oh hell, just for the fun of it, Artie thinks maybe he can prove the Lincoln Continental is hot.'

'Car theft, now that's really shocking. Is the girl all right? Vicky?'

'Mostly. They didn't have time to do much.'

But he knew that voice. 'But what?'

'Well, she's undocumented. And her prints are on file, it's a third offense.'

'Oh-shit-oh-dear. She'll never be eligible for citizenship.'

While she polished off the last of the picnic she told him about her realization, on the way home from Phoenix, that wanting to make total slaves of his women had been a pattern with Frank Cooper. 'I couldn't be absolutely certain Phyllis was Cheeks, but it stood to reason she was, and that she'd have the most to lose if Frank got fond of somebody else. So I tried reading her one of the emails, and it shocked her so much she showed me I was right. I was guessing she still didn't know about the contract with Laura, and I was right, that blew her out of the water.'

'Very clever, Sherlock. She give you the LadySmith yet?'

'No, she's lawyered up now, we'll need a warrant. I think, though, we can point out to her defense attorney that killing Frank might be framed as second degree, but lying in wait for Lois so she could stage the scene as murder/suicide makes it Murder One for sure. When reality sets in we'll get more cooperation, I think. Is there any more of this chicken?'

'Lots. You want some more potato salad with it?' While he refilled her plate he said, thinking he was joking, 'What else did you do today?'

She laughed. 'Well, that was about all for me but Jason went down to the ME's lab to observe while José identified Chuy Maldonado's head.'

Dietz watched, bemused, as she laughed some more. 'What?'

'Well, he, you know, flunked his first autopsy. So we all asked him, you know, how did that go for him?' She laughed again.

'Having your own party or what?' Dietz said. 'Tell me.'

'He said, very cool, that Chuy didn't look much like his photos any more. So I said OK, but did José ID the head? And Jason said, "Right away, with no hesitation. But I think he was mainly trying to get away while there was time to stop by the In-N-Out Burger place on the way to the plane."'

'Sarah,' Leo said the next afternoon, 'what were the Cooper siblings doing in here just now?'

'I called Nicole yesterday to tell her I was taking her store manager away to booking. I thought she should hear it from me. But she wasn't in when I called, so she came in to talk about it today.' She cocked her head. 'Why are you dodging her?'

'Just keeping my shirt clean. Was that her brother with her?'

'Yes. Did you notice how friendly they were acting? I said I suppose it's a relief to have this settled and they both looked kind of embarrassed. Remember I put in the report how they didn't look at each other or speak? I realized just now they must have each thought the other one killed their parents. I guess they were hoping very sincerely we'd stick with the murder-suicide theory.'

'Really,' Leo said. 'Don't people realize how scientific we've become?'

'Right,' Sarah said. 'Also it helps when the perpetrator goes nuts and confesses.'

Sarah told Denny that Vicky had been rescued from Freddy but she had no other details as yet. Denny, anxious but help-less, went off to the new school every day, came home and did homework, chores, bed like a good little robot, trying to earn points enough on some cosmic chart to keep Vicky safe.

When Tía Luisa's van came to clean the Bentley Avenue house and Denny saw that Vicky was no longer on the crew, she tried to ask Ana about her. Ana shook her head and said, '*No sé nada,*' and after that wouldn't talk at all.

After they left, Denny asked her grandmother if Tía Luisa said anything about Vicky. 'No, honey, and I didn't ask because I knew she wouldn't answer. If Vicky's an illegal, Luisa could lose her license for having hired her.'

'Boy, we sure know how to punish poor people, don't we?'

'Denny, you can't fix everything, so fix what you can. Do your homework.'

A couple of weeks later Sarah came home on time for once, got into soft clothes and came out in the kitchen where Denny had just finished browning chops in a pan, and was laying them over Aggie's sliced potatoes and roux. Aggie said, squinting at the control, 'Is the oven hot?'

'Yeah, here we go,' Denny covered the dish and slid it in the stove.

Aggie went to watch the news and Sarah said, 'Denny, let's take a cold drink and sit outside a while.' They went out to their new favorite place, in the shade under the eucalyptus trees, and Sarah told her about the awards ceremony she'd been invited to, on Hilton Head Island. 'There'll be speeches and awards. From a grateful nation for apprehending the Soltero gang, breaking up their drug-smuggling operation, nailing them for the stash house murders, all of that.'

'Oh, neat. Are you excited? When will you go?'

'Oh, I'm not going. I don't want to leave Mom yet. Phil Cruz is going to collect my plaque. And my boss is actually pleased about that case finally, because our share of the confiscated loot will help a lot. Looks like I can quit saying "I just happened to take the call" every time it comes up.'

'I bet I'm the only kid in fifth grade whose aunt is a hero. Can I take you to Show and Tell?'

'Why not?' They rattled the ice in their glasses. 'I got some news about Vicky, finally. Her case is being handled by ICE, because there was a criminal act involved. It's kind of complicated, because Freddy O., while he's charged with just about everything but mass murder, is a US citizen, whereas Vicky's undocumented, so . . .'

'Does that mean he can kidnap her and beat her up?'

'Of course not. It just makes prosecuting him for that particular crime very awkward, because they'd have to grant her temporary asylum or something so she could stay here and testify at a trial . . .'

'Yes!' Denny lit up. 'Good idea! Let's do that!'

'Well, nobody's much inclined to, because we've got a ton of other stuff to pin on Freddy O. Including the houseful of other illegals he was harboring, many of them also under-age. So . . .'

'What?'

'It looks like Vicky's going back to Mexico very shortly.'

'Oh, *no*! Aunt Sarah, you can't let that happen! This is her home just the same as it's ours!'

'Unfortunately that's not true. Vicky's not a citizen and she's been deported twice already.'

'I don't care! Vicky loves this country and she's willing to work to support herself! Isn't that the kind of American we're always saying we want?'

'Yes. But Denny, all countries worth living in have laws they enforce.'

'They don't have to have that one. She could have stayed.'

'Maybe so. But tell me this: when those bad guys were putting her in the car, who'd you call?'

'You know that – I called you.'

'Why?'

'I knew you'd help her. But—'

'No buts. You called the cops – that's what everybody does. Help her, you said. And you knew I *could* help her, because I'm a law enforcement officer so the law's on my side. Look at me, Denny. The law's on my side because I'm on its side.'

'Well, sure, but—'

'No buts. Every time. You can count on me to enforce the law every time because that's my job. I like my job so I'll always do it as well as I can. You know that joke about it's a tough dirty job but somebody's got to do it? Well funny or not, that exactly describes a cop's job.'

'So if the law says send Vicky back to Mexico, you'll do it.'

'That's right. And if you don't like it, don't yell at me. Yell at the people who make the laws.'

'Come on. I'm just a kid,' Denny said.

'And I'm just a cop. We all have some excuse, don't we?' They sat still a minute, listening to the doves. 'You'll grow up fast though,' Sarah said. 'I can see you're going to be one of those early bloomers. Study hard, will you? We're looking for a few good kids to grow up and change the world.'

Denny gave her one of her patented dubious looks and drank the rest of her soda. Just before they went in she said, 'Thank you for rescuing Vicky from that terrible man.'

'You're welcome. It's what I do.' She took Denny's hand and they walked in together toward the good dinner smells.

When the bus doors hissed open just south of the gate, Vicky climbed down and walked wearily toward the sign that read 'Frontera de Cristo.' The patio held the familiar cluster of tired-looking people, mostly men, talking softly. A couple of volunteers smiled at her, offered her water and coffee. She took some water and found a seat among the returnees.

Most of them were sharing their stories – how long they had been in Estados Unidos, where they'd gone and what jobs they had found. Vicky was very tired and she had a little money, so she knew she would get up soon, eat something and find the cheapest place to stay. But first she wanted to sit a while listening to the stories of the dispossessed. Maybe somebody here had a new idea.

She began to ask the ones who would talk to her, 'What's next for you? You got any plans, know anybody to call?' She was looking for a small, energetic group to join – people with experience, ready to try anything reasonable. No more crazy chances like Freddy, though.

She moved to a chair near a young, quiet woman who was also listening to the stories. She looked strong, her face was grave but not defeated. Someone worth considering as a friend, Vicky thought. A traveling companion would be a comfort and improve the odds of success.

She smiled at the young woman, who asked, 'Do you intend to try going back?'

'I will always go back,' Vicky said. 'Tucson is my home.'